the
PRINCIPLES
of L♥VE

the
PRINCIPLES
of L♥VE

Emily Franklin

nal
jam
books

NAL JAM
Published by New American Library, a division of
Penguin Group (USA) Inc., 375 Hudson Street,
New York, New York 10014, USA
Penguin Group (Canada), 10 Alcorn Avenue, Toronto,
Ontario M4V 3B2, Canada (a division of Pearson Penguin Canada Inc.)
Penguin Books Ltd., 80 Strand, London WC2R 0RL, England
Penguin Ireland, 25 St. Stephen's Green, Dublin 2, Ireland (a division of Penguin Books Ltd.)
Penguin Group (Australia), 250 Camberwell Road, Camberwell, Victoria 3124,
Australia (a division of Pearson Australia Group Pty. Ltd.)
Penguin Books India Pvt. Ltd., 11 Community Centre, Panchsheel Park, New Delhi – 110 017, India
Penguin Group (NZ), cnr Airborne and Rosedale Roads, Albany,
Auckland 1310, New Zealand (a division of Pearson New Zealand Ltd.)
Penguin Books (South Africa) (Pty.) Ltd., 24 Sturdee Avenue,
Rosebank, Johannesburg 2196, South Africa

Penguin Books Ltd., Registered Offices: 80 Strand, London WC2R 0RL, England

First published by NAL JAM, an imprint of New American Library, a division of Penguin Group
(USA) Inc.

First Printing, July 2005
10 9 8 7 6 5 4 3 2 1

NAL JAM and logo are trademarks of Penguin Group (USA) Inc.

LIBRARY OF CONGRESS CATALOGING-IN-PUBLICATION DATA:

Franklin, Emily.
　　The principles of Love / by Emily Franklin.
　　　p. cm.
　　Summary: After moving to a Massachusetts boarding school where her father is the new principal, high-school sophomore and aspiring singer Love Bukowski learns some lessons about
friendship and romance.
　　ISBN 0-451-21517-6 (trade pbk.)
　　(1. Interpersonal relations—Fiction.　2. Singers—Fiction.　3. Music—Fiction.
4. Boarding schools—Fiction.　5. Schools—Fiction.　6. Massachusetts—Fiction.]　I. Title.
　　PZ7.F8583Pr 2005
　　[Fic]—dc22　　　　　　　　　　　　　　　　　　　　　　　　　　　　　2004026840

Set in Bembo with Hoosker Dont
Designed by Daniel Lagin

Printed in the United States of America

For Elliot, Sam, and Nathan

ACKNOWLEDGMENTS

Thanks to Faye Bender—the definition of good agent—and to Anne Bohner for seeking me (and Love) out. For their continued support, love, and encouragement, I thank my parents and grandparents. For enthusiasm, my in-laws (and RS)—if I could wrap you in tinfoil, I would. And to Kathy Franklin, aka The Namer, I give thanks and a roadkill bunny slipper. To Plumpy, the perfect blend of Watts, Blaine, and Duckie, thank you for the tidbits. Thank you also to Sara Woods. And a special thanks to Heather Swain, writing confidante and friend.

To the kids—thanks for not touching the computer (too much) and for the daily source of love, fulfillment, and laughter you bring to my life.

Most of all, thanks to AJS, Gold Medal husband and father (if only there were a Sandwich Olympics!).

CHAPTER 1

Just to get this out of the way: yes, it's my real name. And no, I wasn't born on a commune (not unless you consider Boston, Massachusetts, circa 1989, to be a commune). In the movie version of my life, there'd be some great story to go with how I got my name—a rock star absentee father who named me in his hit song, or a promise my real father made to his grandmother in the old country. At least a weepy love story of two people so happy about their daughter they had to give her my name. But there's not—there's just me.

Love. My name is Love. Maybe this makes you think of your first kiss (mine = Jared Rosen, who managed to knock out my top left tooth at the beginning of the summer and provide my first kiss—a peck—by August's end). Or maybe you cringe when I introduce myself, wondering if I come complete with a tacky poster of cuddly kittens tangled in wool (I had one in third grade that showed a tabby clawing the wall, saying HANG IN THERE! Thank God for paper recycling).

Trust me: Despite what my name conjures up, I am not the sort to have a bed piled with fluffy kitties or well-loved stuffed animals. I actually don't even like cats all that much, not since I hugged little Snowball, my old neighbor's cat, right before the freshman formal last year and wound up sucking down antihistamines and nursing facial hives in my gown. Not pretty.

Then again, pretty's not all it's cracked up to be—or so I hear. I'm not what you'd call pretty, not the even more tantalizing *beautiful,* though maybe I've got potential. Right now I suppose I could fall into the category of appealing. My Aunt Mable's always saying the girls who peak in high school show up looking downright average at their tenth reunion, so I'm hoping (hoping = counting on) that my best years are still ahead of me. I don't want to look back on my life and have soph-omore year of high school stand out as a blue ribbon winner, though the chances of that happening are slim at best. Part of me wouldn't mind trading places with the shiny, perfectly blond and still summer-tanned girls who probably emerged from the womb with a smile as wide as a Cadillac and legs from a music video. But since my life isn't one of those Disney movies where the heroine gets to swap places for a day and learn the secret to life, I have to be content to know only what it's like in my own life—and all I can say is it's too soon to tell.

We've been here (here = the Hadley Hall campus) for four days. Four days and six hours. And still not one decent conversation, not one promising smile-nod combination over mushy tuna sandwiches and lemonade outside, courtesy of FLIK, the school food supplier. When my dad told me about orientation for Hadley, I guess I imagined days spent lounging on the quad, soaking up the last of the summer rays while meeting cute boys, bonding with my two amazingly cool new best friends, and somehow forgetting that I have a forehead label—New Girl. Love, the New Girl. And not only that (here I'm imagining some lowly freshman pointing me out as someone who's even more lost than they are); I have the privilege of being the principal's daughter.

When my dad and I arrived on campus, typical trunk loaded with boxes, laundry hamper filled with my still-dirty duds, some overly en-thusiastic tour leader showed us to the faculty housing. I followed my dad up the slate pathway toward the front door of a yellow Victorian house. Huge, with a wraparound porch, the house overlooks the play-ing fields and the rest of main campus. I stared at it, thinking of the card my dad gave me for my seventh-grade birthday—one of those 3-D cards that you unfold into a whole building—a large house with a turret and a carousel. I used to stare into that card as if I could get sucked into its landscape and experience some magical life for a while. This is what I thought of when I saw our new digs . . . minus the merry-go-round.

"This is Dean's Way," the tour guide boy explained, his hands flailing as he pointed out the features of our new abode—porch, view of central campus, door knocker in the shape of a heart. I stared at the metal heart and wondered for a minute if this could be an omen (heart = love = me), but then I rolled my eyes at myself. I hate when I give myself Lifetime programming moments.

"This is for you," Tour Guide said, and handed my dad a large manila envelope and reached out to shake my hand. It still feels weird to shake hands as an almost-sixteen-year-old (almost = just under eight weeks until I'm highway-legal). Plus, Tour Guide never even asked my name. Around here, I guess I'm just a faculty brat.

My dad took the keys from the envelope (an envelope labeled, by the way, PRINCIPAL BUKOWSKI AND DAUGHTER, as if I have no other identity), and began to fumble with the front door lock.

"Ready?" he asked, and smiled at me.

I nodded, excited. Dad and I have lived in some pretty grim places before—the apartment on Yucca Street that lived up to its name, the rent-reduced properties on the campus of Seashore Community College—so I never planned on living large. We've moved around a fair bit, actually, and one of the reasons Dad signed the contract with Hadley Hall was to make sure we could stay in one place. The thought of living here, of calling this home, or not peeling up anyone's old apartment buzzer labels and slicking ours on top, feels both comforting (stability = good) and trapping (sameness = confining)—or maybe I just mean revealing.

Dad rushed in, ever eager to explore new places and see what problems (kitchen bulb out, bed in the wrong place for optimum light) he might fix. That's what he does, problem-solve and rearrange. Me, I'm more cautious. I lurked for a minute in the doorway, holding on to the heart knocker and wondering what I'd find.

And I don't just mean that I stood there wondering what my new bedroom would look like. It was like right then, at the front door, I knew everything had changed—or would change, or was changing. The morphing process of leaving freshman year and the already hazy memories that went with it. Soon, sophomore year at Hadley Hall— *the* Hadley Hall, with its ivy-coated brick and lush green lawns, its brood of young achievers, lacrosse-playing boys, and willowy girls— would begin. And I'd be in it.

CHAPTER 2

*I*n the made-for-television movie of this day, I'd wake up in my new house and while sipping my milky coffee, I'd meet my new best friend. We'd bond over loving the same sappy lyrics to 1970s songs (example = "Brandy (You're a Fine Girl)"—lame but awesome song from sometime in the late seventies). Then, later, I'd be getting ready to go for a jog (and by jog I mean slow, but hey—it's something), and the Kutcher-esque hot guy I saw yesterday by the track would happen to be running by and take time out of his exercise regime to give me a guided tour of campus . . . and of himself. Heh. Unlikely— but then, it's a movie.

The reality of my life is this:

Outside, I can hear the buzz of bugs and the grunts from soccer and field hockey players from the fields near the house. I am decidedly un-motivated to get out of my bed—even though it's eleven o'clock. Last night, I caught my second, third, and fourth winds and wound up flip-ping stations between a *90210* rerun on cable and some infomercial that nearly convinced me to order that bizarre brush/hair-dye combo thing that supposedly makes it easy to home-color. Not that it'd be useful for me, since my hair is different enough already: penny-hued, with some bright bits at the front (not so suitable for highlights or lowlights—more like dimlights). I think about adding some wild streak of blue or something, but mainly this is when I'm PMSy. As my Aunt Mable always says, Let No Woman Attempt Hair Change When Hormonally Challenged. This was, of course, after the Miss Clairol mishap that took her three trips to the salon to correct.

Actually, I kind of pride myself on never having ordered from TV before—not that there's a fundamental flaw with it, but there's a principle there. Maybe I feel like if I started, there'd be no turning back, and pretty soon I'd wind up with that weird mop and the orange goop that strips paint and the hair-braiding contraption that I know would create such tangles I'd need to cut off great lops of hairs. So I avoid potential psychological damage (and smelly fumes) by refraining from any and all made-for-TV offers.

Plus, Aunt Mable already signed me up for the Time-Life Singers & Songwriters discs. They arrive each month. She wants to edu-ma-cate me on the finer decades of rock and folk, long before OutKast and Britney. Most of the songs sound like an advertisement for deodorant, but I love the cheesiness of the lyrics, the mellow strumming of the guitars. Instead of John Mayer introspection, there's just old-fashioned lust or odes to seventies fashion. Half the time the guy's singing about making it with his lady or the woman's crooning how her disco man done her wrong—what's not to appreciate there? Plus, sometimes Aunt Mable will listen with me and tell me how a particular song makes her think of being a cheerleader, eating grilled cheese, and making out with Bobby Stanhope in the back of his Camaro.

With so much late-summer sunshine streaming in my window, I can't stay in bed any longer. It's harder to be a lazy slob in warm weather—hiding under the covers is much more gratifying in winter or heavy rains. I slide out of bed and onto the floor, pressing PLAY so I can hear the latest disc—it arrived yesterday, my first piece of mail to this new address. The typed label proved that I don't even need a street number anymore—just my name, Hadley Hall, Fairfield, Massachusetts, and the

ZIP. Fairfield is "just outside Boston"—that's how the school catalog describes it, although my dad and I clocked it in the car and it's nearly twenty-four miles, so it's not as if you can walk it. Probably because of my own moniker, I am name-focused and tend to overanalyze place names, so when my dad announced ("Love, pack your bags—we're going to prep school!" as if he'd have to endure the mandatory school blazer with me) we were moving to Fairfield, I couldn't help but picture green expanses and fair maidens traipsing around in long dresses, books carried by the same guy who'd throw his blazer over a mud puddle for easy-stepping.

Anyway, I was partially right. Fairfield is easy on the eyes, as are most of the Hadley students I've seen so far. Doing my usual shower routine, lathering all parts and hair while lip-synching, I wonder for a minute what life would be like here if the town were called "Hellville" or "Zitstown"—but when I emerge, clean and wet, and wipe the steam from the window, I can still see the soccer players and beautiful full elm trees. No ugliness here.

"She's going to be here any minute," my dad yells up from his post in the kitchen. I know his routine so well that I can tell he's already come back from the gym and eaten the first half of his multigrain bagel. He doesn't use jam, he squashes fresh fruit onto the bread and munches away. He will have already set aside the last cup of coffee for me in the microwave, which he will nuke for forty-six seconds prior to my arrival in the kitchen. We have a system. It's what happens when you live with just one parent—either you don't know each other at all or you're way too familiar.

"Hey," I say, right as the microwave beeps to signal my caffeine is ready.

"Big shopping day?" Dad asks. He flips through a book. I shrug. I'm not Prada-obsessed or anything, but I enjoy looking around at what's out there. Mainly, it's an excuse to get off campus and be with Aunt Mable, who gives me regular reality checks.

"What's that?" I lean over his shoulder. Dad smells like strawberries and the original Polo from the green bottle. Dad smell. "Or, better yet, *who* is that?" The book in front of him contains black and white photos.

Dad puts on his game-show announcer voice, "The Faces of Hadley Hall!" I reach for the book. He holds it back and says in a regular voice, "I'm just trying to familiarize myself with the rest of the faculty. You'll get your own copy later in the year."

"And the IPSs?" (IPSs = Issue Prone Students—teacher code for screwups.)

"Maybe," Dad says, and bites the rest of his bagel. "Eat something."

A car horn beeps. I can see Aunt Mable's car out the front window. She emerges from the driver's side and sits on the hood of the rusting black Saab 900. With jean cutoffs, black tank top, and Ugg boots the same camel color as her ringlets, Aunt Mable always looks like a rock star herself—Sheryl Crow's lost sister or something.

"I gotta go," I say. "You know I'll eat more than my fair share with Mable. She's taking me on a culinary tour as well as showing me her personal fashion finds."

"Here." Dad hands me a key. "Your name here."

"My name here," I say back. This is our "I love you."

I take the house key and head outside. He could ask when I'll be home and I could answer that I don't know or make up some time frame, but the truth is, Dad doesn't set rules like that for me. He knows I'll call and tell him where I am and what I'm doing, and it's not a big enough deal to bother setting up some structure that I have to follow. Besides, I'm a lousy liar, and I never want to lie to him. It's his Jedi mind trick: He figures if he gives me enough freedom, I won't actually want it all. Here's the thing: Up till now, it's been true.

Before I even reach the Saab, my senses are overwhelmed. Mable's new carfume wafts from the rolled-down windows, and my aunt sits cross-legged on the hood of the car, singing along to Guns N' Roses ("Sweet Child o' Mine") at the top of her voice.

"Skipping decades?" I ask, and join in on the chorus.

"After you are thoroughly informed of the 1970s, you will pass Go and move on to obscure eighties tunes," she says.

"Axel Rose is not obscure," I say.

"True." She nods and slides off the hood to hug me. "But this is a classic."

Mable drives the twenty-four miles into Boston using back roads, and explains the various towns and subway stops along the way. We pass suburbs and slumburbs, a country club or two, industrial buildings, and a huge water tower splashed with brightly colored paints.

"Supposedly you can see faces and words in the mural," Mable says, pointing to the tower. "Personally, I think you can see Clapton's profile in the red part."

We make our way over Mass Ave., where hipsters and homeless people mingle. Passing by Berklee College of Music, I watch as students heft guitars, keyboards, and massive drums in the late summer heat. Aunt Mable watches me absorb the scene.

"Here we are, the mecca of vintage apparel," she says, sweeping her arm toward a storefront like it's a new car on display.

"Baggy Bertha's?" I'm skeptical. Let me state that my own personal style is not fully developed. Not that I don't know what I like—I do, and I'm well aware of what makes me gag—but I'm sort of all over the place when it comes to picking out clothes. I have no trouble finding items that appeal (a pair of black flip-flops with plastic red flowers on them, faded Levi's 501s, two close-fitting tops—one electric blue, one layered white and gray), yet I have no idea how to put them together. It's like I'm a crow drawn to shiny things. After shopping I usually get home and sift through my purchases only to find there's not one presentable outfit in the lot. It's why I tend to stick to music instead.

"Perfect," Mable says of the suede jacket in front of her. "This, too. And let's try this."

She collects clothes, and I wander around the vintage shoe section, agog at the array of coolness and crap up for grabs. Next to thigh-high pleather boots (think Julia Roberts in the hooker phase of *Pretty Woman*) are Mary Janes and saddle shoes, Elton John disastrous sparkly clunkers circa 1976, and then—the black ankle boots I've longed for, like a riding boot only not in a dominatrix way. Plus, the heel would give me an extra couple of inches (I'm what the pediatrician called "on the smaller end of the growth chart"—better known as five-foot-two). I hold up my footwear find to Mable, who's clad in a bonnet and purple boa yet still manages to be sexy.

Mable makes me try on the Aerosmith-inspired Lycra outfit she's picked out, and I make her don a dress out of a fairy tale—not a Drew Barrymore kind of fairy tale; the Little Bo Peep kind. We stand in front of the three-way mirror, looking at the flipside images of ourselves.

"I'll never be this kind of rock star," I say, toying with the fringe on the sleeves. Mable smoothes her frilly petticoat. "If I placed an online personals ad with this picture of myself, would I find the love of my life?"

As I wait for Mable to get changed, I look at the old posters for Woodstock (the real one, not the Pepsi-mudfest) and *The Rocky Horror Picture Show,* the framed black-and-whites of Mod girls in thick eyeliner and go-go boots standing by their Vespa scooters. Was life better then? More fun? Simpler? Sometimes I think of life-as-told-by-a-Robert-Doisneau poster (you know, the master of romantic photography, who took those pictures of people kissing in Paris or the woman walking down the street in Italy), and how the days must have felt—I don't know—bigger somehow, more important. But then, I know I'm fantasizing, because in these imaginings, I'm never in high school or doing dishes or tying shoes. But even the posters of hippies hanging out in front of the Metropolitan sign in Paris seem cooler than the midriff-baring teens we passed near Harvard Square. Maybe the past is bound to seem better, because it's done with.

Reading my mind, Mable pays for my boots with cash, glances at the hippy posters, and says, "It wasn't any different than today." Then she tilts her head, reconsidering. "Okay—a little bit. No email, lots of polyester, and too much patchouli and smoke."

Boots in hand, I suddenly wish I were someone who felt that back-to-school shopping were the start of the rest of her life. But I'm not. I can't help but think it'd be easier if I gained redemption or enlightenment with a new purchase, or that getting a cool outfit meant my year would work out. I think of my dad, fortysomething and still picking out his ties as if he were presidential, as if superficial coatings mattered.

"Hey, lighten up, Brick," Aunt Mable says. She calls me Brick when, in her opinion, I'm thinking too hard or weighing down an otherwise pleasant moment.

"Sorry," I say, shaking my head to shrug off my thoughts. I roll down my window, rest my arm on the door frame, and let the wind wash over me.

"Look at us. We're like that Springsteen song." Mable smiles. I don't have to ask which one. She means "Thunder Road." She mentions it all the time: She loves the line about not being a beauty but being okay just the same. I always wait for the one about how highways or roads can lead you in whatever direction you choose—forward or back, able to take you anywhere.

Just like that, I'm out of my small funk and say, "I can't wait to get my license."

"That's right! You should be practicing. Drive. Hop in."

We swap sides, and I attempt to drive standard in the highway hell better known as Downtown Boston (hell = one way meets merge meets six lanes and a blinking red = huh?). Once she's fairly certain I'm not going to kill or maim us, Mable starts a round of RLG.

RLG is the game we devised—basically a musical Magic 8-ball. The rules for playing Radio Love God are elementary (though open for discussion and warping depending on how desperate the situation). The idea stems from the fact that we all do those stupid little tests with ourselves like "If I get this wrapper-ball into the trash on the first shot, so and so will like me," or "If the song ends by the time the light turns green, I'll get the job." Sometimes the tests work, but of course the odds go down if you start doing the "It's 11:11, make a wish and touch something red" and then you wish to become Paris and Nicky's other sister (but, hey, if that's what you're wishing, you have other, worse problems).

Anyway, to play RLG, you have the volume down and say something along the lines of "Whatever song comes on next is from ____ to me," or "The next one is how my summer will go." We make sure the volume-down rule is strict, because otherwise you can sort of cheat and, in the middle of "Your Body Is a Wonderland," say, "Oh, by the way, this is from that campus hottie to me." And that's just plain wrong.

The best part of this slightly loser game is that you can twist the lyrics to suit your particular situation. For example, even if it's an ad for Jolly Jingle Cleaners and you've stated that it's from your long-lost summer love, you could interpret "We'll clean you, steam you, get the wrinkles out" as "See, he's wiped the slate clean from when I kissed that other guy. He's steaming—meaning he's still hot for me, and the wrinkles of our relationship are gone." And then you can go home and email said boy, only to humiliate yourself when he doesn't write back. It's brilliant fun.

Mable takes her turn playing RLG and is saddened when she asks how business will go tonight and the reply is "Alone Again, Naturally." Mable runs her own coffeehouse, Slave to the Grind, with comfy couches, a laptop lounge, and amazing lattes, so she's constantly surrounded by people. I couldn't take that much face time. I like my alone time—balanced, of course, with a good friend or conversation.

Mable lets me parallel park (parking = getting it on the second try!), and we go for greasy cheeseburgers and sweet potato fries, splitting a vanilla frappe (frappe = East Coast milk shake).

"Are you thinking about the scene in *Grease* when Olivia Newton-John and Travolta hide behind their menus in the diner?" Mable asks.

"No," I say, sliding two fries in my mouth, whole, and then using dentist office–speak for a minute. "Ibuzthinknboutthishotguy."

"What hot guy?" Mable asks. She has an uncanny ability to understand dentist-speak.

"Someone at Hadley . He's probably an idiot."

"A really gorgeous idiot?"

"Yeah, that. Plus, I was thinking how much I miss singing."

At my old school, I was in a band. Maybe not the best band, but Baby Romaine ("Baby" as in the girl from *Dirty Dancing* who won't be put in a corner, and "Romaine" as in lettuce, as in *let us* play—hey, it was freshman year) gave me an outlet aside from Mable's car and my shower for singing.

"Well, you've got an incredible voice. What about Hadley? There's got to be—what—an octet group or something . . . like in *American Pie*." Yet again, Mable references movies and songs to prove a point, but this one's lost on me.

"Yeah, I know. But I don't want that—"

She cuts me off. "Then write your own songs."

I want to protest or crack a joke, but I don't. I just eat my burger and nod. I'm so afraid of sounding cheesy in songs, or derivative, that even though words sometimes swirl in my head, I don't write them down.

Bartley's Burgers turns out to be this famous place. Harvard undergrads, former presidents, movie scouts on location all come here for the grub. The walls are blanketed with peeling bumper stickers (ENVISION WHIRLED PEAS, ELVIS HAS LEFT THE BUILDING) and NO NUKES signs.

Mable sees me checking out all the paraphernalia and wipes her mouth on the little paper napkin. "Your mom and dad used to come here."

My hand freezes before my mouth, a quivering sweet potato fry stuck in midair. No one ever mentions my mother. Ever. Not even in passing.

"Sorry," Mable says, and quickly slurps some frappe. "It was a million years ago."

By my quick calculations, Mable's overestimating by about 999,987. "No—wait—go back."

Mable shakes her head. "Never mind, it's late. I should drive you home."

"It's not home, it's Hadley," I say, annoyed at how teenagery I sound. "Seriously, Mable, I'm not being Brick, I just have to know something. Tell me anything."

"Fine." Mable takes a breath and looks around. "Once, I saw your parents sitting in that corner over there, sharing some sproutburger or whatever alfalfa mojo your mother liked then. Your dad drummed the table, as per usual. He's done that since we were kids. And your mom put her hand on his like this." Mable flattens her own fingers and leaves her hands resting on each other. "And . . ."

She looks at my face. Probably I look too eager, too desperate. She cuts herself off. "And that's all."

I open my mouth to demand further details, but Mable's gone up to pay the bill.

The car ride back to Hadley Hall starts off stilted, with no conversation, just the radio's declaration, over and over again, that summer is over. WAJS plays tributes to this effect, with songs talking about empty beaches and seasons changing. This, plus the sight of the Hadley campus makes me cloud up again.

Chin on my hand, I stick my face partway out the window like a dog. In front of the house—our house—my house—Mable stops the car.

"Listen, forget what I said back at Bartley's. Say hi to your dad for me, and just enjoy the here and now." I know she's not just talking about movies and songs and decades-old hippy posters. She means for-

THE PRINCIPLES OF LOVE 15

get the maternal mystery, don't dwell on what could be—just live in the present.

After dinner, I sit on the porch while my dad commits to memory student names from the face book. People here have names that seem more suitable to towns or buildings: Spence, Channing, Delphina, Sandford. I mean weren't Pacey and Dawson enough of a stretch?

Outside, I can't get comfortable—first too hot in my sweatshirt, then too cold in just my T-shirt. Then the porch slats cut into my thighs, so I stand up.

"It's less windy on the other side," says a voice from around the turret-edge of the house.

I go to discover the person to whom the voice is attached. Sitting on one of the white Adirondack chairs in the front of the house with her knees tucked up to her chest is:

"Cordelia, as in one of King Lear's daughters, and a fac brat just like you."

She rattles off other information—about me, my dad, the house (turns out the heart-shaped door knocker was put on by some old headmistress who died a spinster, so not a lot of romantic omen there).

"I'm Love," I say, even though Cordelia knows this already. And before she can make some joke about it, I add, "Bukowski. Love Bukowski."

CHAPTER 3

*T*hat's the trick of my name. I say Love, visions of cuteness—but when followed by Bukowski, I'm safe from cliché.

"Bukowski as in Charles?" Cordelia asks. I'm impressed: Most people don't know who he was.

"No relation to the poet, although I like his stuff."

"Love Is a Dog from Hell." Cordelia twists her fingers into her messy ponytail of dark curls and recites Bukowski in a poetic voice, proving she's not just making an empty reference.

I grin. "Nice to meet you, too."

The next morning, Cordelia's at my bedroom door knocking before nine, courtesy of my dad's attempt at getting me a new friend.

I let her in while I'm washing my face. Dressed in low-slung khakis, tiny T-shirt, and flip-flops, Cordelia's the essence of preppy casual.

"I've been here forever," she says. "Born here—not in this room, but down the street. Never lived anywhere else but campus." She looks at me. "Not that I'm going to name my first kid Hadley Hall or something, but I do like it here."

I nod, rummaging through my as-yet-unpacked bags for a clean shirt.

"Dress sexy." Cordelia puts on a voice. "Today's the Welcome Picnic, after all. I'm totally kidding, of course. No one gives a shit how you dress—that's the plus side of boarding life." I layer a T-shirt over my tank top and then strip it off, grabbing a faded blue zip-up sweatshirt instead.

"All set?" I say, hinting we should leave my room, though I have no idea where we'll go.

Cordelia stands up and stretches, eyeing my sweatshirt. "Ooh, looks like a castoff. Do tell." I stare at her. "Castoff. You know, as in used to be your boyfriend's clothing but now yours?"

We walk through the living room and the kitchen, and I peer into my dad's empty study. On his desk, papers are already heaped into mini-skyscraper towers, folders piled up, and the photograph of me as a sticky-faced kid holding a lollypop graces the middle of the mess.

"Yes," I say to Cordelia once we're outside. "This is a castoff." I tie the shirt around my waist and explain the bland nature of my freshman year unromance with Paul Paulson.

"What were his parents thinking?" she asks when she hears his name. "I mean, vulgar poets like Bukowski and clichéd Shakespearean fodder not included, don't they know they were dooming him?"

"I know. It's worse—just like his name, everything about him was the same. Day in, day out. He called every night at seven exactly, sent me notes twice a week, emailed and IM'd on Wednesdays and Fridays."

"Jesus, were you dating or playing secretary?" Cordelia leads us down the trail through the shady woods in back of the gym. "Boring."

He was so boring that once when we were kissing, I thought of all the synonyms for boring: uninteresting, tedious, dull, lackluster, dreary, mind-numbing, monotonous, humdrum, uninspiring. Not words I'd like to associate with romantic aspirations of lust, love, desire, flirtation, or connection.

The smallest girls' dorm, Fruckner (common campus slang, according to Cordelia = frucked her. Commonly accepted question: "Did you two fruck?"), sits perched on the edge of campus. Cordelia brings me inside, and I meet a gaggle of girls readying for the picnic. Without makeup and in old jeans, comfy sweaters, and mere slicks of lip gloss, they all look beautiful, and I wonder if I stick out. Maybe a bit. Maybe it's just in my psyche. I need a sign to warn visitors or just myself, BE-WARE OF OWN BRAIN.

One girl, Sienna, marks something in her magazine, and Jessica speaks up. "I'd go with answer B—definitely."

"Me, too," says another.

I look to see what they're doing. It's a glossy magazine quiz titled "Are you happy?" And I can't help but feel that if you need to take a test to find out, you probably aren't.

"We'll see you guys later!" Cordelia says. I smile and nod, following her outside and back onto the dorm path that connects one side of campus to the other. We walk in silence for a while and Cordelia says, "There are lots of different types of people here, Love—some brains, some Lip Glossers, some alternas, some preppy kids who are the fifth Hadley Hall generation—but the boundary lines are blurry."

I wait for her to say more. She doesn't. She's given me some basics, I guess, and I have to fill in the blanks.

I stop to tie my sneaker. Through a clearing in the brush, I can see Whitcomb, one of the boys' dorms. I haven't had a chance yet to commit to memory the vast number of academic buildings and dorms, but I know Whitcomb, since it's the closest to my house, directly across the street. Near the patio in back, two guys fling a Frisbee back and forth.

"Hurry up," Cordelia says.

I finish tying my lace, but notice that one of the Frisbee tossers is the incredibly beautiful guy I've seen around campus. He's got that prep school hair that refuses to stay out of his eyes, full mouth, but not so full he'd Saint Bernard–kiss you, and the physique of—I'm pathetic. I need to stop. I stand up, wishing I were alone so I could stare and long from afar.

"Where are we going, anyway?" I ask.

"Whitcomb, for a small matter of business," Cordelia says. "Then for a brief appearance at the Welcome Picnic." Every time she mentions the picnic, Cordelia puts on a Stepford Wife face and semi-salutes.

The boys' dorms face east, making one half of an arc on the far side of campus. The girls' dorms are flush on the other side, with all the dining hall, theater, arts center, and academic buildings in the middle. It's as if whoever planned the property had the segregation of sexes in mind, even though the school used to be all boys. Whitcomb is the largest of the dorms, three floors of testosterone, shirtlessness, cell phones, and various musical tastes blaring from the windows.

Cordelia marches over to some boys in front and motions for me to come with her. There's a bunch of gesturing I don't understand, a couple of hello hugs, including one for me from some guy Cordelia will later describe as a MLUT, one of the Hadley Hall Male Sluts. Still, it feels nice to be included. We're in the common room when Cordelia announces she's "getting parietals" from the dorm parent. I know from going over the Hadley Hall handbook with my dad that this is a fancy way of saying she's getting written permission to go upstairs into a boy's room. There are really funny/stupid rules, like you can be in the room but not have the door closed, and you have to have three feet on the floor at all times (obviously, not one person's three feet—that'd be highly unusual—but I suppose this is meant to keep two people from, uh, lying down).

I'm left sitting in a worn-in leather chair. In front of me, the empty fireplace looks like a hollow mouth. Logs are stacked next to the grate for far-off winter nights, and I wonder what life will be like then. Just as I'm thinking this, the hot guy comes into the cool darkness and rushes over to me, leaning down to give me a slightly sweaty hug. Yum. He backs up and looks at me.

"Sorry! My eyes are out of whack in here . . . I thought you were someone else." He stands there for a second, politely waiting for me to introduce myself, but my mind is flipping through inappropriate responses (oh my god I love you, do me now; hey, get some Right Guard—no, wait, don't) and my body is still reeling from his sweat. I'm not so much being cool by not saying anything; it's more like I've had the emotional wind sucked out of my lungs.

Cordelia comes down the stairs two at a time, and hot guy wanders off, playing catch with his balled-up shirt. "We're all set," Cordelia says, and pulls me up from the chair and my hot-boy stupor. I can tell without touching my cheeks that they're probably red. I think about explaining my brief but intense crush-brush to Cordelia, but I don't. I just save the hug so I can replay it later, dissect it, and maybe even let myself love it.

"Get ready for a J. Crew catalog montage," Cordelia says, and I don't know what she's talking about until I see the Science Center lawn, bannered and bright with plaids, khakis, shrunken cable sweaters, and tank tops, faculty in their Hadley Hall blue blazers. Perfectly highlighted blondes ("I used some lemon juice at the beach" is a line I hear not once but four times in an hour) and well-formed guys high-five and catch up on summer situations.

"All we need are a bunch of slobbery dogs," I say. And, as if on cue, shaggy golden retrievers and muddy brown Labradors weave in and out of our legs in search of hot dog ends and burger buns. "I see my dad."

"Meet me by the creepy fish statue in an hour," Cordelia says. I know the landmark she means. It's at the back of the old health center. Some alumni artist famous for his murals finally succumbed to the Hadley Hall pressure to donate his work, only he gave some sculpture he'd done while actually at Hadley. My dad says the kids make fun of it and that seniors decorate it every graduation, but I don't mind it. It's like a metal fish trying to jump out of its iron ocean. The times I've jogged past, I've wondered if the fish is meant to be escaping from its metal pool or jumping up in a vain attempt to capture some prize that's nowhere to be found.

"This is my daughter, Love," Dad says over and over again, and I try to eat watermelon while being introduced. Several students say hi, and I'm half in, half out of conversations, mainly floating from group to group, swatting mosquitoes away.

I hate the feeling of being on show. It's like I'm a pet or a diversion, like a newborn or something. The academics have to pay a little attention to me out of politeness to my father, but I can tell most are none too fascinated by yet another young woman starting out at Hadley, even if she—that'd be me—is the headmaster's daughter.

"Love, this is Mrs. Gabovitch," Dad says, and I shake hands with the nearest conception of a hippy I've ever encountered.

"Wow," Mrs. Gabovitch says. "What a great vibe you have." She waves her hands over the air in front of me, and I wonder if she's kidding, then decide quickly she's not. "I expect great things from you, Love." She tucks her silky scarf into her gauzy blue-and-green mottled top. Five of her could fit in the outfit. "I'm Dance, by the way."

This is how all the teachers introduce themselves. "George Philanopolous, History." "Margie Kempner, Physics." How would I sum up myself?

I notice that little by little certain kids drift away from the picnic and don't come back. There's still a big crowd, some parents, kids, and teachers, but I tell my dad I'll see him later. He nods and mouths *your name here*. I say it back.

Cordelia grabs me and tells me to run, our ride's about to leave. Without asking where we're going, I pile on top of random laps in the back of someone's Volvo. Against highway safety recommendations and my own recent Driver's Ed knowledge, we hunch untethered, driving past the campus outskirts until right when I think my head will pop through the ceiling, we stop. Everyone filters out.

Our destination turns out to be Josh Bradenford's house, some upperclassman who hosts regular parties. I wander from room to room, with Cordelia alternating back-to-school hugs and explaining the Hadley Hall dating chain to me: who dated or hooked up or slept with, or wants to date, and so on. Beer sloshes from plastic cups decorated with out-of-date slogans: Happy Birthday, St. Patty's Day Charm, Aloha, etc. I take a couple of sips from a Happy Fifth Birthday cup and feel decidedly un-fifth-birthdayish.

"Hey." This plus a nod from the hot boy who hugged me.

"Hey." I say back. I managed to speak! I'm improving.

"It's starting, you guys!" comes a voice, and instantly herds of people make their way to the back deck, where four Twister boards are set up. I watch as simultaneous games of Drunken Twister are played. Excuses for the stray-hand-on-breast routine, the occasional break in the game to puke over the rail, and lots of sitcom-style laughter and groping.

Later Cordelia finds me in the house, getting juice from the fridge. In the summer, I used to babysit, and after the kids were asleep, I'd make some dinner and hang out like I lived in the house by myself. I had sort of the same feeling now, minus being in charge of toddlers. I felt the urge to clean up after people, to put the house in order, to do *something* other than make an ass out of myself.

"What's up?" Cordelia's swaying slightly, and tips some beer on her hand. "Good for the skin, don't you know."

"I thought that was oatmeal," I say.

"What's oatmeal?"

"No, oatmeal being good for your skin," I explain. Cordelia stumbles into some guy and it's clear she's more than a little drunk. "You okay?"

Cordelia gives an exaggerated nod then slowly shakes her head. "No. Actually, no."

I look around for anyone I vaguely recognize and find hot boy, whom I pull aside and ask for a ride. "I'm a boarder," he says. "No car." But when I explain he just says to meet him out front. I pull Cordelia along and load her into someone's car. During the quick ride, hot boy sings along to Crosby, Stills and Nash, out of tune, but with the right lyrics, even the Spanish ones. Impressive. Though not quite as impressive as his physique. I believe the word I'm looking for is *luscious*.

"Hey," he says, suddenly looking back at me. "Don't worry about Cordelia."

"Okay," I say, aware that I still will.

"She does this every year." Hot boy shakes his head. "Never learns."

I take this to mean he disapproves of binge drinking (good) and hasn't fallen for Cordelia's feminine charms (also good), but thinks of me as Brick—a worrier (possibly not good). We arrive back at the faculty housing ten minutes later. Cordelia stumbles to the lawn and lies down.

"Thanks," I say to the driver. And then I look at hot boy. In the movie scene, he'd get out of the car and stay with me, and after we'd cleaned up Cordelia, we'd sit on the night lawn and talk and connect and kiss. But he gives me only a nod. "Get some sleep—have a good one." I always wonder what that means. A good day? A good year? A good soda? A good life? We'll see. Then they drive off.

After I set Cordelia up in her room with a trash can, water, and Tylenol, I head home. From outside the house, I can see my father in his study. Does he look at the photo of me as a kid and wonder where the time went? Or does it feel natural as you get older, that days slip by until everything you know seems different, and suddenly you're you—in your life, with a kid or not, a job or not, love—or not. I'm being Brick here, I know, and Aunt Mable would tell me to take a breath, but when I do, I inhale a mosquito and need to hack it up. Typical.

"I'll have the pound-and-a-halfer, boiled," my dad orders.

"Corn on the cob, potato salad, regular salad, and the blue fish," I say, and hand over my red plastic menu. We're sitting at wooden picnic tables that overlook the harbor, enjoying our Last Night of Summer dinner and feeding the seagulls that dart and land. "Don't crap on me," I say to one that's too close. Dad laughs.

"What's Cordelia like?" Dad asks, but before I answer he continues. "Nice? Someone you like? Anyway, there'll be lots of new kids to meet tomorrow. And some great musical talents on campus, I hear." This is Dad's Hadley Hall pitch for me—he's trying to sell me on all the private school life has to offer.

Dad drums the table and I reach over, like Mable said my mother had done, and press my hand down so he'll stop. My father says nothing, but I know he registers the gesture.

When the food's set down on the table, I use the small pad of butter to slick the corn and start eating. "My opening address tomorrow is about *change*," Dad says with dramatic emphasis. I wonder if he's thinking about the hand-drumming or my mother. Or just his lobster. Or me.

"Yeah?" I ask. "Like adaptation change?"

"I suppose," he says. "I like the idea that we all start off one place in life and wind up somewhere else. But how when you're in it—in the day-to-day—you can't really feel the morphing process."

"I totally know what you mean." I tell him about how the French say, *Plus ça change, plus c'est la même chose,* which I'm sure he knows—but he seems happy to know my two-week exchange program in Paris this past July at least garnered some vocab.

The more things change, the more they stay the same. I watch my single dad eat his lobster. He cracks the claws and dips them in melted butter. Out on the harbor, boats rock against the tide, squeaking their bumpers on the docks and pilings. In the movie version of this (hell, I'd take the *Dawson's Creek* or *OC* version), a boat would pull up, and I'd never have to deal with high school. I'd just sail off into the dark water. But the reality is this: Summer's over, and as of tomorrow, school's in session.

CHAPTER 4

*I*n back of the round theater on campus and the first library, Maus Hall (local moniker = Eek! Hall), is the huge expanse of green that begins North Campus. Perched way to the back of this, on top of the hill near Whitcomb, is the quaint stone chapel. Clusters of us, the Hadley Hall students, the supposedly brainy elite, head toward the sound of ringing bells like cattle. I watch the blue-blazered youth (me included) and feel like a girl in a prep school movie. This, of course, makes me know exactly whom I would play if I were in fact cast in such a film, since there are only five girl-types ever portrayed.

There's the standard pretty girl role (examples = Molly Ringwald in *The Breakfast Club* or Jennifer Love Hewitt in *Can't Hardly Wait*); the pretty girl's best friend, who is decidedly less pretty, but cool enough (examples = Sarah Jessica Parker in *Footloose* or Maggie Gyllenhaal in *Mona Lisa Smile*. The BF of the PG is either supernice and winds up with the quasi-loser guy in the movie, like Seth Green, or the BF of the PG is kind of slutty and betrays her BF). Then there's the classic UG, the Ugly Girl, who is, of course, gorgeous underneath her shaggy frizz of hair and baggy clothes (examples = Ally Sheedy in *The Breakfast Club* or that girl from *The Princess Diaries*). She winds up with the stud at the end, thanks to her now-Lycra-infused dress and eyeliner, and thus swaps roles and becomes the PG.

This is not to be confused with the subgenre Crossover Girl, who—like Lindsay Lohan in *Mean Girls*—starts off the UG, becomes the PG, then realizes what a total bitch she's become and becomes a lovely blend of the two—a FUGNPBNG (formerly ugly girl, now pretty but nice girl).

And then, there's me. I am the lesser-dealt-with cliché of girldom: the Friend-Girl. No, that's not a brush with dyslexia. Friend-Girl as opposed to girlfriend. The best example being Mary Stuart Masterson in *Some Kind of Wonderful*. Like Watts in what happens to be one of my favorite viewing experiences ever, I am the girl who is most likely to become friends with the hot guy while pining for him in the secrecy of her journal/song lyrics/blog. Maybe I have a way of putting guys at ease, or maybe I'm so nonappealing sexually that our conversations end up being actually good rather than mere flirtations, but either way, being the FG is a blessing and a curse. I get the closeness, the proximity that people long for with far-off crushes. But I also get the heartache of knowing what I'm missing, all the while being too scared or dumb or supportive (supportive = sorting out Hot Guy's relationship troubles while wishing he'd notice me gazing at him) to act on anything.

So this is what I'm thinking about on the way to the opening day chapel ceremony.

"What's up? What're you thinking about?" Cordelia asks. She's my unofficial chaperone for this event.

"Nothing." I shake my head. "Just that it's pretty here." This, while being dishonest, is certainly a shorter answer, and true to some extent. Everywhere I look, smiling faces and summer-streaked hair abound. Healthy, toned students and distinguished faculty members all amble up the hill and through the cavernous arched doorway to settle into pews. Dotting the back wall are symbols from a plethora of religions, informing us yet again that this is a nondenominational place of worship, that all are welcome. All are welcome provided they are smart enough or wealthy enough or connected enough to get into Hadley Hall in the first place. I am too snide for opening day.

"Welcome," says the first of several blond-turned-gray women to speak. Cordelia whispers everyone's role or name to me: head of the trustees, English Chair, History Chair, who happens to be Cordelia's mother, until finally my father is introduced and Cordelia says, "That's your dad. Principal Bukowski."

"Yeah, I got that, thanks." I smirk at her. Probably because he's my dad first and my principal second, I actually listen to the speech, to the words about truth and striving not to just fit in, to blend, but to dare for greatness, even if being different is harder. As my father leans into the dark oak podium, he clears his throat and gets ready for the closing remarks. I listened to him practice while I attempted (in vain, I might add) to script a song of my own. I sat poised with pen in hand, but wrote nothing. Now, my dad has rewritten his speech, apparently stealing (stealing = borrowing with honor) my French expression from our dinner last night. He comes out from behind the podium and talks about how change can be daunting, but in the end, a good thing—and that the more we change the more we stay true to ourselves. Students applaud and stand up, immediately filing outside into the still-warm air for a brief social pit stop prior to rushing to first period.

There's clearly a system, an order to life here that I just don't know yet. How everyone knew to leave by the back door and lounge on the stone steps, draping their jackets over their shoulders like a Polo ad, how it's clear who the upperclassmen are and who the freshmen are, painfully green and nervous, keeping their blazers not only on but buttoned.

Cordelia pulls me by the cuff out the back door and over to the side steps where a jumble of people, some of whom I recognize from the drunken Twister debacle, mill around.

"This is Love," Cordelia says to no one in particular. I feel like I'm on display for the group. Various nods and hellos, and then, just as I'm about to feel seamlessly integrated and semi-part of something, a tap on my shoulder produces an instant hush of the mingle-chatter. I look to see my father standing behind me, doing the I'm-a-fun-principal thing, smiling and saying "Hey" rather than "Hi" to the students near me. Cordelia raises her eyebrows. One ruddy-cheeked cute boy nudges the one next to him.

"Hi, Love," Dad says. "Mind if I steal her away for a few minutes?" It's as if he's cutting in on the dance floor, but no one cares. I let my dad direct me to the faculty horde, who stand with coffee cups and briefcases, talking about diversity and Dante, and—already—exams. Exams aren't administered until late fall.

When I free myself from this-is-my-daughter-dom, the first period bells are chiming away, playing the school hymn, "Green Though Yet It May Be"—no clue as to what that means yet, except that some old rich guy who was in the class of 1801 or something and gave a shitload of cash to the school decided "Green" would make a good school song.

And so it is ringing and chiming as students flurry to their classes, and I start to pick up the pace because I have math first and don't know where it is. Or where my schedule printout is that contains vital info such as the name of the buildings where my classes are, my student ID number, my name, my brain, my life. I wind up booking it over North Campus, past Whitcomb, home of the hottie, and back to my house, where I've cleverly left the schedule on the kitchen table, directly under my ring of orange juice. Out the door, I run toward main campus and stop only when I reach the front of Maus Hall. Eek! (Eek = Oh, my nondenominational God!) My schedule conveniently tells me I was supposed to be in Rollinson Hall for math eight minutes ago and yet conveniently denies any map or plans as to where I might find said building out of the sixty-some-odd brick and ivy structures on Hadley Hall grounds.

"Excuse me," I say to the nearest person. "Do you know where Rollinson Hall is?"

"I'm a freshman," the kid says, shrugging a sorry and walks off.

"Excuse me," I say to the next person, a girl in a twinset with a tan so evenly distributed it's got to be a mist-on. "Do you know where math classes are held? Rollinson Hall?"

She pauses on her cell phone and looks at me. "Math?"

Yes, I want to say, as in arithmetic, simple or complex equations, reckoning of inequality in numerical form, but instead I just cut to my already infamous chase: "Rollinson Hall."

She mutters into her tiny phone and says, "Probably that way. Go to the basement of the rectangular building there and look in the lab."

Suddenly I have visions of myself being on *Hadley Hall Survivor,* where I have to outwit and outplay the preppy masses, using my wits as my guide. In this ridiculous vein, I set off to the building where tan phone girl pointed, and take the stairs two at a time.

In the basement, the air is cool, the walls thick concrete, decorated with student art and murals. I search for signs of mathematical life, but find only a sculpture gallery (Note to self: Naked male sculptures of people currently enrolled at Hadley Hall = sexy and disturbing at the same time), a huge auditorium presumably where FRIDAY FILMS! are shown, and then a blue metal door marked LAB. Finally. I open it up, prepared with my "I'm new/sorry I'm late" excuse already forming on my lips, but when I get inside, there's just tables and paper cutters and black and white prints and another doorway marked LAB 2. Now I really feel like I'm on a surreal game show and decide to just open the next door to see if a dragon or faded pop star will pop out and explain the rules to me.

But instead I hear, "Didn't you see the developing light was on? Close the door, quick."

My eyes take a minute to adjust to the dark, and when they do, I can make out a tall figure in the corner.

"I'm looking for Rollinson Hall," I say.

"Robinson," the guy says.

"No, Rollinson," I say. I step closer toward him, watching him slip a large piece of white paper into a shallow tray. While I wait for him, an image seeps onto the once-blank paper. Ah, I may be slightly slow, but at least I know where the photo lab is now. Not that I take Photo. Not that I'll be allowed on campus if I get expelled for cutting classes on the first day. "Sorry—Rollinson?" I ask again. My voice goes up, too girly, and I annoy myself.

The guy flips his hair up and I see that he is no other than hottie himself. He comes over to me and speaks slowly, like I'm an exchange student. He points a finger into his chest, "Me, Robinson."

"Oh, your name is Robinson." *My name is Loser,* I think, but don't utter.

"Yes, Robinson Hall. How can I help you?"

If the room wasn't dark, he'd see my red face and red hair, my whole self a blend of embarrassment. "I thought you were my math building."

Even in the dim lighting I can see his mouth twist, half smile, half dumbstruck by my weird comment. I start to back out of the room. "Sorry to bother you."

I'm back at the door of the naked-man sculpture gallery when he—Robinson—reappears and says, "Hey, wait up. You must be late for Trig with Thomspon, which means you're in trouble. I'll walk you over."

Oh, my God! is what I'm thinking when he actually starts to accompany me to class, but what I say is, "Great T-shirt." Smooth, Love, smooth. Robinson's got an old General Public shirt on, the one with the eyes and weird wing logo.

Robinson glances down to remind himself what garb he threw on this morning. "Yeah?"

"Yeah," I say and then, "I really like 'So Hot You're Cool.' " It's my favorite song on that disc. Another gift from Mable.

"I don't actually know their music," Robinson says, semiadmitting lameness. "A friend in New York gave this to me." From his voice I can tell he means a girl, but I don't ask for details and he doesn't offer any up either.

Short from carrying my books in a satchel, Robinson's escort service (I wish) proves to be very gentlemanly and helpful. It's the first time he's been mistaken for the math building, despite the only two-letter difference in spelling. But the error is in my favor, I feel, as he deposits me at the threshold to Trig and actually shakes my hand. Skin on skin contact. I try not to melt into the floor or blush or barf. For now, I'm successful.

"Thanks for being my personal map," I say, leaning up against the wall, wishing the world would fade into the background and Robinson and I would have all day to talk.

"Sure thing," he says, slicking the hair out of his eyes. His white shirt is untucked and stained on the sides. He notices me notice this. "The curse of photo fluids. I have a habit of wiping my hands on my shirts. Shouldn't wear white, I guess."

The door opens and a slim, brown-bobbed lady appears with her arms folded against her nonexistent boobs. "If you're done socializing, I have some trigonometry to explain." She eyes me up and down as if inspecting for turds. "If it's not too much trouble."

Robinson shakes his head, clearly having dealt with Ms. Thompson before. I follow her inside but turn back just in time to get in, "I'm Love, by the way."

Robinson smiles his Cheshire grin, his eyes slightly sleepy. "I know who you are," he says in a near-whisper and walks away.

Inside Trig Hell, I proceed to be lectured by Ms. Thompson, who doesn't understand the overwhelming size and scope of the campus confusion I've had.

"I'm sorry if the campus seems large to you, Ms. Bukowski, but I sincerely hope you'll familiarize yourself with the maps provided in your new student handbook." Yeah, okay, bitchy lady, except I didn't *get* the handbook and new student welcome package because the administration office just assumed I'd be fine, what with being the principal's daughter and all.

"Sorry," I say for the third time.

Thompson fiddles with the yellow stick of chalk in her hand. "If your tendency toward tardiness should present itself again . . . Well, let's just try not to have this happen."

She doesn't say I will most certainly be sent to the principal's office, but I can hear it in her voice. Um, Hi, Dad. After what's left of class, Thompson gives me another blurb about how "that boy" isn't worth jeopardizing my academic future. It's the first damn day of class and already I have apparently succumbed to the evils of the male student body. Robinson Hall is "that boy." Can't say her warning made my interest in him dwindle.

Second period is Great Works and Performances. In Hadley-speak this means English, and luckily for me, a girl from my math class looks over my shoulder at my schedule and swivels my body so it faces a set of stairs. "Up two floors and third door on the left."

Unlike the math and science rooms where chairs with those little bubble desks are set in neat rows, the English rooms are straight out of the catalog. The room is sun-filled and warm, with hanging plants and stacked books. In the center of the room there's a large oval table and sturdy wooden chairs. I find a seat and slip my backpack under the table, following suit with everyone else. Ancient graffiti pocks the surface in front of me, quotations from 1960 (CLAPTON VS. HENDRIX = THE ULTIMATE SHOWDOWN, OUT OF VIETNAM!, LOVE YOU—ah, the irony of my name yet again), obsolete initials, a tiny perfect star someone—maybe many students over the years—has traced again and again. Around me, students sit down and chat to the familiar faces (total sum of familiar faces for me = 0), leaving the obligatory empty spaces next to me—New Girl cooties. The last to arrive is a guy in a gasoline attendant jacket that bears the name Gus across the left breast pocket. I assume this isn't his name, but I could be wrong: Dad is always saying not to go on assumption but on fact merged with feeling. He's also prone to using sports analogies despite not being particularly inclined toward athletics. Go team!

"If I am not for myself, who will be for me? If I am only for myself, what am I? If not now, when?" Mr. Chaucer writes "Hillel," presumably the author of this quote, on the wall-sized blackboard and slugs his worn leather case onto the table. "Welcome to my class. I'm Mr. Chaucer, as you may know—and yes, I've heard the jokes before. You might think that I was destined to become an English teacher due to my name. Possibly." He looks around the table at all of us, and we follow his gaze. "Names introduce us but aren't ours by choice usually, so they may not reveal as much as we think."

He asks us to go around and say who we are without using our names, just bits and pieces of what we do, what we like. For once I am free of being Love Bukowski. With four people to go, I suddenly feel scared shitless—if I'm not Love with a capital L, who am I?

One of the field-hockey-playing girls goes next. She's got car keys in her hand, and fiddles with the Tiffany key chain as she speaks. "I play defense, transferred last year from Andover, and I like long walks on the beach." A boy in a ripped Hadley Hall sweatshirt says in a fake-cough, "Not just walks," which lets us all know that he's personally given Ms. Tiffany a sandy night to remember. She smiles and shrugs.

Long walks on the beach? I'm in a beer ad, minus the bikini and hot twin sister. I have to come up with something more than my shopping tastes or food preferences. These kinds of exercises always make me nervous. There's clearly a cool response, or at least one that flies under the collective student radar but is still truthful.

One more to go. The guy next to me, not Gus the gasoline man but someone who will reveal himself in a minute, sits silent and hunched down in his seat. Then he sits up. I catch a glimpse of him from the side. Beautiful. Not hot; beautiful, like one of those English guys in a historical movie. Dark coils of hair dip into his eyes. Green? Hazel? Can't tell. And he's kid-caramel brown from the summer. He looks around the table, unafraid, and says, "Man of words, man of music. A voice like sandpaper and glue." He stops.

Mr. Chaucer's grinning, and for a second I'm puzzled—then I click into action. Before I can introduce myself with saying "Love" I say to Quiet Boy, "That's a David Bowie quote."

"Quotation," interjects Mr. Chaucer. "And she's correct."

"Yeah." Quiet Boy nods, not ashamed at being found out. "It's what he wrote about—"

"Bob Dylan," I blurt out. "Whose real name is—was—Robert Zimmerman."

Mr. Chaucer stands up. "Which brings me to my next point. Do we think that the great Dylan, the infamous poet of a generation, the father of music as we now know it, would have gotten all the accolades if he'd kept on being Robert Zimmerman instead of *the* Bob Dylan?"

Mr. Chaucer segues into name-changing as a cultural and societal measure of something—something I'm supposed to be following but really I'm sidetracked by Quiet Boy and his slightly obscure Bowie knowledge. I decide to test him after class. We're given an assignment: to read the first half—not the first chapter, the entire first half—of *The Scarlet Letter* by Monday. The first paper's due at the end of next week. What happened to that beginning-of-school grace period?

Quiet Boy stands up and I swallow and cough to get his attention. He turns to me. "Did you know that "man of words, man of music" is actually not a quote—quotation—of Bowie's, but a title?"

"Oh, yeah?" He's smirking so I can't tell if he's humoring me or impressed.

"It was the original name for the *Space Oddity* album," I say, and he opens his mouth to respond but Mr. Chaucer interrupts him.

"Jacob, let me steal Love away from you for a moment." The corners of Jacob's mouth turn up and he slides out of the room. Jacob.

With a tiny bit of irony, I remember that Bob Dylan's son is Jakob with a k.

"Love?" Mr. Chaucer, who no doubt can tell I'm in a hundred other worlds, yanks me back to the here and now. "Don't think I didn't notice that you talked your way around the nameless introduction." I shake my head back and forth and sling my bag onto my left shoulder. I can never get a book bag or purse to stay on my right shoulder, ever. Another mystery of life. "Do it now."

"Huh?" I ask, eloquent as ever.

"Don't say 'Love'—say anything else."

I'm halfway out the door at this point and I pause, balancing on the threshold. "I'm on the threshold," I say, not entirely bullshitting.

"Of . . . ?" Mr. Chaucer waits for me to continue.

The hall bell rings, the campus chapel bells chime, and I'm officially going to be late—again—and I shoot a pleading look at Mr. Chaucer, who shoos me out the door with a *next time*. And maybe I would've had something to say, found the right words, if the bells hadn't sounded, but I think—no, I know—that I'm not sure enough of who I am *with* my name at this point to be able to blurt out who I am without it.

CHAPTER 5

I' ve seen pictures of New Delhi streets teeming with people, I've dealt with one horrible Manhattan rush-hour commuter train ride. But the mass of bodies in the Hadley Hall dining hall makes those places feel calm. You'd think that people had never had factory-enhanced macaroni, never experienced the wonder of fro-yo (I'll admit, I was psyched to see a coffee-vanilla swirl on offer today, but still, I didn't scream or butt anyone out of my way to get a taste). Being the unfamiliar one in the dining hall sucks for so many reasons. With no clue what line to get in, I stand for twelve minutes, salivating at the thought of a tuna sandwich, only to find I'm in the utensil line. Nice. Salad stations; hot meal lines; drinks, hot and cold; dessert table; cold-cut bar. So many choices, I hardly have time to throw together a turkey wrap before rushing to my next class.

I do, however, manage to have enough time for said turkey wrap to unroll and empty its contents onto my lap (shredded lettuce = my accessory of choice right now) and look lost as I wander around with my tray-as-shield looking for a seat. Not even my father, who takes advantage of the mayonnaise-laden potato salad, acknowledges me as I drift and bump from one place to the next. I find a chair in what is surely considered the arctic of the dining hall social sphere, but which offers a good view. While pecking at the remnants of cold cuts on my jeans,

I watch bouncy girls and their clots of friends nibble at noncaloric broccoli 'n' salsa combos. I notice guys shoveling fistfuls of deli meats as if they are contestants on a new reality show, and see the other aimless newcomers straggle between bonds of old friends.

Four tables away (an acre in high school dining real estate), two girls eat sandwiches and frozen yogurt, talking and laughing. I want to be them. Not them personally, but part of their friendship. The closest girlfriend I have right now is my Aunt Mable—and she's got decades on me. Someday I'm sure I'll meet someone my age who can be as funny, freakish, and cool as Mable is—but so far, I haven't met her.

"What'cha doing?" Cordelia shoulders me outside the dining hall where I'm breathing in the fresh air, just glad for a hint of personal space. She reads over my shoulder as I check my schedule. Free period. Cool. Except I don't know where to spend it. Without structure, I'm left to more Love-as-a-pinball, rolling my way around campus (Beep! Bling!).

"Me, too," Cordelia says, and motions with her chin to the building directly in front of us. It's the newest of the bunch—glass-faced and tall, with multiple doors and Starbucks-style hanging lights. We are student center–bound, and—just like with movie stars in L.A.—the whole place turns to look at us when we walk in, and then goes back to what they were doing.

"Were they expecting Julia Stiles maybe?" I ask.

"Too classy. Tara Reid—way hotter," Cordelia says, and grabs us a spot on the couch near the foosball table. We watch people compete for control over the Lilliputian soccer players, and sip lukewarm coffees Cordelia procures from the snack bar.

"Anyway," she continues, as if we were just speaking of it, "I hear you have No-Ass Thompson for math. Sucks to be you."

"Pretty much," I say. "Tell me the highlight of your day so far."

"That'd be drama workshop with Herr Fritzman." She sees confusion waft over me. "Herr Fritzman, aka German Drama God. Gay, but totally Pitt-worthy, and so great at making you get to this . . ." Cordelia gestures to her chest.

"Your bra?" I'm not even trying for humor. It looks like Cordelia either has a rash or that the German Drama teacher is doing decidedly unteacherlike exercises in class.

"No, fool. Herr Fritzman—Claus—gets you to, you know, reach inside yourself and figure out what's there. That way, your performance on stage is—an in-depth article."

"Sounds, um, deep?" I say. I just can't stomach one more *who am I, reach inside and feel my innards,* blah blah blah. I'm sinking farther into the grimy couch and a moodswing sponsored by my alter ego known to Mable as Brick. Then Cordelia yanks me out of my sandpit of despair and gloom.

"Someone's checking you out," she whispers, and toes my shin. I look up and see none other than my photo lab buddy, Robinson Halll—so cute he deserves an extra *l* on his name—who guy-gestures at me with his head and takes his place at the foosball table. Nothing hotter than a rousing game of mini-soccer, I tell you. Who knew that spinning a handle and yelling "Dude, score!" would entice me to near-fainting extremes.

"Earth to Love, tune in! Do you need epinephrine, or will you survive?" Cordelia rolls her eyes.

"Clear!" I yell, electrocharging my own heart like a gurney-bound patient on *ER*. "I'm back now. Sorry for the delay."

"No problem." Cordelia tips the rest of her coffee back into her mouth and sighs. "He's totally taken; he and Lila Lawrence are practically conjoined twins. But I completely get the vibe—what's not to like?"

Taken? I try to have this not register. I want to be the kind of girl who doesn't care. I'm fairly good at that, since with my claim to fame as Friend-Girl (Friend-Girl = me as a superhero, minus the tights) I get a lot of practice at lusting/loving from afar and never admitting to it. Lila Lawrence? No idea what two-by-two photo claims her in the face book, but damn sure I'm looking her up.

"I'm not into him or anything," I say, taking a huge interest in stirring invisible grains of sugar into my coffee. "He was just nice to me earlier today—that's all."

"And you practically fell at his feet at Whitcomb." Cordelia throws this in, sharp as a tack, a hawk, a needle—whatever is too sharp for its own good. "Besides, he's a senior, you're a new sophomore, and despite the age-old senior-sophomore hook-up scene, it's never gonna happen. He's, like—and no offense . . ." (of course, this means take offense) "—he's out of your league."

"Sure," I cover. "He's cute, but not really my type." Out of my league? Am I the NFL? The ACL? The ACLU? In my head I think: a) I am not a league and b) Just say I were a league, who's to say what guy is out of it? Another way of responding to that would be "screw that— I can get him if I want to" but since I'm not Tara Reid in the latest teen flick, I just shrug.

"Oh, yeah? What is your type?"

"Eyes of David Bowie, grin of John Mayer, coolness of Elvis Costello circa 1979, and . . ."

Cordelia cuts me off. "So basically, obscure musicians turn you on."

"John Mayer is *not* obscure," I say, clearing our paper cups and reaching, yet again, for my schedule.

"Whatever." Cordelia stands up. She does what I call girl maneuver #2 (#1 being hair flip with a giggle), the yawn-stretch combo that makes her sweater ride up just slightly so it shows a good three inches of midriff skin, then coyly tugs it down. Up until right then, I'd wanted to invite her to come to Slave to the Grind, Aunt Mable's coffeehouse, this afternoon, but I decide against it. Cordelia is fine, and I'm grateful for her company and Hadley Hall expertise, but she's never going to be the friend I've always wanted. "See you later?" she asks.

"Of course," I say, and head off in search of French III, then American History, and then a subway ride to relief—the latte lounge at Slave to the Grind.

"You again?" Robinson Hall gracefully claps my airborne schedule between his palms (oh, to be born a piece of paper) and hands it to me.

"Thanks! I'd be lost without this." I stick the schedule in my bag and pull a couple of strands of copper-colored hair in front of my eyes. A nervous habit. Robinson waves to a group of girls— Cordelia included—who wave back and clearly make note of him talking to me. Great. Now I can be the subject of Hadley Hall tongue-wagging without any of the glory and fun of actual tongue-wagging.

"Let me know if you need me to be your map," he says, and walks off, feet shuffling along the brick-edged path. Be my map? He could be my foot fungus and that'd be swell.

The language classes are held in the rotunda—a huge, yes, round building with an open top (where the biweekly conversationals take place) and rooms on the bottom (where the thrice-weekly classes are held). While waiting for French III (Imagine! *J'attend!* = Imagine, I'm *waiting* rather than showing up late) to start, I check out the bulletin boards. Announcements for the literary magazine, band tryouts, play auditions, and senior-taught electives flutter in the open-door-inspired breeze. I'd like to do something extra, and not just for college applications (since you can't list the 1970s lyrics I've committed to memory as counting for extracurricular activities).

I miss being in a band—I miss singing. I'm humming to myself (Chicago's "Baby, What a Big Surprise," if you must know—an Aunt Mable hand-me-down song that rocks) when I see the fine print on the senior elective ad. Extra credit, one night a week, cool subjects (Art as Metaphor, Chocolate for Beginners, Fiction into Film—that one, I notice, is conveniently taught by R. Hall. Must be Robinson Hall, my hottie, right?). So I put pen to paper, determined not to be "cut from the team"—out of my league indeed. We'll see.

Friend-Girl, step aside. Girlfriend wants a shot at wearing the cape. Just for kicks, I also take down the email of a couple band members searching for lead singers. They all sound vaguely lame if you go by cheesy email monikers: Pianoman4, SinginDiva, GeetarGod, DrakeFan. I rip one off anyway, then I head to Français.

At Slave to the Grind, mellow tunes drift from the speakers, and hot cocoa laced with espresso drifts into my stomach. Aunt Mable sends over a caramel-coated graham cracker (she makes them herself) dotted with tiny chocolate chips and baby marshmallows—my own indoor s'more.

"Do you mind if I take this?" A girl I recognize as one of the shiny field hockey players gestures with the sugar shaker. Quite frankly, it's a relief to see a female other than me have an interest in real sugar as opposed to its various substitutes (I will puke if I hear one more thin girl mention the caloric deficits she's managed to accrue throughout the day—Look, ma, no fat! No fun! No food!).

"Sure," I say. "Sugar away."

"It's just so much better than the other fake shit," she explains.

"Seriously." I nod. "Nothing splendid about Splenda."

She sits near me and we proceed to make up alternate names for sugar-substitutes—*Tasti-lame*, *Air-honey*, *BullSugar*—then progress to Hadley Hall and what we did over the summer.

"I volunteered full-time at this shelter, The Umbrella Project. You know, like everyone deserves to be under one umbrella, dry and with a home."

"Sounds interesting," I say. "Was it a good experience? I think if I did that I'd have a really hard time separating at the end of the day."

"Tell me about it." She swallows hard and plays with a strand of her perfect hair. "I'd be around these girls with nothing, no one, no support, and then I'd go home and my slightly psycho mother would be like, 'Do you want to get a massage this weekend or a pedicure?' and I'd sit in my room feeling guilty."

Hard to believe she's so untrue to her stunning blondness and tall-glass-of-water body. If she weren't so genuine and nice—at least so far—she'd be hugely annoying.

She tells me about the young moms, the street life, the fastest way to make lasagna in bulk (don't precook the noodles, just add a big can of diced tomatoes).

I tell her about moving to Hadley. "I got totally lost this morning."

"Campus hazard, without a doubt."

I reminisce with my own sad self about sexy Robinson and then reenter reality. "Luckily, someone showed me the way."

"Oh, my God—I love this song!" she blurts out, and then hits herself in the forehead. "Could I sound any dorkier?"

" 'Perfect Way,' " I say, to let her know I know the song, too. "Now this is truly an eighties classic—so underrated."

She agrees, and we sing along for a verse or two and then she stands up to go. "You have a really good voice."

"Thanks," I say.

"Don't say 'You do, too,' because I know I suck." She does, but she's fun. "You can't have everything."

Later, when she's left to go to varsity practice, I realize I haven't even asked her name. But at least she's proof that good conversation and potential good friends are out there. And that, no, you can't possibly have it all. Right?

When the caffeine-crazed crowds thin out, Aunt Mable comes over and plops down next to me.

"Ah, Hester Prynne." She eyes my *Scarlet Letter*. "The ultimate in misunderstood women."

"It's good so far," I say. "My enjoyment is only slightly marred by the fact that I have to finish almost the whole thing in a matter of days."

Mable nods. As the light outside starts to fade, I'm suddenly glad Hadley Hall has the somewhat moronic policy of starting classes on a Friday. Maybe the administration knows just how fatiguing first days inevitably are, and how a weekend is necessary to regroup.

"My dad's working late tonight," I say. "Any chance of getting a ride back?"

Mable looks around, and nods. "Sure. But let's order Chinese first. I have a General Gao's craving like you wouldn't believe."

"And lo mein?"

"But of course," Mable says. "But you'll have to sing for your dinner!" She does this all the time—makes me belt out embarrassing show tunes (example = "You're Never Fully Dressed Without a Smile") or Miss America–style ballads in the voice of her choosing.

"If you insist." I dramatically clear my throat.

"Do the Mattress Discounter's ad, but in faux British!" I put on my Gwyneth Paltrow as Emma voice—all upper-crust and flouncy dress—and sing the bargain sleepware tune. Mable's so impressed she begs me for more. "Make up one about this place," she commands. So I improv jingles about Slave to the Grind, alternating vocal style somewhere between Stevie Nicks and Gwen Stephani in the early days of No Doubt. Mable claps and goes to the back of the cappuccino bar to call Peking Dynasty for delivery.

When she comes back, a man in a coat and tie approaches us. First I think he's going to ask Mable for her number, which would be great, since she totally deserves a love life, but then he turns to me—which I first think is pervy—until he hands both of us his business card, which reads blah blah blah VOICE-OVER PRODUCTIONS, WAJS.

"You've clearly got what it takes—or will," he says to me. "Call me if you're interested in recording some ads." It's my very own *American Idol* moment, with no Simon in sight—me, Love Bukowski, on the radio! Hawking pizzas, selling shoes—singing my little inexperienced heart out about dog food. Sign me up.

In the car ride back, Aunt Mable and I drive in comfortable quiet. Then we play a quick round of Radio Love Gods in the driveway. I turn the volume down and say, "This is from . . ." Mable waits patiently. "Robinson Hall to me." When the volume is up again, the station is in the middle of an emergency broadcasting test—one of those offensive, loud, insistent beeps.

"Oops," Mable says.

"Forget it," I say. "It's not worth it." I switch it off. She won't ask, and therefore I offer up my who-is-Robinson tale. This leads us into a brief discussion of senior-sophomore love and lust.

"I loved dating seniors!" Mable gushes. "Burke—Burke, um, wait—I'll remember in a second."

"Burke Fredrillo," I say, reminding her.

"How pathetic! My niece has more of my memories than I do."

"You've told me a bunch of times," I say smiling. "Burke, Burke, first prom and then a jerk." That was the little song Mable had made up to get over her dumpage after said prom.

"Yeah, fine. You tell me your news then."

"Nothing, really. Maybe nothing. Maybe potential."

"Oh, check out the vagueness with which Love speaks! Means trouble's a-brewing."

I push her shoulder and grimace. "No, no, nothing good."

"Well, speak for yourself!" Mable smacks her lips and turns to me. "I just might have a fix-up. My bean supplier . . ." She looks at my face and interrupts herself. "Shut up! Seriously, it gets harder to meet people when you're older. I don't have a hottie in a dorm to drool over. Anyway, my bean supplier has a bean supplier and blah blah blah, the coffee connection is strong. We're all wired from too many shots of espresso."

"So, who is the lucky latte lad?"

"Miles—Miles something or other. God help me remember the current names."

We drift into quiet, each envisioning our own happy endings to imaginary dates, and then I say, "I wish Dad weren't alone."

"Yeah?"

"I mean, I wish he'd date people."

"He will," Mable says, confident. "He needs time."

"Hasn't he had, like, a decade and a half?"

Mable doesn't answer. Inevitably, because I poke and prod, the conversation turns to my mother. Or rather, my attempt at info-gathering about said non–maternal presence in my life.

Forever, my father's point of view, and thus Mable's (though I believe she would crack if given the chance), is that out of sight is out of mind. Either dead or gone, the woman who birthed me serves no role now, so the past isn't worth dredging up. I should remind my dad of this when it's American History exam time and he goes on and on about how the past is so important. Apparently, only where dumping tea into Boston Harbor is concerned, not in matters of maternal mystery.

Lying in bed, digesting the lo mein and the lowdown on the day's events, I think about identification: radio station IDs, name tags, nameless intros, building names, and emails for potential bandmates, and then drift off into a nameless void.

CHAPTER 6

O ne of the weird parts of high school, and maybe this continues when you leave education or pre-twenties life behind—I'll have to see when I reach that stage—is the feeling that each day takes forever. The minutes from first light until the last IM at night stretch out like an eternity, and yet, when I think back on entire years (freshman, for example), I can only recall one or two vivid moments, or a generic feeling that sums up the whole twelve months. Emotionally, each day brings cause for me to run the gamut between relatively calm and collected (not necessarily cool) to head-in-a-gray-cloud funk.

Each day can produce a huge range of feelings: security (Dad and I walk to school together), anxiety (still not entirely sure of where things are, so am either late or too eagerly early), hormonal surge (Robinson waves from across the quad), minor depression (Robinson fails to see me two feet in front of his face at the snack bar), excitement (A- on *The Scarlet Letter* paper), confusion (where will I be in ten years, will I really need trig to function there?) . . . and so on.

And then there are days like today that seem minimally invasive to brain function and emotional well-being. Thor the golden retriever (and when I say "the," I mean one of the plethora of retrievers that constitute the canine population of Hadley) has been barking at the acorn-gathering squirrels that congregate outside of my window, and now I'm used to it. I'm used to my view, too, of campus and the red- and gold-hued leaves, the gentle smoke that wafts from Whitcomb's chimney, the early runners—sometimes I am one of these. Classes are good, and slowly I'm learning the lingo (DSG = day student girl, BG = boarder girl) and the codes of conduct (everyone dumps their bags under huge signs that say DO NOT PLACE BAGS HERE). Cordelia flits in and out of my daily routine, again—not the friend for life, but fun.

And I even have my first real confidante. As of two days ago, I am in cyberspace with DrakeFan@hotmail.com (and yes, I'm aware of the hot male/Hotmail potential—then again, who signs up for free email at vileboy.com?). After staring at the emails I'd written down on the back of my French notebook, I chose to email DrakeFan, a musician whose email I plucked at random from the many on-campus bands. Actually, it wasn't totally at random: It was the least obviously cheese- induced of the group, and I like a Drake's Cake as much as the next person, so I figured I'd go ahead and see what music DrakeFan is into.

Even though my email was of the uninspired "I'm a singer" form and I doubted I'd get a response, DrakeFan wrote back nearly instan- taneously (praise be to the Internet Gods). And not only that, Drake- Fan managed to genuinely entice me to write back to him (also right away) with his verbal quips and tales of world travel. At this point, I don't care who he really is—it's just nice to have a daily (or more true to fact, nightly) email to look forward to. With just wires and ENTER buttons between us, it's been easier (so far) to let my guard down—and a relief to be faceless, known only for my words.

I'm thinking about what I might write to DrakeFan tonight while I jog. Past the health center and funny fish statue and the lower day school, I cut across the back of the science center and make my way towards the real track, even though I have no intention of hauling ass around the blue oval like a track-star wannabe. I like the feel of my sneakers on the cold morning pavement, then how my ankles get icy from the fall dew on the grass. I make the high-jump poles my end mark and sprint the last quarter mile, hoping there's a bench or some-where I can have my asthma attack in peace when I'm done. Winded and wiped out, I get to the poles and find the ultimate in resting spots (not as in graveyard, I am not Goth enough for that); the three-foot thick blue mesh pole-vaulting mat that's just starting to warm in the sun. I lie flat on it, staring up at the sky and trees, and catch my breath.

"Which is exactly why the roles of women throughout much of liter-ature condemn females to be either saintly or—for lack of a better word—slutty," Mr. Chaucer continues, and keeps us all captivated. He's that teacher I imagine looking back on as an adult when someone asks Who's the best teacher you've ever had? He drops movie references (*Caddyshack* yesterday, *Freaky Friday*—the original one—today) to make points that resonate. He knows everything from TRL to MSG, and, if I must say, has the Harrison Ford circa *Raiders of the Lost Ark* good looks (minus the whip).

"But don't you think the dichotomy of virgin-whore is overplayed? An academic male construct?" says Harriet Walters without raising her hand. Actually, few people raise hands at Hadley Hall—it's like some unwritten code that the quasiintellectual debate we're capable of doesn't warrant a kindergarten-style Q&A. Harriet is most likely to go to Smith or Mount Holyoke, where she'll dominate the women just like she tramples the guys at Hadley Hall with her pseudofeminist rant-ings. Actually, she's not too annoying. I like her knowledge of Anaïs Nin and her Dorothy Parker quotes, and the way she changes the un-derside of her hair every other week: blond, maroon, blue—this week she's got Kermit-green poking out.

"Interesting point," Mr. Chaucer says. "One you might explore in the next essay. I'd like everyone to try to investigate the parameters of being female in Jane Austen's *Pride and Prejudice* and *One Hundred Years of Solitude*." It occurs to me that half of the books that are assigned in high school have titles that convey my typical fears. Heh. "And, if time allows, feel free to watch *Fast Times at Ridgemont High* and *The Piano,* and throw those in as focus points, too." Ah, a mere seventy hours of reading and viewing.

"What about the portrayal of women in teen movies—you know, either the hot girl or the less-obviously attractive friend," Jacob the Quiet asks from under his lovely shaggy mop of curls. He looks up. "Isn't that pretty much the same thing as the virgin–whore scenario?" A) Very cool point and B) Was it my imagination, or did Jacob look at me when he said *virgin*?

I complain about the amount of work I have to my dad, who does the understanding smile 'n' nod combo while circling a beat-up Hadley Hall handbook with his infamous red marker. He's had the two-sided (thin for mere incidents, thick for massive fuckups) felt-tip for a long time.

"Finding spelling errors?" I ask, tucking my feet under my thighs for warmth.

"Changing some language, actually. There's some outdated stuff in here, and some that needs reiterating, like parietals." He gives me a look when he says this, as if I've even had *one* occasion to go to a boy's room so far.

"Don't worry about me, Dad," I say. I reach for *One Hundred Years of Solitude* (aka Love's love life).

"I don't," he says, and gives my hand a pat. "You've always known how to be—you don't need a guidebook." He gestures with the Hadley Hall manual. "And I'm proud of how you've done settling in. It can't be easy."

"I'm totally overwhelmed by the amount of work." I gesture with my book to make my point. "It's like each teacher thinks they're the only one assigning reading or problem sets." Problem sets make me think of Trig and Thompson and how my heart sinks every time I even go near the entryway to her room, but I continue. "Did you have this much to do when you were my age?"

Dad ponders for a second, chewing on his pen cap. "I'm not really sure. I don't remember, but maybe we did," he says.

"Well, obviously not enough to make an impact." I smirk.

"I blocked it out, I guess," he says, and thinks of something but doesn't say it.

"What?"

He shakes his head and pats my knee. "Nothing. You keep reading."

I nod, and get back to Márquez and the author's surreal descriptions and dreamlike images. Part of me wants to keep talking with my dad, find out how *he's* adjusting to prep school principalhood. He'd no doubt tell me, and even let me in on some behind-the-faculty news and information, but I know that if I neglect my reading I will lag behind and not be able to catch up. And I know that if I attempt to slide into the subject of my mother, he'll rebuff me.

Plus, according to Cordelia, I *have* to go to the next off-campus bash that falls this Friday, before Columbus Day, which will still give me the rest of the long weekend to immerse myself in fine literature, Blockbuster rentals, and lattes at Slave to the Grind.

Dad looks over at me as he recaps the red pen. "Need anything?"

I think for a minute before responding. "Dad—"

"Love, you know full well I mean from the kitchen," Dad says, already defensive. Crap—his Scooby sense is very strong when it comes to times I'm about to ask about my mother.

"Wait—Dad. Just one thing. When she, Mom, was in school, what was she good at? You know, like did she get all As or try out for plays?" I hate myself when I unintentionally rhyme. "Sports?"

"I didn't know her in high school," Dad says, and his face lets me know that this case is closed for the night. You'd think that with Google and Internet-related answers I'd be able to find out more about the woman who got me into this mess of a life in the first place, but to be honest, I haven't even tried that route. Okay—maybe I typed in my name a couple of times, hoping (hoping = totally panicked about) for an easy link to "from Love Bukowski to birthmotheroflove.com," which of course there wasn't. Which was and is kind of a relief. I guess I know that there's a reason or plural thereof as to why my dad and Aunt Mable don't fill me in. But there might come a time when I need to know, when just poking around for clues (did she have copper-colored hair, too? Did it go white in the front in the summer like mine when I've been at the beach? Did she love artichokes?) isn't enough.

"Correct, correct, incorrect, correct," my math teacher (doesn't math teacher sound a bit like ass teacher?) hands out our equation sets, each with a check or check plus or, in my case, a check minus (minus = minus the fun). The only comfort I have is in noticing the red marks are scripted in the same red that my dad uses.

While listening to another go-round of sine and cosine, I rummage in my bag for a Swedish fish. I'm slightly addicted to the chewy red fish, despite their tendency to get jammed in my molars. My candy-fishing leaves me empty-handed but produces the WAJS card from the voice-over guy. I decide to call him and spend the rest of the class (rest = twelve minutes) scripting the conversation in my head. I'm bad that way—I'll imagine the way a day or interaction will go and thus be disappointed when it goes differently, or I'll try and map out what to say and it comes off sounding so sure and determined that it's more like a speech. Note to self: must mellow. That said, I don't mellow and proceed to call WAJS from the hallway phone that resembles a Superman-style booth, but made of wood circa 1915.

I emerge from the booth as my own superhero—no, not Friend-Girl—she's been skulking down in the depths recently—but Voice-Over Woman, able to sell zit cream and bowel cleanser like no other. Well, maybe. I am set for an audition on Saturday. That means I can't stay too too late at the party tonight, lest my lungs suffer from second-hand smoke and screaming so as to be heard over the obligatory high-decibel music. Plus, I've been falling prey to that midfall syndrome of wanting to sleep the shorter days away, waking only for meals.

"Left foot, red. Left hand, green. Oh, Cordelia's lookin' good," some guy working the Twister spinner narrates.

Cordelia's board game (or, in my case, bored game) partner is one of the MLUTS (Hadley Hall male sluts) of whom I've been debriefed (as in given the info on, not as in anything remotely connected to underwear—although, given the guy's current position on the board, ass-up, hands in an army push-up mode, it's clear he's a boxer boy).

"Oh, shit!" Cordelia says, unsteady. Spence Stiller Heller (aka SShhh . . .), the back end of the cow in the Hadley Hall fall production of *Into the Woods,* comes to join the fun, sloshing beer (pumpkin-flavored in honor of autumn) as he literally bends over backward to be near Cordelia. "Love, Love! Come on!" Cordelia shouts when she sees me leaning on the railing, watching safely from the sidelines.

"No thanks!" I say, trying for cheery and upbeat, not at all snubbing, even though I wouldn't want to be caught dead playing Drunken Twister. First of all, I'm not drunk. Second of all—

I cut my own thoughts off when I notice I'm leaning my ass on a wet patch. Please be just beer, I wish silently to the growing splotch of wet on my backside as I take off my fleece and tie it around my waist. I'm like that girl in the old tampon ad who happens to wear white pants at an inopportune moment, but rather than looking menstrual, I look incontinent. Yummy! I make my way inside in search of a bathroom, but have to go upstairs to find one that's unoccupied (what is it about bedrooms and bathrooms at parties—wait, I'm not an idiot, I know people like the idea of getting it on in small spaces. Nothing more romantic than left foot, toilet, right foot, sink).

"Hey—Love, right?" I bump into a guy I vaguely know is friends with Robinson Hall. Luckily for me, Robinson is not here to witness my peed-in-pants look, and his friend knows my name!

"Yeah, I'm Love," I say.

"I'm Channing." Another one of those only-at-prep-school names, but he's adorable in a *Real World* way (as in he'd be the nice, cute guy who hooks up with the cute girl and then drops her in week five of the show). "And this is Chris."

Chris, the top MLUT at Hadley, is apparently notorious for marking his conquests with a special hickey (he's English, so he calls hickies Love Bites—an omen?) on the belly. This is all courtesy of Cordelia, who has received the belly-mark on two separate occasions.

"Hi," I say, copying my dad's nod 'n' smile.

I make my way past Channing and Chris, finally get to the bathroom, open the door, and turn on the light only to reveal Harriet Walters, the English class feminista, straddling Spence Stiller Heller (aka SShhh), which is bizarre for any number of reasons, not the least of which is SShhh's rather back-end-of-the-cow-like stance on the floor. It's unclear whether they're rehearsing for a scene in the play or hooking up.

"Sorry." I blush and back out. Never underestimate the power of a keg and high school hormones to override any burgeoning political views. SShhh is one of the MLUTs on campus, and I'd have thought that Harriet would steer (Ha! Steer—as in cow!) clear of him, but I guess not.

Outside, I begin the long walk back to campus. The noise of the party seeps out from the house and dwindles as I get farther up the road. It's funny how far away the party house seemed that first time, but now that I've gradually been learning my Hadley Hall geography and getting to recognize the various Victorian and ranch houses on the outskirts of campus, clocking the distance from my house to the T station to Slave to the Grind, the walk back is only about twenty minutes.

Ten minutes into it, with my underwear officially stuck to my butt cheeks, I'm nearly to the intersection near the very south end of campus.

"Hey, Love!"

I spin around. If this moment were a John Hughes movie, Robinson would be sauntering up toward me, hands shoved deep in his pockets so I wouldn't see him shaking, and he'd cup the back of my head, tangle his fingers in my hair, and pull me into him so that we could—

"Oh, hi, Chris," I say to Hickey MLUT.

An ambulance whizzes by, sirens breaking the quiet campus night. Chris points to the blaring and says, "AP—bad scene."

"Excuse me?"

"Alcohol poisoning—some freshman. Pretty lucky for her someone found her passed out in the master bedroom and called 911."

Chris shuffles along next to me. Life is so weird sometimes. I know it's useless trying to plan out conversations (even though I'll probably do it forever) or predict what will be. I sure as hell never pictured walking along in the brisk night, my feet scraping the sidewalk, heading home from a lame party with a MLUT for company. Chris talks and talks, his English accent alluring and distracting. He talks about English sweets (candy = sweets) that he misses from home and whips out—no, not that—a Curly Wurly, a sort-of braided caramel rope covered in chocolate. He walks me back up to my house and we sit in the circle of the field hockey playing grounds.

"You'd look good in one of those little skirts," Chris says, chewing and miming a field hockey face-off.

"I don't think so," I say, not in the way that says *bad body image,* but in the *that's not gonna happen* way.

Just as I'm thinking Chris isn't such a slut after all and our conversation is good, he tries to feed me the remaining bit of Curly Wurly, sliding it into my mouth in a decidedly un-Wonkalike fashion.

"Whoa, there," I say, as if I've somehow stumbled into a Western flick.

"What?" Chris has that guy dopey look on his face, and is leaning in to kiss me when I stand up. He follows my lead like what I'm really saying is *I prefer to be tongue-kissed standing up.*

"I have to go," I say.

"Suit yourself," Chris says Englishly, and then adds, "You'll be back." Unlike a regular dissed guy, he insists on walking me to my front door (proper, or just very clever?). He stands waiting for me to get my keys out.

"Thanks for the candy," I say.

"Sweets," he corrects.

"Sweets," I say, and something makes me want to cry. I wish I wanted someone like Chris, who is nice enough and cute enough, but who doesn't register on a gut level (or below, I might add). Life would be simpler if I could just accept what was put in front of me. I touch the heart-shaped knocker and go inside.

I walk into the kitchen and Dad hangs up the phone quickly.

"Who was that?" I ask.

Dad pauses. "Just faculty stuff," he says. It could be that he's already been alerted to the blood-alcohol incident, or something else entirely. "How was your evening?" "Evening" always connotes a dinner dance with gloves and hair tendrils that intentionally fall from their clasp, but I don't say this.

"Okay, I guess." I poke my head into the fridge in case, magically, a pastry has decided to move in.

"I got you coffee syrup," Dad says. He stands next to me, bumping me out of the way and moving the broccoli and bag of apples (he likes them cold) to the side so he can get at the bottle that's been lying down at the back.

I smile. "Thanks." Since I was little, I've always loved coffee milk. You can get the syrup only in Massachusetts and Rhode Island, where it's made. I've even been to the factory (is there any wonder I am single when I freely admit this shit?) and, as with my Swedish fish fanaticism, I'm quite the coffee syrup advocate. No caffeine, just a sugary coffeelike flavor, like ice cream in liquid form.

I take my milk and watch *Buffy* in rerun. Sipping as Sarah Michelle

Gellar (note to self: Should I have three names? Is that really the secret to success?) ass- and groin-kicks her way to safety, I suddenly know what I'm going to write my English paper on. I'll write about how when women have power they have been seen as scary, like witches in Salem or Henry Miller's plays, or Buffy, or even the sisterly power on *Charmed.* If we are financially or emotionally secure/dominating, breaking out of our molds like in *Pride and Prejudice,* we are somehow dangerous. I climb the spiral staircase up to my tower room and humor myself by thinking I'm somehow mystical myself, that I can snap my fingers or wiggle my nose to get what—or whom—I desire.

After kicking radio butt (a weird image, I admit), I am riding high. I started by meeting Richard Markowitz at WAJS, and instead of a summer job type interview (i.e., Have you worked at The Gap previously?) we went right into the recording room and he put headphones on me. Dad waited in the lobby while I learned not to pop my *p*'s and bust my *b*'s, and smooth talk about pizza and the Marshfield Garden Center. I find out on Tuesday if I get to do a real ad. The money's not bad, but the best part is getting to sing and feel professional in a completely different arena. No school, no dramatics, no crushes or papers—just using my voice.

I blathered my way back to school with my dad, and went for a run, needing to get rid of my nervous energy. With each step, I re-created the pizza jingle (Extra sauce—sure thing! Bet you can't pick—just one thing!). Now, I'm sitting on the steps outside the student center. Saturdays are empty on campus. Day students are home, boarders are either signed out to some DS's house, or studying, or at a sports-related event, or pretending to study while getting felt up in the library. I am none of those things, none of those places.

Before I even realize where I'm going, I find myself outside the naked men statue exhibit. I wander in, shyly gazing up at the rather daunting bronzes. I pause by one lean statue, and crack myself up imagining all the nakedness coming to life. A funny and creepy *Dawn of the Dead*-gone-porn image. As I'm laughing, who should walk in but—

"You could give a guy a complex," Robinson says.

"Oh," I say, steadying myself on a statue's thigh. "I'm less harsh when presented with the real thing." Oh, like I'd know.

"Glad to hear it," Robinson says. I'm afraid he'll walk away, so I search through the brain files trying to find a topic. All I can do is focus on him, his mouth, his eyes, and then his shirt—a white one. No stain.

"You're going to get stained," I say, and point to his oxford.

He looks down. "True," he says. "Any chance you want to be my hands?"

Huh? Whatever that means, yes. Yes, I do.

"I mean," he clarifies, "do you know how to develop film? I've got a roll from August I want to do today."

And so begins my first photography tutorial with Robinson Hall. He leads me into the dark room and shows me the various trays of fluids, the light-exposing machines, the strips of film. My whole body registers every word he says.

"Lay the developing paper in the bath," he instructs. Oh, why not us in the bath together?

"Hey, cool! It's turning into a real picture." He doesn't make fun of my excitement. He nods and smiles.

"I know, isn't it amazing. It's like learning to drive—or how to make an omelet or sex or something . . ." I'm somewhat baffled, but the mere mention of sex and I'm a heart-thumping mushy wreck. But only on the inside. "You know?" he asks.

"Sort of," I say. "You mean how when you don't know what something is, or how it's made and then you find out and it's like *oh, that's what it means.*"

"Exactly," he says.

He explains how to slick the photo to the wall to let it dry without curling, taking my own hand into his, allowing little drops of water

to turn warm between our fingers and run down my arm. I give a little shiver.

"You cold?" he asks. I shake my head and expect him to do the guy
thing, offer me his sweatshirt or something, but he doesn't.

We do test strips to see how much light each picture needs, and I
get to feel the warmth of Robinson's body behind mine while seeing
gradually developing images of him playing in Central Park with his
dog (thank God he's not a cat person—I'd have hives just looking at
the feline), on a beach (the Hamptons, it turns out), and then, the picture to end all of them, a shirtless Robinson working outside as a car-
penter (à la *Trading Spaces*), building bookshelves for the guest cottage
at his parents' summer house.

"What a cool house," I say, pointing to the photo I just slicked to
the wall.

"Dad's pet project," Robinson says. He flicks through other images
to show me another picture. "This is the view from the deck." Rolling
surf, litter-free beaches, and perfect tufts of sea grass. I'm invaded by an
army of romantic and domestic images of the two of us playing Frisbee with the dog, spending the summer in the guesthouse.

And then, when five near-perfect images are done, Robinson says,
"You're good." Heart into mouth. "A good student I mean."

"Thanks," I say. "It was fun." Bland comment on my part, but better than faltering over how he's a great teacher or such bullshit that
only barely covers up my extreme lust. Only when I'm walking back
to my house after leaving Robinson at Whitcomb do I realize I didn't
see any trace of his supposedly serious girlfriend in the photos. There's
hope yet.

CHAPTER 7

I wake up from one of those dreams where your teeth fall out. Not the entire mouthful, but one at the front or a molar. The feeling is similar to the whole Naked in Class Dream phenomenon that everyone has at some point (in my case, I was actually naked on stage prior to performing a song I'd written—doesn't take Freud to figure that one out—not that I've ever been in the buff publicly nor penned my own lyrics . . . yet!). Shaking off the witch-toothed vision of myself takes nearly all day.

In an attempt to better myself and live up to my full potential (I like to sound like old report cards when I lecture myself), I take my journal outside and sit on the porch, alternating between writing down lists of things I like and gazing at the swish of purple skirts as the girls' field hockey team scrimmages on the same spot where Chris the MLUT tried to gargle with my tongue.

Faint cheers and words of encouragement ("Yeah, go for it! You can do it!") make me think of Nike ads and fluorescent Gatorade drinks, but what I write on the unlined pages of my navy blue book ranges from Songs I Will Always Love to Words that I Find Creepy/Annoying (phlegm, itsy-bitsy, nefarious). I also like to jot down words that rhyme or slant-rhyme or somehow flow into each other in case I ever get the guts to write a song in its entirety. And I say entirety, because it's not that

I am so scared or insecure that I've never tried to pen an original tune, it's just that I am the Queen of Unfinished Lyrics (if I am demoted from my superhero Friend–Girl position, I can assume the throne). Earlier pages of the journal reveal songs titles and phrases such as:

> *Wherever Eye Hide*
> *Sleeping softly waking light*
> *Keeping tabs on you tonight*
> *You say you're*

Insert abrupt ending here, only to skip a couple of pages and, right next to a perfectly peeled French beer label from when I first saw the Eiffel Tower this summer:

> *I've heard spring in Paris is the time for love*
> *But here it's August and nearly the end of*
> *Summertime, without you again, streets emptied of their remembered kisses*

And then STOP.

My point is: I try. I just don't get as far as I'd like, and when I go back to see if I can finish the stuff I've started, I feel dopey and whatever feelings I had at the time have dissipated.

Now I write:

> *In the movie of this hour, in the theater I'd have the power*
> *To forget myself and find my scene with you*
> *You'd be cast as Leading Male, I'd be more than just a walk-on*
> *And we'd—*

And just as I'm making progress, I see cleats in front of me. Connected to said shoes are the long, lean, and tan (will they ever fade?) legs of the cool field hockey girl I talked to at Slave to the Grind.

"Hey, Love," she says. And if she hadn't used my name, I might have been able to figure out a way to ask for hers, but we've clearly gone beyond this get-to-know-you point and I'm obviously supposed to know her ID, but I don't, so I have to make do.

"Hey, you," I say, making a note to add myself to my list of things that are annoying.

"Mind if I sit?" She rests her stick on the porch and smoothes her skirt underneath before sitting next to me. I take a good look at her— yup, she's very shiny—and pivot, closing my journal. She asks what I'm writing and tells a story about how her grandmother was a writer but didn't publish her first collection of poems until the age of eight-two.

"I hope it doesn't take me that long to write a song," I say.

"Hey," she points out, "you already rhymed." I smile then twist my mouth. "I'm sure you'll do anything you want." It's so bizarre to hear this from her, not just because we hardly know each other, but because she is *that girl*. That girl that roams the hall of every high school as the human equivalent of a dog in those Purina ads—silky hair and bright teeth and perfect bones. And no doubt a luscious older, probably foreign boyfriend waiting for her to accept his offer of eternal love in his castle. Plus, she's probably got two parents and a life vision.

As the afternoon light fades, she unlaces her cleats, rolls off her socks, and steps onto the still-green grass. "This feels amazing," she says, and pads around.

I'm leaning up against one of the pillars on the porch. "You look like you belong on a beach in the Bahamas or something."

"Really?" Her hair swings as she spins like a kid, dizzying herself until she falls and laughs.

"Don't you wish you were in a tropical paradise?" I say, conjuring up the scene.

She thinks a second and shakes her head. With her arms around herself, hugging against the cold wind, she says, "Not really." When I shoot her a look that suggests otherwise, she explains, shrugging. "I guess I'm always fine where I am. Like, I don't try to be somewhere else, because I know I can't be—so what's the point?"

Her words resonate with me and we part ways and I head inside for dinner with my dad. He's on a multicultural kick that means pad thai, many different bean and grain combos, and tofu sautéed, braised, and grilled.

"Tonight," he says, trying to flip some sort of substance around in a pan like a Food Network chef, "it's garlic and chicken kebabs with couscous and spinach."

"Sounds great, Dad," I say. "Let me clean up and I'll be right back down."

I pull my hair back and wash the grime of the day off my face. I managed only to dot myself with mustard at lunch (as opposed to the more frequent splotch 'n' spill), so my shirt is decent enough to wear out tonight to study at the library. Then I remember that I have my first Robinson Hall–taught senior seminar tonight and whip my shirt off to try to find something more appealing. And then I reconsider—if a clean shirt is what would make Robinson like me, then he's a superficial loser and not worth it. So I put my mustardy shirt back on. Then I think, but if my self-worth is such that I value treating myself well and wearing clean clothes, and *that's* what catches Robinson's subliminal attention, then that's okay. So I get topless again. I'm sure Lila Lawrence, Robinson's supposed amazing girlfriend, would never wear something with lunch hall remnants on it. I walk around my room, poke into my closet, open and shut drawers, and then rationalize again. No guy would ever change his merely slightly dirty shirt just to go to a seminar, a class where the girl he likes *might* notice him. So I put the mustard shirt on again, just in time for my dad to yell up.

"You okay up there?" he bellows. I yell an affirmative, but feel like I'm bonkers just the same.

My footsteps echo in the night-empty corridors. Just being in the building after dark feels illegal and makes me excited and edgy. What if there weren't any other people in the seminar and Robinson became my private tutor? And what if space aliens landed and abducted my brain—oops, apparently that already happened. I open the ridiculously heavy A/V door and go inside to the screening room.

Already there are eight, maybe ten people—mostly underclassmen like myself, mostly girls and film freaks. Harriet Walters gives me a feminist salute and waves me over. I sit next to her down toward the front and compliment her newly silver-fringed hair.

"Very Debbie Harry," I say.

"Cool," she says. I drum the beat to "Heart of Glass" on my knees, picking at the mustard drops on my shirt hem.

Enter Robinson (no, not my plea for virginity-loss, though it could be—more a stage direction). He comes in from the emergency exit (or as Prince or Led Zep would say, *in through the out door*) and pushes up the sleeves on his woolly sweater. He's got that guy in autumn look down, with worn-in jeans and an oversized knitted sweater (probably listed in the catalog with a color name like *storm cloud* or *Atlantic gray*). The kind of top that's made for girlfriends (not Friend-Girls) to steal.

Robinson gives his intro about the translation process of making a novel into a film, and gives some examples of success (*The Godfather, The Age of Innocence, Lord of the Rings*) and, in his opinion, some failures (*The Remains of the Day, I Capture the Castle*). I'm right there with him, listening, and even forgetting that he's the best-looking, most magnetizing person I've encountered thus far until he—in the middle of deconstructing a clip from *Gone with the Wind* (a battle scene, lots of rotting bodies in a field)—slips his sweater off, balls it up, and chucks it to me with a wink. All thoughts of film, literature, and coherency are momentarily out the proverbial window. I hold the item of clothing in my lap like it's a gift from an onstage rock star, then feel pathetic and discard it. Then I think that's rude, so I pick it up and drape it carefully on the seat next to me. Would he care if I took it? I picture myself somewhere, some cobblestone street in London, some cityscape in New York, wearing the sweater while holding his hand.

And it is of course at this very moment that the door swings open and down the steps trots field hockey girl. I wave to her but she's past my aisle already, past all the rows of seats, right up to the front. She doesn't stop until she reaches Robinson and with mercury-style fluidity, puts her arms around him and they kiss. Deeply. And then a peck to seal the deal.

Field hockey girl is—

"Hi, sorry." Robinson pseudoblushes. "I'm sure you all know Lila Lawrence, my girlfriend." We sure do. Now.

Then, as I'm sitting with a sweater I'm sure Lila's been naked in, she comes and plants herself in the chair next to me. She takes Robinson's sweater, drapes it over her shoulders twinset-style, and says, "Thanks for saving me a seat."

Reading and underlining my Howard Zinn text for history class, I'm taking advantage of a free period and relishing what is sure to be one of the final warm days of fall. Soon the leaves will drop and so will the temperature, banishing us to indoor studying. Right now, though, the scene in front of me is perfect prep school, with guys draped over their sophomore girlfriends, heads in laps, fingers in hair. Couples sunbathe back onto their backpacks. Pro-SPFers shield their faces with books and marked-up papers, and I sit observing all this. Not apart in a bad way, just slightly distanced. I count how many senior-sophomore couples there are and come up with eleven.

"Fourteen," Cordelia corrects me when she slings her bag onto the lawn next to me and perches herself on top. "It's the perfect situation, really."

"Home court advantage?" I say, not entirely sure what this means in this context, but my dad's always using sports analogies to get his point across.

"Yeah, kind of. Like, it's just really typical, because in the end, the senior goes away and is free and there's no real thought of being together past the graduation parties. Pretty much Crescent Beach is the breakup point."

"Sounds superficial, but not totally bad," I say. "And what is Crescent Beach?"

"Ah." Cordelia raises her eyebrows. "A beach on the North Shore—it's where many a final party, and a final fuck, takes place."

Got it. Note to self: Would I go, given the chance? Sex on the beach, aside from being a cheesy bar drink, sounds, well, grainy. But I digress.

With Cordelia, and of course now with Lila Lawrence—and Robinson—I haven't really let my guard down. Maybe I've taken a couple of bricks off the top, but no crumbling. That is, except with my email pen pal, DrakeFan, who is a daily part of my life even though I have no intentions of trying out for his band. Being completely natural around Hadley Hall campus comes in fits and starts: A joke slides out unedited or I just blather away about books and movies in Mr. Chaucer's class, but there's still my inner feeling of being on the periphery of it all. And maybe this isn't something that's done to me; rather, I've been wondering lately if I do this to myself, either as a coping mechanism or safety measure. This is what I write tonight to DrakeFan. As usual DrakeFan writes back long enough afterwards to let me know he's read my mail and digested it, but fast enough to reassure me that I didn't bore him too badly.

"Love," Mr. Chaucer says when I go to collect my Buffy meets Powerful Women paper from him today. "I'd like you to consider applying for the Hadley Hall English contest." He explains how it's an annual thing with two prizes, one a series of books about how to find your writing voice and the top prize of having an essay published in an alumni's magazine. I thank him and say that I'll think about it, but I know I won't. The whole thing sounds too blue-blazer-bound and old-boy-networky to be for me. Probably the essay gets published in *WASP Weekly* or *Old Money Magazine,* read by no one but Hadley Hall trustees.

Just when I need a pick-me-up, I get news that I might have a life, a glimmer of hope in my small high school world. No, I didn't win a date with Robinson Hall (or any other would-be glam Hollywood-esque boy), but I rock. I rock and record and am now the official local voice (at least for this one ad) of Pizza Plus, the chain of *thin-crust in half the time* pizza places around Boston. At WAJS, I stand with headphones on and sing the opening line.

"Ohh . . . sausage," I say, and it comes out kind of like a moan. Hard-core blushing on my behalf. Then I talk my way to extra cheese (*oh, it's melting!*) and special toppings (*roasted red peppers, just like in Tuscany!*), but then I fuck up the part about double-size, half-time, golden brown, and have to start over. After four takes, I get it, but go back and "sultrify" the talking part. During playback, I cringe, listening to my voice sound like I want to be naked with the dough. But the studio head pipes in on my headphones with, "Nice work, Love," and gives me a nod. For a second I feel like I'm on my own reality show!

Ohhhhh, cheese! I think to myself on the way out of the station. Yeah, that's perfect. I could be the only woman to have her first serious sexual experience with a bread and mozzarella product. Charming. But since WAJS seems pleased with my work and I'm going home with at least one commercial on my demo reel, I just don't care about giving innuendo to carbs. If all goes well, next weekend I'll come back for another advertisement. This time for—yes, say it with me—*feminine protection* . . . the blessed maxi-pad ad.

I stir the granules of sugar into my decaf (decaf = don't want to be tossing and turning at night any more than I already am with impossible thoughts of stumbling upon Robinson in a half-dressed situation, what with the outline for my history term paper due in two days) and manage to walk my overfilled cup to my favorite spot in Slave to the Grind. The double-sized chair is wedged into the front right corner of the shop, and from where I sit I can see the other coffee customers and still have a street view. This time of year, people are picking up their paces, hurrying from one store to the next, tucking scarves into their coats. The leisure feeling of summer and early autumn has drifted away with tan lines.

I watch a woman with a girl I assume to be her daughter. The daughter shows the mom how to loop her long scarf through and tuck it like in a Benetton ad, and the mother returns the favor by fixing the girl's hair. Tiny moments like this make me feel like I'm stealing something from strangers—maternal comforts or efforts. Not that I know what I'm missing, because I really don't. And when I'm honest with myself, it's more the idea of not having a clue as to the story of me that is bothersome rather than, say, not having a mom to listen to my guitar strumming or tell me about dating in her day. I have my dad, and he's more than enough—plus Mable—and they've both been with me from overalls to my first date. But there's something to be said for missing what you don't know: a mom, a certain boy you like but can't have, or even a part of yourself.

I go for a refill and burn my wrist on the huge brass cappuccino maker. The welt comes up in the shape of a distorted pumpkin smile, crooked and eerily grinning up at me. With Halloween two days away, I wonder whether this is an omen of some kind.

CHAPTER 8

*S*ong of the moment: "Fooled Around and Fell in Love," the 1976 classic by Elvin Bishop. From the first twangy chords, I know I'm going to love this next Time Life CD—they never fail to disappoint. Unlike certain other aspects of my teenage life. I have neither fooled around nor fallen in love (lust, maybe) with Robinson Hall despite numerous encounters in the hallways, lawns, and academic centers of this fine institution. Sadly, I am now in the bizarro-world position of being sort of friends with him (hall friends, no pun intended—the kind of friend you talk to in passing but aren't calling to talk to at night) and getting to know Lila much better. And I wish her arachnid legs and Sleeping Beauty locks betrayed her, but they don't. She's still fun and cool and great at making an ass of herself (for example, she will stuff her shirt with oranges at lunch and look like the citrus Pamela Anderson or, on a dare, write a paper on the erotic undertones of the Gettysburg Address).

All this friendship leaves me and my chest organ (that's heart to the biological-knowledge-impaired among us) in a state of palpitations. So far, I've opted for the Love Bukowski technique of doing . . . nothing. Three cheers for being proactive! Good thing there are no cheerleaders at Hadley; they sure as hell wouldn't seek me out for the squad (short for squadron, which I find weirdly militant and army-based for something that's supposed to be about building people pyramids and school spirit—Give me a B for Brick!).

Not only are there no cheerleaders, there are no pep rallies, no typical high school things. No lockers. There are antique desks in two enormous social halls (segregated by sex, but only for morning assemblies) that were built in the early eighteen-hundreds, and at the beginning of freshman year (or whenever you start Hadley) you get assigned a desk that remains yours until graduation. Actually, until precisely two hours after the graduation ceremony, at which point the campus cleaning crew (the CCC, as in, "Shit, I spilled my beaker of semipoisonous liquids in IPS lab—better call the CCC!") comes and empties the contents into a massive pile outside Grainsburg Hall. According to Lila, students wind up ravaging the remains for CDs, textbooks, and incriminating evidence—love notes and such—and then all that's left are rectangles of stale gum and dried up pens; the debris of all the years of academic gain and sweat.

So for the moment, I am sitting at my desk (halfway back and toward the window side of the room), studying the black streak I've put at the front of my hair in honor of Halloween. Lila and I went to the drugstore yesterday and, on a bit of a chocolate and marshmallow pumpkin high, bought one of those spray-on costume dyes. I could say it looks lame, but I think we both look kind of cool. Not that I didn't notice the eye-rolls from her field hockey teammates, whose idea of nonconformity and fun is shaving instead of waxing.

When morning assembly starts, Cordelia and Lila and Harriet, accompanied on guitar by Mr. Chaucer and Quiet Jacob from class, do an acoustic version of "Birthday" by the Beatles.

"You say it's your . . ." Lila starts. Lila's in the girls' octet group and has a great voice, despite what she said to me originally back in Slave to the Grind when I didn't know who she was.

"Birthday!" Cordelia chimes in. Cordelia's strength is her stage presence, and Jacob and Mr. Chaucer ham it up—and all for me! At the very end, Robinson Hall makes a guest appearance and does a ridiculous falsetto, and smiles broadly at me. It's so weird to see these people I've only known for a couple of months acting silly and singing for me. But I'm glad—relieved, to be honest, since it was entirely conceivable that I'd wind up friendless or forgotten amongst the prep school mobs.

"Happy birthday, Love!" The group ends their skit and assembly resumes with notices of sports and language sectionals, required attendance at various functions—I'm not listening, just thinking about being born and being here.

I am sixteen. Sixteen and seven hours, having been born (according to my dad) at two-thirty in the morning during a windstorm that swept electrical wires onto the streets and caused one of the biggest power outages in East Coast history.

"So in honor of all the energy that went from the city of Boston's supply right into you," Dad says in the dining hall, "I give you your own mode of power . . . sadly nonelectric, but . . ." He reaches into his pocket and produces a small box. I carefully tear at the paper and open it up. On top of the square of cotton wool are three T tokens.

"Subway fare?" I ask, trying to sound grateful.

"Look underneath," Dad says. I lift up the cotton and find one of the most beautiful items in the world—a car key. And not just any car key, the black-topped Saab key that's dangled from Mable's key chain forever.

"The Saab?" I ask.

"It's rusting and has nearly a hundred thousand miles on it, but it's all yours," Dad says. I can tell he's proud of himself for fooling me with tokens and keeping this a surprise. "The tokens are just in case you ever need to leave the car or want a reminder of your past transportation mode."

I hug my dad hard, twice, and do a dorky little I-have-a-car dance.

"I'm going out this afternoon. Or maybe . . ." I look at my watch. Only one more class left today. "Maybe right now."

My dad's face sours. "Love, you know that there are no car privileges during the day." With all the handbook rules, it's impossible to keep them straight: You can drive to and from school, but you can't leave campus during academic hours; you must get written permission from a dorm parent to drive a boarding student anywhere; blah blah blah. I have a car! I can tell he's about to go into principal mode, so I skirt around it by nodding so vigorously I nearly do whiplash damage and thank him again.

I eat my sandwich next to Cordelia and fade in and out of Halloween conversation (not really bobbing for apples so much as bobbing for boys), all the while thinking of myself behind the wheel.

After I finally complete my ten-page outline for my history term paper (the paper itself has to be twenty-five pages long. I can't even write *one* song and yet I'm supposed to produce a tome on treaties and taxes—oh, well), I skip the pumpkin pie dessert my dad's offered and head over to main campus—courtesy of my new car—for the midweek All Saints' Social. The title is from back in the 1930s when Hadley Hall still had a boys' school and a girls' school, separated by geography and academics, but united by dating potential.

Just like back then, the rotunda is turned into a sort of barn dance meets horror show, with blindfolded apple-bobbing and donuts strung up on strings that you have to jump up and try to catch. Masked students (only partially masked these days, due to safety concerns) and vampire-fanged faculty members stroll around offering punch that looks like blood. Rumor has it that the broom closets and music practice rooms fill up on social nights such as these—people hook up underneath pianos or while leaning up against cleaning supplies. I have to say, I've never fantasized about getting together with anyone with the scent of ammonia and Lemon Pledge wafting in the air. Then again, the opportunity hasn't really presented itself.

"Candy apple?" Robinson asks, stretching out a silver tray dotted with bulbous red and caramel McIntoshes. He's dressed in peach-colored long underwear (who ever thought long johns could be so sexy?) with green silk leaves sewn over the crotch. He notices me staring.

"I'm supposed to be Adam," he says.

"Oh, I get it," I say, and divert my eyes. "Thus the apples?"

"Yes," he says. "They're three dollars—to raise money for the annual class gift."

He sees me rummage in my pocket for money but come up empty-handed of change or cash, only my license. Robinson sets the tray down on a bale of hay (the campus clean-up crew will have their hands full later) and studies my photo ID.

"Not bad," he says. Hey, just like the Springsteen song I like—she isn't a beauty but she's okay. In this context, it's not what I'm hoping to hear. Then he reconsiders his word choice. "Just kidding. It's a great shot." He hands me an apple from the tray. "Don't worry about the money. I'll chip in for you."

"I'll owe you," I say, and it comes out suggestively, at least to my ears.

"And I'll hold you to that," he says. "You can give me a ride some time." I nearly choke on my caramel until I realize he means, of course, in my car. He gives my license back and I slip it into my back pocket.

Thursday in morning assembly, Lila Lawrence strides over to me and crouches by my desk.

"I heard you got the forbidden fruit from Adam last night," she says. When I ask her what she means and worry that she overheard my slightly flirty apple conversation with Robinson last night, she says, "I was Eve, but I had too much work to actually put in much of an appearance in the garden. I must've just missed you at the end."

"It was fun, but you didn't miss anything huge. Just a couple of your teammates dressed as the Hilton sisters, which didn't require much costuming," I say. The Nicky and Paris wannabes also made some snide comment about my showing up costumeless and refused to believe I didn't know about the dress-up factor (which I *didn't*). They insisted that because my dad is the principal, I feel I'm somehow outside of the rules and regulations (um, is wearing a costume a regulatory situation?).

Before we can get shushed by my awful math teacher, Ms. Thompson, who lords over the assembly with her checklist of attendance and discipline records, Lila tells me Robinson wants a date . . . with me. And I'm sure I'm going to puke until she explains.

"So, are you up for it? Robinson'll be so psyched—I guess Channing has sort of admired you from afar. He's Robinson's best friend—well, at Hadley anyway." Boarders always make the distinction between their lives at Hadley and their home lives, like the realities are totally separate.

"Oh, Channing. His friend. A double date." I nod. "He'd be my date?"

Lila nods, eyes wide. She's clearly eager for this to happen. "He's so sweet—and pretty cute, don't you think?" I hadn't really noticed, but sure. She senses my hesitation, but I doubt she knows why. Do I really want to subject myself to a first hand account of Robinson and perfect Lila drooling all over their mutual flawlessness? "Come on, it'll be fun."

"Okay, sure. Why not?" I say, and before I know it, I've agreed to drive.

"And you're sure your dad will let you?"

"Pretty sure. Yeah."

And can the maxi-pad ad I recorded make its debut during the date? You bet.

Me, Lila, Channing, and Robinson are parked outside Bartley's Burgers, the place I went with Aunt Mable, and are about to head inside when Lila's like, "Wait a second—can we just listen to the end of this song? I love it." The guys think this is semiannoying but humor her, and I completely understand—you can't leave "Helplessly Hoping" in the middle.

Unfortunately, the song leads seamlessly into me singing "If protection's what you need, maxi-pads are friends indeed . . ." and so on. I reach for the volume but Lila swats my hand away.

"Wait a second . . ."

I try again to get to the volume button, but Lila has inserted herself in front of the control panel. "Shh—you guys, listen!" she says. Channing and Robinson lean forward, and soon Robinson is cracking up.

"Love, this is you, isn't it?" Robinson asks. The guys begin to laugh.

"Maybe," I say. I'm not one to cower based on some menstrual marketing.

"No, it is," Channing says. "You have a really distinctive voice."

I make light of the potentially heavy flow of comments—heh. "Yup, that's me, cramp girl."

"I think you mean Cramp Woman, no?" Robinson asks.

Lila laughs hard and then chokes on her own giggles. "Hey, when you're famous, we'll hear this clip on *E!* when they dig up your past."

Robinson pokes my waist from the backseat. "Hey, if you get lucky, you think they'll let you hawk hemorrhoid creams? They take away the swelling . . ."

I turn around and peer at him from between the seats. "How do you know so much about rectal ointments?"

Lila smiles. "Foiled again, Rob," she says, and we go inside for our burgers.

Lila and I share fries and swap burgers halfway through, which the guys find funny. Channing, Lila, and Robinson are all boarders and they talk about Thanksgiving plans that involve going home to the Upper East Side of Manhattan (Robinson) to visiting his dad out in Denver (Channing) to spending the first half of the day at the teenage shelter where she worked over the summer (Lila) and the second half of the day with her mother at Elizabeth Arden Day Spa to prepare for the formal dinner at her ancestral home in Newport (also Lila). The house is, in Robinson's words, kick-ass, with phenomenal views of the harbor. Hearing this makes the reality of their relationship hit me—they've probably had sex in the water, in her mansion, under the crystal-and-china-set table in the dining room of Robinson's parents' "flat" (for some reason, he uses the British word for apartment, which could be affected and maybe is, but still strikes me as cute. The guy could vomit on me and I'd still be attracted to him). I say how I'm destined to be marooned on campus, trapped in faculty housing with multiple turkey dinners and the English exchange student (the school gets one per year from St. Paul's School in London) who has to stay with us until the dorms reopen.

After we drop the guys off at Whitcomb, Lila and I drive around the campus for a while before I circle in front of Fruckner House, where she lives.

"You think you can do me a favor?" she asks.

"Sure," I say. "Of course. And thanks for tonight, by the way. It was actually fun."

"Oh, shock of all shocks, Love has fun! Anyway, I have an, um, appointment in the center of town tomorrow afternoon—can you drive me? If I walk, I won't make it to practice in time."

"Yeah, just meet me at the back parking lot," I say. "And don't forget to sign out." Lila makes a face that says *duh* but doesn't say it, and gives a wave as she walks to her dorm.

Winded and with that simultaneously hot and freezing feeling (freezing thighs, hot face) of a nearly-winter postrun, I collapse onto the high-jump mat and tuck my hands into my sleeves for warmth. I'm wearing a Hadley Hall sweatshirt—my first—and I let myself drift ahead in time to when the thing is worn and faded. How many days and years will have passed? How many kisses delivered to my mouth? Tears wiped on the sleeves?

Suddenly, the mat dips behind me and makes my head tip back.

"What the hell?" I ask, and prop myself up.

"Oh, hey, Love." Robinson exhales and breathes hard. "Quite the coincidence."

"What brings you to my special running recuperation place?" I ask. "Stalking me, are you?"

"Yes, you found me out, I am obsessed. . . ." He makes a crazy face with wide eyes and claw-hands, and then we lie in silence as the wind whips the empty-limbed tree branches back and forth. "I love it here."

"Here, Hadley Hall or here, the blue squishy mat?"

"Both, I guess." Robinson keeps his body still but turns his face so it faces mine. We're maybe two feet away from each other on the mesh surface. "I mean, my whole family's gone to Hadley Hall—four generations. So, yeah, I think it's pretty cool. Even though it's too much work and I hate my dorm parents."

"I thought the Von Tausigs were supposed to be cool," I say.

"In theory, but not to me. Somehow they got it into their heads that I'm this uptight New Yorker with a chip on my shoulder about listening to authority. Which is complete bullshit, since, if anything, I'm way too play-by-the-rules."

"So they're out to get you?"

"In a word, yes. I think it's their goal for this year. They're placing bets: Will Robinson fuck up before he graduates?"

"And what are the odds?"

He shrugs. "Don't know." He moves his arm so the edge of his jacket brushes my sweatshirt sleeve. He sits up and looks down at me. "Wow, it's so bright." He stops short of touching the Hadley Hall lettering on the sleeve of my sweatshirt.

"I just got it at the bookstore," I say. "It's very, very new. Like me."

Robinson smiles and tilts his head. "You're not as new as you think," he says.

"Oh, really?" I look up at him and wish the rest of the world would sink into the ocean and I could reach up and pull him down to me.

"You play up the New Girl thing, but I think you get it. You have your place here."

I think about asking what place that is, what my role is in his mind, but I don't. For once, I don't prod and poke, I just enjoy my few minutes of morning with this incredible guy. This incredibly taken guy.

I lean up on my hand. "I've got to go," I say and roll my way off the mat. Robinson doesn't move. He just does what guys do really well: watch you walk in such a way that lets you know they haven't taken their eyes off you for a second without saying anything.

CHAPTER 9

*I*t's not without irony that I am offered the holiday series of ads for Mattress Discounters. I belt out their jingles and pump up their slogans, enthusiastically record the slashed prices and pre-Christmas deals with my best future-singing-sensation voice. The manager at WAJS calls me after the double session with some news. I figure my run is up and I'm fired, but instead, the bedding big shots are so psyched about my performance that they give me a bonus of . . . no, not money. No, not fame. The mattress of my choice.

I take Mable with me to pick out my first queen-sized bed and we're given the spiel about different coils and ticking (ticking = the thread color on the mattress—um, who cares? I do, I pretend, since I'm now a mattress world insider).

"This one's cushier," I say flopping down on a sheetless bed.

"But this one is firm. And as you get older—don't look at me like that, Love. As you get older—and you will—a mattress with support is key," Mable says.

"What's the point of even having a queen-sized if I'm destined to spend the rest of my life alone?" I ask, full of mock woe-is-me. The store manager asks if I've made my decision. I tell him I need a minute.

Mable says, "It's not so bad sleeping alone, Love."

"Hello? I have *always* slept alone," I say a bit too loudly, drawing attention from nearby shoppers who flee from me.

"Speaking of which, I want you to meet my coffee distributor." Mable has a goofy look on her face. "You'll really like him. I do. I think."

"Has he made it over the three-date hurdle?" I ask. Mable has a habit of chucking men out after the third date when she says they stop listening and asking questions and just wait to, well, count the coils on your mattress.

"Actually," she admits, "we're way past that."

"Sounds like I should meet him," I say. At least this explains why Mable's been slightly less available of late. She's busy having a love life. While I, Love, have none myself.

I wind up choosing the semifirm queen-sized with the extra layer of quilted padding on top and need to then spend money on deep-fitting sheets. Sheets that might only ever know me. The ticking is aqua-colored.

"One, two, three, four!" Harriet Walters leads in with the bass and Jennifer with Some Unpronounceable Last Name drums. I follow the lead guitarist, Chris the MLUT, of all people, and miss my cue. Again.

"Sorry," I say, and tuck the still-Halloween-black strand of hair behind my ear. I bite my lower lip at a dry patch and wince when I do it too hard. My face, hands, and lips are already chapped from the dip in temperature this past week.

"From the top," Harriet says, and counts again. We're supposed to be doing a cover of Cyndi Lauper's "True Colors" (you know, the pretty ditty about everyone being beautiful like a rainbow? I seem to remember catching the video on late-night VH1 Classic and she's gazing into a puddle or something. It's kind of cool), but with a massively hard edge, loud guitar. As the lead singer I'm meant to be raspy and wild, but it's not going well.

Harriet offered me an audition when she heard me singing "Old

Man" while waiting for Mr. Chaucer. Quiet Jake was listening, too, I could tell, but didn't give me any opinions or trivia about Neil Young. Harriet started TLC (Tastes Like Chicken) as a freshman, but changed the format last spring having decided that "the post–Lilith Fair/Amos/McLachlan thing was over and exclusionary." So she got Chris to join, and he's not a bad guitarist, I have to say.

I, on the other hand, am sucking hard-core. Carrying the tune— fine. Remembering lyrics—absolutely. Being harder-edged and rocking out—not so much. I'm just more folk rock than TLC wants, and no matter how much I contort myself, it's clear to all of us that I'm not a good fit. Chris, Harriet, and Jennifer La Shnonignalfreusen (or whatever her name is) are nice about it, complementing me on my voice, but we leave it at that.

I walk back from the music building and—not surprisingly—take the route back home that leads me past Whitcomb. I count the windows up and over until I can figure out which one belongs to Robinson, give myself a thirty-second grace period of lusty longing, and move on. If only the rest of my emotions were that easy.

As I'm walking away, the front door of Whitcomb squeaks open and I take a glance over my shoulder. Channing, pea coat–clad and lankily appealing as an Irish setter (and I do like dogs), bounds out to greet me and offers to walk me home.

"Good thing I didn't drive," I say and let him. He's pleasant enough company and attentive, guiding me around a fallen branch and asking me about my classes—which ones I like (English, Art, Ethics, History, Intro to Chemistry, Senior Elective) and which ones I don't (Math, Math, Math).

"You like your elective with Robinson?" Channing asks, seemingly agenda-free.

"I do," I say. "It's fun. I mean, pretty much we get to watch movies and talk about them and compare them to the book—what's not to like?"

"I'm not a fan of the *Emma/Clueless* connection," Channing says, in reference to last week's lecture. "I'm more of a *Heart of Darkness* into *Apocalypse Now*."

"Wasn't that only loosely based on the book, though?"

Channing looks impressed. I may not be hard-rock chic, but I know my movie scoop. "True. But I'm just saying that I like those kinds of movies better. Actually Robinson was the one who first made me sit down and watch *Apocalypse*—he's way into it."

We debate the merits of *The Maltese Falcon* in print versus on screen, and then I'm on the top step of the porch and Channing's on the bottom. Before I can even think (let alone overthink) about the romantic undertones of his chivalrous walk home, Channing and I are kissing. With his arms around my back he pulls me in, and I can't help but respond in kind. This lasts for a minute or two and ends with the porch light flicking on (thanks, Dad!) and me rushing inside.

Dad gives me a short but pointed lecture on public displays of affection and how I'm really a representative of Hadley Hall by way of his principalhood and I need to monitor my behavior, etc. Fine. Then, just as I think my good dad has been replaced by the prep school body snatcher, he stops me halfway up the spiral stairs and interjects, "Do you like him, though? I know Channing a little through the student government. He seems upstanding."

It occurs to me that this is Dad's way of trying to deal with his daughter getting manhandled (okay, lightly pawed at), making the boy attached to the lips seem great. He's never really had to come face to face with my face to face, so to speak. And it must be strange.

"I'm okay, Dad," I say.

He nods, and for one second I think he might cry. Which would make me feel horrible. *Please, don't,* I think. He doesn't. "Just . . ." I assume he's going to say *be careful* or something, but he adds, "Just be sure to be yourself. You're . . ." He doesn't complete the thought, but butts in on himself. "Channing would be a lucky guy to be with you."

"I don't know what I think yet," I say. "Too soon to tell. We've just begun filming." Dad is well aware of my camera-mind tendencies.

"Well," Dad says, "let me know when you make some progress— you know, when you're past the first shot."

"Establishing shot," I say. "And, in case you're wondering, I am not part of Tastes Like Chicken. I'm too Fiona and not enough Benatar."

"Whatever that means, I hope you're okay with it."

"Getting there," I say, and take the last steps two at a time.

The slight puffy-lipped postkiss feeling fades after a few minutes in my room. I sit on my bed and look out the window at the dark campus. Whitcomb lights are on. I try to redo my kiss with Channing, dissecting his moves and touches—both up there on the sliding scale of physicality, but something's off. I'm not Friend-Girl with him, that's a plus. But I'm not sure I want the other side of that. It's all too nice—me 'n' Channing and Robinson 'n' Lila and drive-ins and burgers (okay, not that I've ever been to a drive-in, but still). I feel like a fraud. I like kissing—okay, I *love* kissing—if it's a good kiss and attached to a good person, but even though Channing qualifies as all of that, I feel like I did with the tryout tonight: not really me.

How many words can I think of for sluggish and distracted (lethargic and preoccupied, to name two)? I wish I felt connected to math—I mean, I have before; I like doing algebraic equations and geometry— but this year, Ms. Thompson is the bane of my academic existence. The wart on my hand. The stain on my dress. A callus on an otherwise smooth and pedicured foot. And I mention pedicures because after school today I'm blowing off studying for another math "quizette" (Thompson's lame attempt at making tests sounds cute, I guess), and going with Aunt Mable for a belated birthday treat: spa pedicures. So while my body is in math class, my butt is (uncomfortably, I might add) perched on one of the ancient wooden chairs, and my face is forward toward the blackboard, my mind is swirling with Double-Decker Red, Ballet Slippers Pink, and all of the finery OPI has to offer my toenails.

When I tune in, however, I'm greeted with, "And if Love Bukowski's test is anything to go by, you all need to spend more time than you have been going over this stuff." I so dislike when teachers use words like "stuff" or "whatever" and try to sound young and hip when really their facial hair and cruel eyes and burned-out view on life defy any youthful spirit. Okay, that's harsh. Not every faculty person is like that—not Mr. Chaucer or Ms. Yee in Art and Imagery or Lana Gabovitch (who insists on going by her first name) in Dance and Movement (think dancing with scarves and ocean music in the background). But Ms. Thompson just can't get away with it: She's too bitter. She walks around, handing last week's tests out face-up as if to prove how embarrassed we should be at seeing our letter grades (as opposed to the check-plus system she used in early fall, a grace period of sorts).

And I should find some sort of solace in noting that Katie next to me got a C and Matilda in front got a C+, but Claude Charbonneau (the Parisian import) got a B and that pisses me off, since he's a solid no-effort guy. My own bright-red D+ blares out like a sex shop sign (not that I've really seen too many of these, but it's just as blush-producing and horrid). Not only have I never had a D grade before, I find the "plus" part of it a double insult—like, your tests sucks, but I'll throw a little cross near the letter so you can feel like it "sucks plus." Um, thanks.

Now, I'm self-aware enough to know that even though I might temporarily exonerate myself by doing so, I can't blame Thompson entirely for this screwup. The basic problems are: She's a bad teacher (the kind who when you say you don't get something just goes over the same equation again and again instead of finding a different way to make sense or explain it), and I am not focusing *at all*. It's like the sector of my brain where math functions has been attacked by mad cow disease (too many Bartley's Burgers) and now I'm doomed.

Note to self: MUST DO BETTER IN MATH. Not just so I don't wind up back at the crappy community college at which my dad rotated through various faculty positions. More so that I get into TCOMC (TCOMC = the college of my choice as abbreviated by the college counseling office, which has already begun the pitch for grades, SATs, and extracurricular activities). I refuse to be one of those girls who is all about English and can't string together numeric structures and takes classes in college like "Math for Poets."

Exams are looming in the distance, so I call Mable in between classes from the wooden phone booth and reschedule our pedicures for Thanksgiving Break, when I'll need the distractions. At home, I clean my room, pile and discard, stack and organize my books and notes into neat(ish) sections by subject so I can steadily work my way through each one for exams.

Nights, after a solid five hours or more of cramming, I allow myself the indulgence of emailing DrakeFan, sometimes looking forward to our back and forth too much. He's (and I'm fairly sure he's a he, but I could be wrong) wittier than anyone else (at least on paper—or screen), and I'll admit here that I print out our correspondence and keep the pages tucked into my journal (where I've still yet to finish a song). By now, I have of course spent a bit of time pondering the identity of DrakeFan, but with a student body of eight hundred, it's hard to narrow down. Who's to say it's someone I'm familiar with? Could be Zack the geeky but funny freshman or Darth (not his real name, at least I don't think so) the junior who is too into those *Star Wars* movies. Or someone I've never even thought of. Could be a faculty member, though that's a fairly disturbing thought. Or an eighth-grader from the middle school.

I usually put on one of the 1970s discs and type away, free-associating and telling stories (the time at camp when I lost my shorts while running a race in front of my first real crush) or going over incidents at school (without using names, because I might write that I like someone who has a girlfriend) and DrakeFan gives great advice or makes me smile or tells something from his own life—painful (his grandmother's heart attack right in front of him) or awe-inspiring (the trek he did with his dad in Nepal. And the more this goes on, the more tempted I am to hunt and peck to find out with whom my nightly screen time is spent. But I've stopped short of asking. Mainly because I don't want to stop the communication. And also because I could be disappointed. Maybe part of me thinks it's Robinson Hall. Or even Channing, and I'll be totally surprised to find out that we really do connect.

I've had my morning caffeine fix and gone running with the hopes of bumping into Robinson at the high-jump mat—and a couple of times this has come to fruition. But my guilt is also growing—the sense that I'm betraying Lila even though *nothing* has happened (outside of my lascivious imagination) with him. Just cardio workouts on both fronts.

Dad is flitting around the house (as much as a six-foot-one man flits) making sure the guest room is ready for the St. Paul's School English exchange student. The school alternates sending a male or female, and this year it's a "bloke." I know this because Chris the MLUT is always on top (heh) of the foreign scene. So when the bright clear moon has lured me into staring out my window, I've considered the possibility that English Bloke might be the man of my dreams. A dark, brooding foreigner who will teach me the international language of love. Of Love.

"You ready?" Cordelia asks for the fifth time. She's watching me but trying not to snoop as I finish my email to DrakeFan. She's one of the only faces on campus during Thanksgiving break, and we've been spending probably too much time together driving around in my car and slowly eating our way through all the various convenient food items we've never tried (the pink Hostess cupcakes; gross, spicy Slim

Jim; Cordelia's fave, turkey jerkey—yummy, actually, though you need a Big Gulp with them and I wind up bloated from salt and water retention the next day. Ah, the price of indulging in good-tasting crap).

Today she's coming with me to WAJS to watch me record my next spot . . . or should I say spotless. After maxi-pads and mattresses, there's only one way to go—toilet bowl cleaner (even more cringe-worthy is the name Shiny Hiney Bowl, which is apparently some traditional New England cleanser created by someone named Hiney. There's a lot to be said for what's in a name).

"Scum buildup?" I lean into the mike and deemphasize my *b* on buildup, but then I catch Cordelia's eye and giggle. One more take and she'll have to leave the room. She sits twisting her curls and smearing lip gloss on her mouth, trying to make me crack up. I finally manage to get out the stupid jingle, a long ad that blathers away on the benefits to a sparkling toilet and culminates with me singing 1950s-housewife-on-TV-style "If you want a Shiney Hiney Bowl, reach for Shiney Hiney!" I had to sing the words "Shiney Hiney" so many times that now I've got them echoing in my head.

"I'm so glad you're emerging from your cocoon," Cordelia says when I'm dropping her back at the faculty house.

"I still have so much to do." I fiddle with the radio knobs.

"All work and no play—you know the drill. You need to get out more. Stop using the computer as your social outlet and come downtown with me. I'm meeting some DSGs on Newbury Street for lunch and a movie."

The Day Student Girls have yet to embrace me—not that I've tried too hard, since they scurry back to their suburban homes and reappear courtesy of the bus or their mom's SUV the next morning. Cordelia knows them all from grade school, when everyone was a day student, and easily slides in and out of all the cliques.

"I would, seriously, but I'm meeting my aunt for a pedicure," I say, and hope Cordelia doesn't bring up the email thing again. I know she wants to find out to whom I'm writing, but then it's sure to become campus scandal. She's first (or even if she's not, she says she is) to spread the word about the latest hookup or breakup, even when it comes to faculty gossip. I've been lucky enough to be flying under the radar so far, but it's a conscious effort on my part to go unnoticed.

At the suggestively titled G Spa downtown, Mable and I roll up our pant legs and take our seats on the pedicure thrones, dangling our legs into the blue-tinted bubbling whirlpool water. Mable uses the built-in back massager that works via remote control, but I switch mine off: The rolling and kneading feels too automated and inspires nausea rather than relaxation. The pedicure, however, is fantastic. Massage, snip, paint. All good things.

"Anyway," I say to Mable in regards to Robinson, "I just like him so much it's dumb. He's become this mythic creature in my mind."

"Like the Loch Ness Monster?" she asks, eyes closed and smile on her face from the treatment.

"Well, just as unattainable." I look around at the other customers. Well-coiffed women with fancy bags and spotless (as spotless as a Shiney Hiney bowl) heels flip through *Architectural Digest*. A group of girls my age sit in a cluster, tearing apart model-actresses in *InStyle* photos and debating the merits of lipo and Mystic Tan (as someone with reddish hair, and pale, freckled skin, I would look creepy with an all-over spray tan, but I get why it's popular). One of the girls looks up, and I recognize her as Lila's field hockey teammate, Colorado (that's her name, not her state on a map). Colorado, as Cordelia's gossip vine relates, has a bit of a snow problem herself—as in snorting the white powder, not skiing on it. Possibly because of this or maybe she was like this prior to the drugs, Colorado isn't the nicest person in the world. Or the country. Or the state. Or the room. She's pretty much a colossal bitch.

Unfortunately, she notices me right when I'm noticing her. Cackles and whispers abound, and I'm trying not to laugh at the scrub brush tickling my feet but it comes across as me laughing at them.

"Like, she's totally laughing at you," one girl says and nudges Colorado, who sniffs and stands up. She pads over to me in her paper slippers and tosses her straightened hair to one side. Then she looks at Mable. Then at me.

"Your daughter needs a lesson in minding her own business," Colorado says to Mable, who is practically dozing off in the throne. And to me she adds, "Get a grip."

This shouldn't bother me. I should be immune to the bitch-witch ways of the airbrushed crew. But I'm just not—not completely. I can write them off as dim and dull, likely to be floundering at our tenth reunion (when I have my second album coming out and a Hollywood spawn at my side), but the fact of the matter is right now it makes me feel like shit. I need to Shiney Hiney myself!

"Ignore them," Mable says when the front door of the spa has swung shut and they've left. Our feet are under little heat lamps and fans, and we watch the shoppers outside as we dissect my latest interaction. "They're not worth it. I know—easier said than done."

"No, I'm fine. I don't even know them."

"They're probably jealous of your friendship with Lila, not to mention Robinson," Mable says. She's looking at an old home decor magazine, and I wonder if she's imagining her coffee distributor (real name: Miles) urging her toward domestic bliss. I ask her about this possibility. "It's definitely occurred to me," Mable says. "But then, it's so odd to get to this stage in life and think about being a couple forever, maybe even having a kid."

This last part makes me excited and teary at the same time. Like Mable could all of a sudden drift away from me into Ecuador or Mexico or Sumatra or wherever they harvest coffee beans now and live her life with Miles and a baby. But on the other hand, I'd love to have a cousin-aunt relationship with Mable's offspring. And then my dad could be an uncle—he'd be so cool and helpful. But I'm getting ahead of myself. It's not like Miles has proposed marriage (and I know Mable won't live with him without a ring, having tried that—twice—and deciding that she'd rather live alone than share the bills on a touch-and-go basis).

Mable hasn't offered to introduce us; maybe she just assumes we're both too busy. Or, what I really think, is that she keeps all the parts of her life in distinct categories. Me and my dad on one side—and hey, we don't even see her together much. He'll have dinner with her downtown and I'll meet up with her on the weekends, but we don't all hang out that much together. Thinking about this in terms of Miles makes me wonder if maybe Mable protects herself this way—no overlaps, just different parts of herself and important people spread out over the days of the week.

My dad and the English Bloke come outside to greet me and my newly painted toes (which are sadly shoved away, hibernating for the winter in my pseudo–riding boots). Rather than the dark-haired brooder of my visions, the exchange student is a thin, wiry, orange-haired boy named Clive. So not my image. In the movie version of this, Clive would open his mouth and explain that he's not the real exchange student, it's his older, hotter brother, who would magically appear in the doorway, touching the heart-shaped knocker, and give me a look that in two seconds lets me know we will be together—on the floor, in the woods, near Big Ben when he whisks me back to London.

But the reality TV moment goes like this:

"Hal-lo!" from the very enthusiastic Clive.

"Welcome," I say. "How was your trip?"

"Very nice indeed," Clive says, his sweaty fingers and hand shaking mine. And so on, through a cup of tea that Dad makes us all sip, until I excuse myself, grab my journal, and go to Slave to the Grind.

Some nights, Mable has local entertainment—good acoustic gui-
tarists or folky women in long skirts. Even bands, with skinny sexy
Depp-esque drummers. A couple of times famous bands have actually
come and played under a cover name. Tonight, latte-sippers and
mocha-blended mothers recline and relax to the tunes some guy
strums out. He's pretty good, mixing sixties sounds like Blind Faith
with his own stuff. I drain a couple of chocolate drinks and eat my
way through several s'mores talking to Miles, the Coffee Man. I see
why Mable likes him; he's mellow and funny like she is—not likely to
be upset or flustered, kind of a hippy trapped in the body of a grown-
up boy-band member. And I like seeing him help her, do things for
her, take care of her the way that she's so good at taking care of other
people.

Once most people have cleared out, my dad comes in (minus Clive,
who—thanks to jet lag—is home sleeping) and sits next to me. While
Mable picks up the last of the cups and spoons, and the balled-up paper
napkins, I wander over to the microphone and talk to the performer.
He asks if I want to sing something, and my heart is immediately on
the fast track to exiting my body. Even though I know I can sing, I just
get nervous and have that out-of-body experience where I'm outside
looking at this girl who needs to *get a grip*. I think about Colorado saying those words to me, and take the mike.

With the help of the guy's guitar prowess (I can play chords, but not
fast enough to keep tempo), I sing an acoustic version of the Stevie
Nicks song "If You Ever Did Believe." As the words flow out of me,
first shaky, then stronger, until I'm pulled into the music and not thinking about what I'm doing—just doing it—I feel free. Happy. Whole. I
look out at the people hearing it and wonder what they're thinking.
Am I good? Decent? Totally forgettable? I can see in their faces that at
the very least I'm okay. And I feel it, too. One guy stands up and does
that double whistle—then goes to toss his latte cup in the trash.

Even though the song I sang is kind of sad, I smile as I mumble it again as I make my way home. Later, when I'm back in my room, I wonder if my choice of songs (it's a song about being left behind) has to do with Mable or the snooty girls or Robinson or my mother—or no one. Just a song and a girl who can sing it.

CHAPTER 10

When I do laundry I put all my faith in the Sock God. Mostly, I am let down. I keep all the mismatched, single socks in my laundry bag, washing them over and over again, despite not having seen their partners for months, in the vain hope that a pair will be reunited. Today—an omen?—my olive-green soft ones with the black toes find each other and I wear them back to school. I've gotten in the habit of driving to school and parking in the very far end of the faculty lot where the pine cones and clumps of leaves make it nearly impossible to park straight. From there I cut by the lower school and past the music building. Sometimes I pick up boarders from the very far end of campus and give them rides on cold mornings, and I take Lila into town for doctor's appointments. It's fun to feel like I can just pull over or head to the Gas 'n' Mart up the street for instant nourishment.

Today it's so cold that I go through the music building, lingering, since I'm early for assembly. From one of the rooms I hear beautiful piano music and, like a cartoon dog following a scent, let the chords pull me toward the sound. The practice room door is ajar and I can see a head of hair bobbing up and down to the music, but not the face. I stand for a minute and the person looks up—it's Quiet Jacob from English. He doesn't stop playing, he just looks at me and keeps going.

I didn't know he played piano, and I almost didn't recognize him without his curly mop of hair—clearly a Thanksgiving cut. I want to comment on it—he looks good—but it's way too intimate a thing to say here. I back out of the room without saying anything and walk toward my desk.

On top of my desk, next to the small circular hole where an inkwell used to rest during the olden days of note-taking, I find an envelope announcing the Hadley Hall Awards, including the English essay Mr. Chaucer spoke of. First I think I'm the only one to get the announcement, and then I see that all the desks are dotted with envelopes and I crumple it up. I'm not spending my free time writing some essay based on the school motto, *I am myself, I am of the World,* only to find out I'm not either.

I get through the first day without so much as laying eyes on Lila, Robinson, Cordelia, just classes and home to dinner with Dad and— no Clive! He's been sent to the dorm finally and I won't have to make nice-nice anymore. Not that he was so bad, it's just draining to entertain all the time. I get home and I want to eat, give my dad a hug, take my shoes off, and get my work done so it doesn't hang over my head. My exam schedule was posted today, and though it doesn't sound bad—six exams over the course of an entire week—I'm shitting myself. I feel the pressure not just from myself to do well, or well enough, but not to humiliate my dad. He's hinted at, but wouldn't say directly, that he expects me to pull through and prove myself (myself or him?). The Hadley Hall calendar is strange. You come back from Thanksgiving, have a couple of days of classes, then reading period starts and exams for a week, and then Christmas break.

When I log on after reading about the plethora of ways white men fucked up this country, I find my email empty of DrakeFan mail— nearly a first. Sadness ensues. Then I surf around and check again—only one from Lila, saying she's coming back late from break and *needs* to talk ASAP. Immediately I wonder if she and Robinson have broken up, and then feel like a Colorado-esque bitch so I take it back. Lila could have any number of things to talk about: the way I never confronted Channing but never touched him again after our night walk (and maybe he's asked her to talk to me, to give him another chance, though I doubt it, since he seemed to lose interest in me rather immediately after our one-time kiss. Why do guys do that? It's like they're taste-testing or trying on lipstick at the MAC counter—um, wrong color, thanks anyway). Or maybe Lila had some family crisis come up and needs to vent (her brother is at boarding school, too, but one of those last-shot places before military school), or possibly Robinson is in love with me and Lila's cool with that. Or none of the above.

Just my luck, the first and only of my ads to be picked up for national syndication is the Shiney Hiney Bowl one, so as of today, EVERYONE has had the pleasure of hearing me sing the praises of the cleanser, thanks to *The Hadley Chronicle*, which has its own pseudogossip page (creatively titled "Seen and Scene"). Apparently the ad has been heard enough times that I was the subject of a school skit this morning involving several faculty members and upperclassmen walking around with toilet brushes and mimicking my singing. I am trying to take it all in stride and find humor in myself.

Before my last senior seminar starts, I take a tour of the new sculpture exhibit (bye-bye, naked men; hello, well-endowed naked women. What is this gallery? An ode to teenage libido?). Paused near a chiseled naked woman who lies on her back with her legs slightly open, Robinson finds me and gives me a postvacation hug. I wonder if he can feel my boobs on his chest (they aren't the smallest in the world—in fact, I kind of wish I had less up front) or if he's into the stone lady spread at our feet.

We talk about the seminar and I tell him how fun it's been. He mentions film school at NYU and how his dad is some producer and bits of his life start to make sense. I can imagine his world in Manhattan, his cool friends, and famous-filled dinners in the Hamptons. He takes the time to ask me about my break, my dad, even Mable. Then he checks his watch. I wish I'd thought to check mine first.

"We gotta get in there," he says, and we go to the A/V door. I'm just about to sink into minor blues—no more seminar, not too much running in the winter, no excuses to meet up with him—when Robinson turns and asks, "Love?" He reaches out and touches my arm. "Want to meet at the mat during exam week?" I'm sure my face is betraying my emotions, but I try to nod nonchalantly. "Thursday afternoon?"

"I'll see you then." I spend the rest of the final seminar creating sculpture images of myself and Robinson, interspersed with trips to New York where we mingle with film folk at his house and stroll hand in hand in Central Park. Never in any of these images do I feel the windchill factor, nor have chapped lips, nor feel crappy for sneaking behind Lila's back.

Can I just say that if I have to hear the exotic plans of one more Hadley Hall elite I'm going to hurl up my salad bar and deli meat lunch? All around are winter vacation plans including, but not limited to: Turks and Caicos for scuba-diving, Tuscany, Thailand, Aspen (the place, not the girl who is a freshman), Banff, Miami and Cuba, London (fine, so this is from Clive who lives there and is just going home, but still, it sounds better than staying on campus with Chinese takeout and Dad and watching Friend-Girl movies).

Still markedly absent from Hadley Hall campus, Lila emails me again and tells me she really really needs to talk. I give her my phone number but she so far hasn't called. I assume she'll be back for exams, but maybe not.

My left hand is cramping up, and I have two more sentences, no, wait, three, and then I am done with my second exam, French (*très bien, j'éspère*), and—time's up. History's done, too. I think it's slightly unfair to have an exam and term paper in one class, but at least it gives the hope that if you tank on one, the other could even out the final term grade.

I hand in my blue books—the small, lined exam book with the official Hadley Hall crest on the cover and the motto in Latin—and head outside to sit on the steps of Maus Hall (Eek!) in the cool air.

Everyone walks around with their heads down or plugged into some exam-distracting music, trying not to stress about exams but stressing nonetheless. It's impossible not to, with the lists of exam rooms and furious studying and late-night library hours. I finally see Lila across the street with none other than Colorado and her cronies. She lets me know she's seen me, and when she's a little closer mouths *I need to talk to you* but keeps walking with the streaked masses.

Just as I've found tentative piece of mind with two exams done, a free day to study tomorrow, and a dad who has gone on a dessert kick (read: homemade white chocolate brownies and tiramisù—great for postmidnight cramming—in the fridge at home), said father comes and strides toward me. First I think he's going to do what he did when I was little: pick me up and swing me around and sing a silly song about ducks. But no such luck. He's got his scowl face on, and when I see his green eyes flare, I know it's something I've done.

"I don't know what to say, Dad." I try to focus on inspecting the brownies in front of me. The plate has the Hadley crest in its center, purple and orange, the school colors, rimmed in gold and probably the real thing. We used to have mismatching silverware and dishes: a couple from Crate and Barrel, two glasses Dad brought back from a conference on public school (the letters had rubbed off from multiple washings so they read UBLIC OOL), and various hand-me-downs from our moves around the state. Now our Hadley cupboards are well stocked—stacks of cream-colored plates and saucers and tea cups and side dishes and chowder bowls and consommé dishes. A bit of overkill.

"I don't know," I say again.

"Well, think of something," he says, tone unflinching despite my obvious fear.

"I guess I just forgot that I couldn't give rides—I mean, tell me you at least recognize that it's freezing outside and I was just trying to be nice."

"I don't care about nice," he says, sounding like a pod parent (pod parent = *Invasion of the Body Snatchers* type moment where your parent sounds totally like they've been replaced by a replicant with the same footwear). "I care about rules, Love. And having my daughter follow them."

"I'm sorry, I'm sorry," I say, voice rising high enough to hit a Celine Dion note, "I won't do it again—really."

"Oh, I know you won't," he says, and I'm comforted in the fact that at least he believes me. "I know this because I'm docking your car privileges for a month, and if this happens again, you can look forward to being treated like a boarder, signing in and signing out."

"Oh, my God, Dad—you can't be serious," I say, even though I know he is. "That's ridiculous! You want to be my dorm parent? Do I need parietals to invite friends over?"

"If it comes to that, yes," he says. "In the meantime, no more convenience store runs, and certainly no more shuttling Lila Lawrence to and from her appointments in the city."

"I did that precisely *one* time," I say. Maybe two.

"One time and yet you didn't get permission, an admittedly easy thing to do."

We leave it at that and I'm fuming, too angry and annoyed to study. Or to listen to "Feel Like Makin' Love" or any of the other seventies songs that deny both my experience and freedom. So I lace up and run, but avoid the mat, since I don't want to deal with a Robinson run-in until I am more composed.

By the ugly fish statue, I see Cordelia, who is taking photos of it from odd angles. I jog in place next to her.

"You look happy," she says.

"Oh, yeah, fabulous fucking mood today," I say, and then add quickly, "But I don't want to get into it now."

"Whatever," she says, and clicks the camera. "I'd have thought you'd be psyched, considering the news."

"What? New salad bar? Pajama Monday?" These are some of the headlines from the Hadley Hall newspaper. *The Hadley Chronicle* contains articles written by future Pulitzer Prize–winning journalists, I'm sure, but no one reads those. The students are more concerned with "Seen and Scene," the weekly gossip column that masks itself as "student news."

"Nope." Cordelia turns the camera on me, still focused through the viewfinder. "Your Boy Wonder Robinson broke up with the lovely Lila. He's free for the taking."

My mouth hangs open and Cordelia takes the photo to prove it.

Twenty minutes later, I can hardly catch my breath. Not so much from running, although the sharp air stings my lungs and makes my already red-prone cheeks feel slapped or sunburned, but more because I am now plagued with two thoughts: Robinson is single. I have no car. Who'd have thought I'd get so attached after only a couple of months? Wait—do I mean the Saab or Rob?

Single. That is if Cordelia is correct and did her fact-checking (she once reported that an adventure in rhinoplasty had been undertaken by a junior named Greta, only to find out she was wrong, and Greta had the nose bump to prove it). Instantly, movie reels of me with Robinson in the student center splitting sodas and playing foosball, Robinson watching me sing at Slave to the Grind, Robinson inviting me up to his room (Note to self: Should this ever occur, must get parietals!), and so on until I have jogged my way to a combo of fantasy and frustration, all the while knowing full well I'm on my way to meet him.

In the movie version of this moment . . . it looks just like this. The way it does on the blue mat, under the blanket of Robinson's down jacket, my head near (but not in) his lap. The wind tosses his hair back from his face, and he reaches out to tuck the sleeve of his coat under my shoulder for extra warmth. When I sit up, knees to my chest, sneakers touching Robinson's thigh, he's in the middle of telling me about his favorite restaurant in the Hamptons and how his mother taught him to make clam chowder based on a recipe from there and how I'd like the view from his room at the beach house. Yes, I'm sure I would. Even movie cameras couldn't make this scene better.

Unless, of course, he were to lean in and I— Note to self: They just broke up. I am still her friend. He is still clearly, at best, ambivalent about me. And I just forgot what he asked me.

"What?" I say. "Sorry, I spaced for a second there."

"I asked what you were up to for break—any plans for beach or mountains?"

I shake my head and stick my arms down the arms of his jacket— backward, so I look like a priest, though my thoughts are impure. "Nope, just me and my dad and a big-time date with the video store." I realize after I say it that I sound lame and loserly, but it's the truth, me in a nutshell. "And maybe some singing." I add this to give a more well-rounded image, so I'm not just eating microwave popcorn and talking to the principal in Robinson's mental image of me.

"That sounds great, actually," he says. "Maybe sometime we can rent that movie you told me about—what was it, *The Story*?"

"*The Philadelphia Story*," I say, reminding him it's my favorite and how amazing Katharine Hepburn is in it—and how her men swoon and how poised she is, even drunk.

"Right." Robinson looks at me, really looks hard into my eyes, and I'm dying to know the exact words forming in his mind.

"What?" Should I ask him about Lila? Or no, that would just be a reminder of his past, or his breakup present. I could suggest another meeting, but that's too proactive for me to justify.

"Nothing." This comes with a small smile from lips I want so badly to kiss.

And despite our movie moment, the final credits roll before there's a single smooch—no last-second grab and outpouring of love. Just me, standing up, feeling guilty but thrilled, and Robinson feeling God knows what, maybe *nothing,* as he said. Instead of a hug good-bye, he takes his jacket back and I'm left shivering, wondering what it all means.

Just as I'm rounding the track, past the hurdles and the benches, I turn back and see the tail end of a scarf blowing in the breeze—a red-and-white-striped scarf, a veritable candy cane motif, belonging to none other than Cordelia herself. From where she's standing, down the small hill near the high-jump area, she could have witnessed the entire thing.

With a mind-blender of driving-induced disciplinary action and non-delivered kisses and spies with big mouths (and the ability to twist what they've seen), I arrive back at the house to find my dad has let Lila Lawrence into my room. I figure she's come by to talk about the breakup and to dissect the parting words: who held the power, who cried, who spoke the *it's not me, it's you,* or if another reason was given. But rather than look like she's just broken up with (or been dumped by, I'm not sure which), Lila looks white and drawn, with the female-on-the-verge-of-tears expression.

Her hair is pulled back and she looks more real somehow, less a vision of glamour and golden beauty. Her lips are chapped, too, and she's had no benefit of concealer to mask the plum-dark circles under her eyes.

"Love," Lila whispers. I shut my door and hug her. She clings for a minute and then, as if realizing this doesn't suit her, pushes me back. I go and sit on the bed and she slides down the wall and sits on the floor with her legs splayed out in front of her, her posture slumped.

"What's going on?" I ask.

"Well," Lila looks at her hands. This isn't breakup regret nor is it a stressed-about-exams meltdown. This is something else completely. Lila reaches into her pocket and rummages for something. "Promise you can keep a secret?" she asks.

I nod.

CHAPTER 11

*O*nce when I was about ten we had to watch this educational
film at school that was supposed to enlighten all of the fourth
and fifth graders on the dangers of smoking. Old ladies with
raspy voices spoke about their emphysema and teenagers talked about
having sick parents or not being able to play football because of their
decreased lung capacity. Since my dad lost his own mother to lung can-
cer, I was well versed in the no-nicotine laws of the Bukowski house,
but I watched the movie wondering why they'd chosen what looked
to be some tropical resort for filming it. The backdrop of palm trees and
tiki huts made the serious subject matter seem surreal. I'm pretty sure
there were even cocktails being sipped in the background—pineapple
rum blendeds with giraffe-necked straws. Too surreal to make a point.

This vaguely mimics the feeling I have right now, in my tower bedroom with Lila Lawrence, who leans against the wall, sitting right
under my black-and-white print of the Paris café I latted at this summer, and to the left of the signed framed sheet music from Joni
Mitchell's "Carey"—a gift from Aunt Mable. When Lila tells me she
thinks she's pregnant, she's like a small, balled-up version of herself surrounded by my room props. No tropical drinks, just books and the
hum of my computer, and the empty-tabled image of the deserted café
above her.

"I mean," she says, sweeping a stray hair back and tucking it into the elastic, "I'm on the pill, and this is just not normal."

"Is that why you were late coming back to school?" I ask, and regret my word choice. Note to self: For now, avoid words such as *late, missed,* and *period.*

"I just kept thinking that if I stayed home and chilled out, you know, relaxed—they say stress can make you late—then I'd wake up and find . . ." She puts her face into her palms, and I can tell by the way her shoulders shake that she's crying.

"Lila . . ."

"No—you don't have to say anything," she says. "I know you're probably like, 'How could she be so fucking stupid and get herself in this position in the first place?' "

I sit next to her on the floor. "No, not at all. I don't think you're dumb." I mean, mistakes happen—and maybe we'd all like to think we're above it—me with my little driving excursions for example, but the twists and pitfalls of life have a way of pointing out your derelict mishaps. Your absentmindedness—or your sexual laissez-faire attitude.

"I'm totally being punished," she says. "That's how I feel."

I so want to ask if she means by the God of her choosing or by her own body or by Robinson—and hey, does he even *know*? I think about the fact that an hour ago I was covered by his jacket, windblown, and dreaming of kisses, and feel like I'm going to puke.

"I'm so sorry," I say, meaning more than Lila can know at this point.

"Here." Lila reaches into her pocket and pulls out a foil-wrapped item. "It's an EPT." Early pregnancy test—ironically not invented for early in life, but rather early in the menstrual cycle . . .

"Have you done it yet?"

"I was hoping you could take me to the doctor, actually. I can't face peeing in the bathroom and then, like, what? Calling home? At least if I go to the office it seems more—less bizarre, more—I don't know."

I bite my lip and grimace. "I can't."

Lila looks at me with eyebrows raised. Her lids are swollen from crying and her face is blotchy. She still looks gorgeous, just like the sad girl in an after-school movie about teen pregnancy. "Fine. What, this is too much for the principal's daughter to handle?" Her tone is so mean, she sounds like Colorado and the cruel crew. I can see how in another context, Lila could be just like them, on the dark side.

I jump to my own defense. "Lila, listen. I want to help you. Of course. Tell me what I can do—aside from driving. I got in trouble for giving rides, and my dad's gone ballistic about it, so I can't do that. Why don't you just take the test here? Now."

Lila looks at me. "Well, I'm five days late. I told myself I'd test on day nine—don't ask, it's my lucky number—if I haven't gotten it yet." She tries for a smile. "Sorry about bitching at you. But you know what it's like in times like this." She hugs me and I think about telling her that I actually have no idea, that the concept of conception is totally out of my realm, but I don't. I shut my mouth and mind and just try to make her feel better. We wind up listening to the cheesiest of my 1970s songs and cracking up as we try to count the *sexy mamas* in one hit from 1978.

That night, my dad tucks himself away into his study, out of reach both physically and mentally from me—I'm sure he is backing off intentionally, making me feel bad for breaking rules, but I also get the feeling he's distracted. Maybe he's got a job concern or maybe, at long last, he's considering dating. Lana Gabovitch the hippy dance teacher wouldn't be bad, though I think she smokes pot and that wouldn't fly (heh) with him. Or maybe Mable's set him up with one of her friends (the female coffee distributor or the filter woman?).

I call Mable and start to tell her about Lila, not using her name lest it leak back to my dad (which it probably wouldn't—Mable's mouth is usually a locked door). Halfway through my description of the whole deal, Mable's attention fades and I know from her "uh-huhs" that she's only partially tuned in.

"Mable?"

"Yeah, honey?"

"Are you listening? Do you think I did the right thing? Should I have told her again to take the test right now?"

"Oh, I'm sure exams will be fine," she says, way off base and clueless as to what I'm talking about.

"You're not listening!" I say. I don't go over the details like I usually would have, instead I do punishment of my own and just say, "Forget it. Never mind."

And instead of being peeved, Mable's voice goes up to crush level and she says, "So . . . Miles and I might move in together."

"I thought you didn't believe in that," I say. "You know, without a ring, no such thing . . ." I sing-song her words back to her. See, I pay attention.

"That's what I'm saying—we might go to Tiffany's this weekend." Tiffany's? My hip aunt is more apt to buy a twenty-five-cent ring from a gum-ball machine or shop for a funky antique store emerald-cut stone from the 1920s than head to the blue-box sanctuary of *the* Tiffany's. "Want to come with us?"

I can feel myself in some widening pit with my dad walking away on one side, Mable on the other, and all the spokes of my social life (Robinson, Lila, Cordelia, even Colorado) pulling out in various directions.

"Maybe," I say, and I'm already scripting my email to DrakeFan in my head. "Talk to you soon."

I hang up and log on, confessing my not exactly loneliness but trapped-in-a-bubble feeling to DrakeFan. I reread his early emails for humor and comfort. Just letting myself indulge in this act lifts my spirits slightly. Then I get a new message from him and first I'm happy—

> hey love—
> excuse me if this message is poorly punctuated but I'm holding a
> sandwich with one hand and fending off freshmen with prying
> eyes . . . anyway, I know exactly what you mean. I feel like I live in a
> tunnel sometimes, like I see people on the other side of it, but I don't
> feel a part of the scene. I think one of the worst feelings is to be sur-
> rounded by people—like in assemblies or parties or with friends who
> are not getting you—and just be isolated. Oops—downer alert. All I
> mean to say is that I understand.

I feel comforted and intrigued by DrakeFan, glad until—

> By the way, not to make you feel worse (or to somehow make my
> presence I your life unduly weighted), but—I leave tomorrow for An-
> guilla. We go there every year—and not to complain, but I wish I
> weren't—oh crap—dorm meeting. Gotta go.

Probably numerous educational films are shot on Anguilla (sun
warnings, STDs). He says he'll try to find computer access there.

It's stupid that I care that he's leaving. I don't know who the hell
the guy is, and yet knowing that he's going to be far away makes me
feel weird. Even more alone.

As of thirty-two minutes ago, I am a free woman! Exams (aka Hell
spread out over one week) are finished and I'm fourteen pages into my
history term paper. Plenty of time to finish that fucker during my *Sixteen Candles/Philadelphia Story/Some Kind of Wonderful* rerun fest this
Christmas.

I don't bother searching the campus for good-byes to warm-
weather-bound friends. Even Harriet Walters (hair tinted ultra-blond

on the tips) is headed to Barbados. Some people have left already, with boarders shoving clothes and books into duffels and Lily Pulitzer canvas totes (just how many batik frogs and flowers can one person handle?) and jumping into preordered taxis or onto the infamous New York Bus. The Greyhound leaves from in front of the school and schleps the city folk back to their natural Upper West and East Side environments, stopping ever so briefly at 125th Street and the Bronx. According to Cordelia (whom I've been avoiding since her vaulting-mat spy episode), the New York Bus is a scene: sex in the back row, drinking in the middle, all advantages taken in the consequence-free environment. Kind of like how eating french fries on the road doesn't count, neither does getting felt-up on the bus.

I head for coffee sanctuary—via T, of course, since I still have no car. I sit by the window and watch the world (world = my small, semiurban world) slide by, and end up nodding off, missing my stop, and having to go back through the turnstile and retrace my public transportation steps until I finally reach Slave to the Grind, where I have only a quarter of an hour before I have to head to WAJS.

Mable flits around like she's been mainlining espresso beans, pausing only to tell me Miles has scoured the Jewelry District and presented her with ink sketches of rings (why does this bug me when I should just feel happy for her forthcoming engagement?). She wipes counters, refills biscotti jars, and answers the phone; then, as she's talking into the receiver, writes on a piece of paper:

Love—do me the biggest favor?

I look up at her. She waits for my affirmative nod, but I gesture I'll need further explanation (further explanation = I am not spending break cleaning toilets with or without Shiney Hiney Bowl, or handgrinding beans).

Host open mike night??

I sigh.

Please?????

The five question marks are enough to guilt me into the project, so I say I will, and head out to do my radio spot. On my way, I walk a different route than I normally do and go past a Starbucks. Even with the wintry glare through the windows I'm pretty sure I see Lila (with her telltale shiny blond locks gathered in a neat nape-of-the-neck knot) sitting in the far corner with Robinson. Are they holding hands? I peer in and then, afraid of being caught, I move away and out of sight. As if walking in the now-snowing afternoon wasn't enough, the irony is that the advertisement I'm about to sing and record is for a car rental agency. Between this and the giant mattress, I'm pretty convinced that life is playing games with me.

Two double features and a moo goo gai pan later, I confront my dad. Not with the *When can I have the damn keys back?* but with a white flag in the form of father-daughter outing. We used to have weekly lunches, trying new places (the crepes place in the square, the crab shack by Singing Beach), even activity afternoons of bowling or shopping (I'd make him play a game I call "Is this appropriate?" whereby I show him articles of clothing and ask his fatherly opinion about what occasion the skirt/dress/accessory would work for). We haven't done anything remotely considered quality time since getting to Hadley. Either a sign of the times (his job, my workload) or just natural distance. Or both.

We walk toward the campus squash courts, and my father opens the locked door with his master key. We drop our racket covers and jackets on a bench and head into court two, the one with the glass back wall. I'm decent at squash—it's all pivoting and bursts of energy, but Dad is tall and able to reach obscenely high or far in front and capture my tricky corner shots. I always prefer to play games without a score, just for fun, no set time limit or end point. I still play hard, just not for some number. So when my dad shouts out his current lead, I make a face.

"No points, Dad," I say, and get ready to serve.

"Let's keep it this time, Love." He sees me stop moving and continues. "A little competition is good for you. Scoring isn't a bad thing—it's what the game is based on."

"Oh," I say in bitchy teen mode. "Here I was thinking that it was based on sportsmanship."

He has his "don't use that tone with me, young lady" look on, and adds, "One can have a healthy sense of competition and still be a good sport."

Somehow this smacks me with the Lila–Robinson scenario and girlish competing for a guy and my own unsportsmanlike behavior. And then I'm distracted by counting the days since Lila was in my room. Has she tested yet? Why didn't she call me if she did? Are she and Robinson back together? Did they even ever split, or was that Cordelia's master plan to confuse me? And will a Lawrence–Hall progeny make an appearance eight-plus months from now?

I miss an easy shot and my dad wins.

"Good game," I say, and walk out of the court. We sit catching our breaths on the bench with the empty squash court in front of us.

"Want to go record shopping?" he asks. This is his truce. A couple of times a year we go to the used-records shops in Somerville and flip through the bins, searching for the funniest record (best so far = *Bagels and Bongos,* traditional Jewish songs set to a Latin rhythm). I nod. He smiles at me—a real smile for the first time in a while. "You want to drive?" I accept the sorry and hug him.

I've left two messages for Lila—one on email, one on her cell phone—but who knows if she'll even be checking messages from Val d'Isere, the alpine resort where she goes to ski and sip Champagne in a hot tub. I'd be more focused on hearing from her if my mind and body weren't otherwise preoccupied with open mike night, which is in full swing.

Two bands, five solo singers, and one small gospel choir have come to perform here to a packed house (people are so thankful for something to do in the lag that follows New Year's). Mable's barista, Bella, tends to the drinks and delicacies (enlarged Rice Krispies squares dotted with icing snowflakes, chocolate-dipped pretzel sticks rolled in rainbow sprinkles) while I circulate and work the sound system, ushering the next performer on the small stage until there's no one left and it's nearly midnight. Closing time.

With just the dregs (people, not coffee) of the crowd left, I decide to try my luck again and sing, unaccompanied. The hollow applause doesn't bother me. I didn't do it for the accolades. I just did it for me. When I come down from the stage and start to unplug the mike, I notice a pair of boots in front of me. Familiar boots.

"Hi," Quiet Jacob says. "Mind if I do one quick song?"

"You're back early," I say. He looks cute, windblown. Secure.

"History term paper calls," he says. He looks good. Vacation-tanned and yet New England rugged with his navy blue jacket and gloves, which he takes off and puts on a tabletop so he can unlatch his guitar from the case.

"Wow . . . guitar *and* piano," I say, twisting my mouth to show I'm impressed. "Bi-musical." When he doesn't respond, I add, "A man of many talents." I wonder if this last part came out too complimentary and now I'm the female equivalent of Cheez Whiz. Never mind.

He tunes up, strums, and sings a song I don't know, which he tells me later (later = when I'm complimenting him and trying not to gush, since he's really, really talented, with a voice like the earliest Dave Matthews mixed with Ryan Adams) is called "Which Will," and no, he didn't write it, but it is a great tune.

I ask him to write down the lyrics for me. They're all about which will you choose, this person or that, what roads in life you will set out on. He's jotting the words onto paper while I clean up, and the place is empty.

"You'll love the ending," he says, and I don't question him even for a second. "The whole song is just a great question. It's so well done I feel almost guilty singing it."

"I know just what you mean," I say, looking over his shoulder as he dots the last *i*. "Sometimes I get the feeling that if all the amazing songwriters out there heard all the crappy renditions of their music, they'd cry." Jacob laughs.

"Hey, isn't bad flattery still flattery?" he asks.

"I guess," I say, noticing how empty Slave is. Even Bella has waved her good nights after mopping the floor and shutting the till. Jacob and I bring the glass canister of white- and dark-chocolate-covered grahams over to the double chair and sit facing the deserted snowy street.

"Okay," he says, unashamed of his cookie-full mouth. "Best summer you've had."

I think for a minute and then say, "Hasn't happened yet."

"Fair enough," he says.

We take turns posing questions and responding to real (worst insult) and hypothetical questions (would you rather travel the world or never leave this city but be famous) until we get bored. Then we head to the kitchen and create what we deem to be By Jove (Jove = a combination of the 'J' from his name and the 'ove' from mine), a sickly sweet but tasty concoction of cocoas and colas and hot milk, topped with mini marshmallows.

"I love sweet things." I lick my spoon free of caramel sauce.

"One of the best things in life," Jacob adds.

"What're the other things?" I ask. It's quiet in the kitchen and my question hangs there with extra weight.

Jacob looks down and licks a bit of chocolate from the corner of his mouth. "Love, I guess," he says softly. I assume he means the emotion, not the girl in front of him, and we sit there in not-awkward silence, then clean up.

Back in the main room we sip and sing bits of songs that would feature in the soundtrack of our lives, and then Jacob nearly makes me pee in my pants doing a lounge singer version of "Hey Ya!" mixed with "Jingle Bells." Bizarre and funny and so natural I don't even care that when I go to the bathroom I have smears of chocolate and frosting on my lips like some post–ice skating kid, and my hair's seen better days, weeks, months. I just look happy and am wheezing from laughing.

My final thought before giving way to sleep is how I've been too wrapped up having a blast to think or plan or worry or give directorial camera angles or script edits. This makes me smile and snuggle a little closer—not entwined, but nestled—to Jacob in the double chair, with no sense of the time nor of the consequences of not going home.

CHAPTER 12

Waking at five in the morning with Jacob's head on my shoulder, my arm twisted and cramped on the chair, makes me wince in pain and then gasp with the rush of reality: I never went home. I slept here. With him. Not slept with but next to, and oh, my God, I need to magically fly into my window (Peter Pan, where are you?) and be able to walk down the spiral stairs and into the kitchen where in a couple of hours my dad will be making his traditional Sunday morning shape pancakes (letters, weirdly shaped animals, Pollock-esque designs made from dribbling batter from a fork).

"Shit," I say, and nudge Jacob.

"I know," he says sheepishly, but grinning. It was worth it—I think. I hope.

"We've got to get out of here. Now."

I do a thirty-second tidying up when Jacob goes to the bathroom and then we slink out the side door. We lock up, and book it back toward the T. Of course, the T doesn't start running this early on Sundays, so we're screwed. Jacob saves the day by calling a taxi with his cell phone and we get the car to stop several blocks away from campus. The light is just shifting from night to morning, and soon the smoke will curl from the dorms and my dad will wake up.

Jacob and I stand in the clearing in back of the library and wait for

one of us to do something. My heart is racing from the way he's staring at me—he's got dark blue eyes rimmed with yellow, and he's tall,
so when he hugs me I feel enveloped and safe.

Unlike I do when I decide to tell my first nose-growing whopper
lie to my dad. Sure, I've done the "No, I don't have any homework"
line to avoid being sent upstairs during Thursday night TV, but until
this moment I haven't ever crafted an intentionally big lie. I haven't had
to. Even the car thing was more like an oversight, a part of life I left out
explaining. But this I can't get out of, especially after finally winning
back regular Dad (as opposed to militant principal Bukowski).

I unlock the front door and sit at the kitchen table, waiting for my
dad. First I sit in my jacket, going over my lines. Six-thirty. He'll be
emerging in his robe soon, with his hair sticking up on one side. Seven.
I hang up my jacket on one of the brass hooks that poke out from the
hall closet. Seven-fifteen and I'm changed into sweats, and by seven-
thirty I'm drinking coffee and reading a day-old *Boston Globe*. Then I
reconsider and go out the front door onto the porch and pick up the
blue-wrapped Sunday *Globe*—it gets delivered each week. If my dad
came down now, would he know that I didn't just wake up and trot
downstairs having slept soundly in my bed all night?

I'm weighing the pros and cons of trying my hand at that. It's conceivable that he fell asleep at eleven and figured I'd returned really late
after closing up Slave to the Grind and tiptoed in. But would he have
checked on me? Hard to say.

Before I can decide which tack to take ("Boy, late night" versus "I
slept at Cordelia's"), the key turns in the lock and, instead of coming
out from his bedroom, Dad comes in wearing jacket and hat, fully
dressed. He looks embarrassed and then covers it by taking out the fry-
ing pan and Aunt Jemima mix before even removing his gloves.

"Morning." He kisses the top of my head and gets cooking. The
pancakes are just circles this time, nothing out of the ordinary, and so
is the conversation. No direct lies on my part ("How was the open

mike night?" "Great!") and no clarifying on his part as to his prior whereabouts. Out for a morning jaunt? Out all night? Neither of us says. We just pass sections of the paper back and forth and take turns with the syrup.

In my journal, tiny fragments of what I can only call My Night with J. (why am I so lame that I have to abbreviate him even in my own journal?!) are turning into yet another (probably) unfinished song. But at least I'm writing something. And I know I'll want to look back on this feeling, to remember the way he moved my hair out of my eye and gave me the first bite of his Krispies Treat, the way his body moved on stage. Either I'll look back on this and have a record of the early days of my relationship with Jacob or I'll have notes on a wishful-thinking level of something that never panned out.

The phone rings while I'm sorting laundry (more unmatched socks and a now-pink bra that until I washed it with a red T-shirt was white) for school tomorrow. Lila's voice comes through, and I tell my dad to hang up, I've got it.

"I'm, like, so sore from skiing" is the first thing out of her mouth. She relates the trek to the chalet, the black-diamond trails, the hot Swiss garçon she eyed from afar, and then stops, letting silence fill up a full minute.

"So," I say to Lila, trying not to sound like I'm bursting with news of her possible pregnancy, "are you . . ." I don't complete my question, figuring she'll do it for me. While I wait for her response, I type quietly to DrakeFan, asking how his break was, telling him (without really telling him) what I did—the movies, the squash, the open mike night that I describe as "amazing" but leave at that.

"Lila?" I ask. "Are you okay?"

Finally, after what seems like ages, Lila says, "I'm actually—I gotta go."

"You sound like there's more to say. Did you . . . ?" I start but she cuts me off.

"Shit! My mom's outside my door. I have to go catch the shuttle back. See you tomorrow."

Maybe because of my very early morning before or maybe because my head is going to explode, my eyes open—windows to my state of minor panic—at six. Seventies music fails to chill me out, so I go for a run. I head right for the high-jump mat and lie there, flat, gazing skyward and watching the small flakes fall. I try to catch them on my tongue, but they're too light.

In the movie version of this moment, there are so many songs that could play over the opening shots, so many ways this film could begin: Jacob finds me and pulls me up, we try to stand on the mat but collapse into the squishy mesh and kiss, his hands exploring my hair, my body, sliding under my Gortex. Or Robinson, back from break and searching for me, finds me at what he calls "our place" and without saying anything, just takes my face in his hands and his kiss explains how long he's wanted this to happen. Or maybe Aunt Mable comes and apologizes for deserting me lately, and tells me she's planned girlie time for this weekend, with vintage clothes shopping and burgers. Or my dad, who with a tearjerker song playing in the background, appears to tell me he knows about my tryst (does not kissing but sleeping next to someone count as a tryst?) and it's okay, that he just wants to know me better, know my life.

I'm so crazy-confused right now that I don't even know what I'd pick if I had the chance. I get up and jog home, shower, and scarf a Clif Bar (chocolate chip = the best flavor) and head to assembly.

I prepare for English not by going over the first couple of chapters of *The Moviegoer* (by Walter Percy, our required reading) but by fixing my hair in the huge women's bathroom upstairs and wishing my nose weren't quite so red from the cold. I slather on the Burt's Bees lip balm from my pocket and do an ass check (as in, any VPLs? No. Sit in anything gross? No.)

But in class, Quiet Jacob—just Jacob now—isn't there. Massive let-down and minor gray cloud looming overhead. And just when I'm doodling the lyrics to that song he sang at the coffeehouse, Mr. Chaucer chimes in with the due date for the final essay competition and how—he stands behind me and, I swear, gives a tap on my chair—he hopes some of us will consider submitting.

I lug my ridiculously heavy book bag over to Slave to the Grind and am set with a decaf (yes, easy on the caffeine when the mind is a sea of sloshing worries) and my newly purchased Spanish textbook. I'm in Advanced French but starting Spanish this term with the hopes that since I already understand how to conjugate in one romance language, learning another won't be too hard. But I feel like an idiot starting over with the "my name is" vocab and learning to say useless things like "Señora Velázquez lives in a yellow house" and "Marta likes to purchase peppers at the greengrocer." Our first assignment is to do a collage. A *Family Circle*–inspired craft project involving cutting images from magazines or drawing and filling two halves of construction paper with one side representing *"Me Gusta!"* (I like!) and the other *"No Me Gusta!"* (yes, say it with me, I don't like!).

So far, I have a kitten cut out and pasted on the *No* side and a photocopy of Fiona Apple's first CD cover and a Swedish fish wrapper on the other. A ways to go. Giving me inspiration, however (at least of things to put on the *No Me Gusta* side), is the view in front of me. Robinson and Lila ordering coffees and taking them to the very chair Jacob and I sat in the other night. Fine, so they don't share it, but still. I'm at the back where they don't notice me, and, since they have neither books nor laptops, this visit is not work-related. I sink farther down in my couch spot and try to think of the Spanish words for *jealousy, lust,* and *love*—oh, I know that one—*amor*. It's the same in many languages.

CHAPTER 13

$\mathcal{F}$rom the open window near my bed I can hear a faint chorus of "Walkin' in a Winter Wonderland" as sung by the Hadley Hall Girls' Octet. Lila and the other chirpy singers are no doubt boot-clad and frosty-lipped singing into the microphones that project the tunes campus-wide via speakers. I keep my window open despite the below-freezing temps outside because I like to burrow under my comforter for warmth and still feel the refreshing blast of cold air.

I'm about to leave my room and head to main campus for the annual Mid-Winter Carnival but decide to give in to my email addiction—one last check before tromping through the snow.

This is what I have in my in-box: Spam asking me if I want to enlarge my penis (um, no, thanks), an offer to meet singles in my area (nope, not *that* desperate yet—give me a couple years of this nunlike existence and we'll see), and a message from DrakeFan that reads:

Love—
Enough is enough, don't you think? After months of this electronic friendship/courtship, don't you think we should meet face-to-face? I'm not much for amusement rides, but what about the Grease-inspired shake box at the Winter Carnival? Or the ice sculptures? I'll check my

in-box in a bit and see if you've gotten this message. Hope you're up
to it—nothing ventured, nothing gained.
—DF

Shitshitshitshitshit. Why did I think DrakeFan would let me live in
the comfort of anonymity forever? Granted, he (or, ah, *she*?) is the
anonymous one anyway—I'm Love and they know it, so the problem
is . . . me. I am the rate–limiting factor here, and I shake my way (thanks
to the cold and my nerves) over to the rush of rides and cotton
candy–scented air.

My dad's already in place as the target for tinted snowballs: small
pink, medium orange, large purple for the mere price of five for three
dollars, all to benefit the scholarship fund. Ms. Thompson, taking a
break from rubbing my ass in math and terror, takes aim and whaps
him in the chest. She obviously has it out for me and any friends or relations of mine. I wave to dad but bypass pelting him and head for a
snow cone. Scooping the blueberry crushed ice into my mouth I'm
aware of the fact that I will look like a Muppet soon, sky–hued tongue
and lips.

Robinson comes up to me as I'm standing near an ice sculpture
heart. It stands on the bottom point and rises upward about eight feet,
dwarfing me in its clear, cold form.

"Aren't you quite the vision?" he asks, and gives me a thump on the
shoulder. "I haven't seen you around much lately. What's up?"

"Work—busy—you know," I say, uninspired by my own words but
enjoying my sugary mess. Robinson opens his mouth like a bird and
moves in for a scoop. I feed him one and manage not to drip the blue
goop anywhere (nor to drool on him; a feat in itself). "I would have
been here sooner, but I was online."

Robinson looks at me and winks. "Me, too."

Heart rate = way too fast. Lips = numb. Silence = awkward. I break it. "Really?" I grin at him. "What were you doing?" I stretch out each word so it's clear I know he's up to something and he knows I know.

Robinson grins and chucks my empty dish into the trash, then pulls me closer to the heart sculpture. "Try this," he says, and presses his lips to the ice heart.

"No way," I say. "I saw that movie where the kid gets his tongue stuck to the lamppost." Robinson pulls back from the sculpture and shows me the outline of blue from his mouth. I want to press my own mouth against the mark just to feel the shape of his lips, but of course, that wouldn't be the most subtle thing to do, so instead I ask again, "Robinson—what exactly were you doing online?"

"Ah," he says. "That's for me to know and you—maybe—to find out."

As if I don't know already. Sculptures, online . . . Robinson is Drake-Fan but clearly wants to keep up the charade a bit longer. And so I go along with it.

All the hot cider, snow cones, and cocoa has made peeing a complete necessity, so I go to the bathroom in the science center. On my way outside via the back door, I hear giggles and see four legs wrapped around one another, kicking in the snow. In a decidedly nonangelic position, Lila and Channing roll around on each other, kissing and cracking up. So much for finding and confronting Lila—I'm not about to break up the snow party she's having with my one official campus kiss. Not that I regret not following through with Channing—he's still kind of a wet mop in my eyes—but it feels funny to see them together just the same.

However, one thought that does become clear is that if she's making out with Channing, she's probably not going out with Robinson anymore. But why the coffee talks and her seeming avoidance of me? She's either going to be showing soon and asking me for a ride to the maternity shops on Newbury Street or she's not pregnant or she's been pregnant and isn't anymore. Whatever the situation, I wish she'd tell me.

I ride on the Tilt-A-Whirl with Cordelia and Chris the MLUT.

"How's things?" Chris asks at full volume.

"Fine," Cordelia and I say at the same time.

"I never really told you," Chris says, "but I liked your band audition." I'd forgotten about Tastes Like Chicken and Chris's guitar playing.

"Thanks," I say. "You're pretty good."

"Maybe we can play at your aunt's place sometime," Chris asks when the whirling slows down and we can speak in normal voices.

"How'd you know about Slave to the Grind?" I ask.

Cordelia nudges me and raises her eyebrows, always looking for gossip. Chris stammers. "Oh, just heard about it, that's all," he says and slinks off, hands shoved into his pockets. Maybe there's more to MLUT-boy than I thought—or maybe I'm just slightly intrigued by him having any knowledge of my life outside Hadley. For a brief moment I picture drinking vanilla decaf with him at Slave. Then I try to calculate how many girls he must have shared liquids with, and sigh.

"Much improved," witchy Thompson says to me as she hands back my first test of the year. It's the first time she's spoken to me without so much as a sneer or insult since Robinson walked me to class that first day. I look at my grade. B+. I smile and feel proud of my efforts, then slightly dorky, but still proud.

I have yet to get my history term paper back, but I'm hoping for an A. Not an A minus, just a solid A after twenty-nine pages and endless hours of writing and rewriting. In the meantime, I'm following Cordelia's suggestion and going to a party at some DSG's house. I'm so good I even told my dad that I'm driving, and gave him reassurance (that he insisted he didn't need) that I'm responsible enough not to drink and get behind the wheel.

I play Radio Love Gods in my head while Cordelia puts on makeup in the front seat. I get "Hurts So Good" as to what will happen to Robinson and me, and don't know whether this is some sexual thing I should worry about or emotional or what. Then I play the game with the next song being Jacob to me. He's been noticeably absent from my life since our coffeehouse night, and I'm afraid if I push it, I'll get into a situation where he says something like *well, nothing happened,* and I'd rather just enjoy the memory of the night as it is in my mind—special and untouchable. The radio blares out "I'm Coming Up," some random oldie-but-goodie (um, no?), and I wish I could see into the future to see what this means.

She directs me onto Route 128 and we drive north to some suburb where large houses line wide streets and the sidewalks are cleared of snow. I park on the opposite side of the street at the corner so I won't get blocked in, in case I want to leave early.

The house is a faux-Tudor, hulking exterior and massive front door with a bell that plays "Für Elise" when pressed. Inside, the party's in full swing. Bedrooms are occupied, music filters in, liquor cabinets are open and being taken advantage of. Lila comes over, clearly sloshed already, and hands me a large plastic cup with what looks to be blueberry slush in it.

"BWB!"

"What?" I yell. Lila produces a plastic blue whale from her back pocket (a position no doubt envied by many of the other mammals in the room) and shoves it headfirst into my cup so the animal looks like it's scarfing my beverage.

"Blue Whale Beverages!" Cordelia comes back with hers and we toast. I take a small sip.

"These are great," I say, drinking a larger gulp and getting brain freeze. "Just like Gas 'n' Mart dining."

"Yeah," says Lila, slurring. "But with, like, five shots of liquor in it!" She and Cordelia laugh. All the boarders come to parties like this under the jurisdiction of their in loco parentis—the parents of friends who willingly sign boarders out to sleep over and then don't pay attention to what they do. Lila will no doubt crash at someone's house—Colorado's probably—and wake up hungover there.

And speaking of possible hangovers, my drink is refilled and half drunk again by the time Robinson comes over and tells me what's in it: blue curaçao, white rum, lemon vodka, and a shitload of sugar and blueberry mix.

"I'm supposed to be driving home tonight," I say. Robinson laughs, and sticks a finger into my drink and licks it clean.

"I'd say that's fairly unlikely at this stage," he says. "But relax—never mind—sit back and enjoy." As if my life is finally a feature film after the coming attractions.

I do. Kind of.

"Wanna dance?" I ask some guy in a very faded Hadley sweatshirt. He's probably a senior, since the shirt is so worn in, though I have heard from Cordelia that freshmen sometimes drag their Hadley gear through the mud and wash it to extremes to mimic the seasoned senior garb.

I'm half in my body, dancing with some random guy, and half on cloud liquor. Whatever. I'm beyond caring, just flowing with whatever, whoever comes my way.

I slurp down another BWB and wonder if they ever make other flavors.

"What about raspberry? Or peach?" I ask earnestly of the girl mixing more. She looks at me with sympathy—or disgust—not sure—and hands me another one.

When I tire of dancing and drinking, I snoop around the house, agog at the photos of worldwide travel.

"Hey, there." Chris the MLUT oozes up behind me and puts his hands on my shoulder in the classic guy move of fake back massage as an excuse for touching. "Looks like someone's had more than her fair share of juice."

"Juice?" I say and look around for a second to see if there's pitcher somewhere, like at camp. Or like Juice Newton, that singer on the seventies CD. "Do you know Juice Newton?" I ask, and sing a bit of "Queen of Hearts" to MLUT.

"No," he says and smiles. "But I'd be willing to learn. . . ."

He tries to corner me as I fondle a photo of some Roman ruin, but I squeeze away. A minute later, Channing gives me a "what's up" by the bathroom, where he's already vomited. And Colorado, wasted as can be without requiring emergency care, says, "Like, hey, bitch!" to me and smiles—this is her at her friendliest. Not bad.

And then the Twister starts. For Harvard- and Yale-bound Hadley Hall students, I'm surprised that there's not more creativity among the party games. Sure, in the kitchen some people are playing Bullshit (the wrestlers who can't drink because they need to keep their weight down) and in the living room there's a hearty game of Truth or Dare (freshmen and the sluttier set), but most of the crowd goes to the empty sunporch where the dotted board is spread out and Cordelia's in charge of the spinner.

Colorado and Chris the MLUT wind up knotted and nasty. Lila spills her drink and disappears to the kitchen. From where I stand I can see Jacob talking to some freshman girl in the kitchen. I hadn't seen him before now and I have real pangs of sadness and desire—but I know I'm not all here and I don't want to say something stupid to him or wind up crying on his shoulder about how much I loved hanging out with him (drunk girl crying = surefire way to dread looking at self in the morning).

Besides, he's paying what looks to be very close attention to the girl in the pink cardigan in the kitchen. I turn my attention to my drink, which is a beautiful blue blobbing burst of—hey, what a lot of words start with *b*!

I'm looking at the empty Twister board and thinking of words I like that start with *b* when Robinson comes to stand next to me. He leans in and whispers in my ear, "You up for a round?"

I use his low-down voice as an excuse to do the same back and say, "No—no thanks." And I linger a little longer than I would under normal circumstances. Three girls start singing some moody song about walking through fire (probably a Sarah McLachlan song—aren't all of hers about leading someone through the fire?) and suddenly the whole thing seems mortifyingly obvious and glaringly inane to me. The answer is I should just tell him. Tell Robinson how I feel and it will all be okay. Right? Isn't that what confident women do, follow their hearts and lusting loins and just say it?

I let Robinson lead me onto the dreaded double Twister mat next to Colorado, who is now paired up with SShhh (Spence Stiller Heller, who did such a great job as the cow's ass in *Into the Woods*, he's been cast as the phallic donkey's nose in *A Midsummer Night's Dream*) and liking it. Robinson and I position ourselves next to them and wait for orders.

"Right hand blue." Cordelia laughs, and slugs her drink. Robinson does it. I follow with left foot yellow and right hand red and then back to yellow and then I'm thinking about Robinson's lips and the ice sculpture and the blue snow cone and the blue drinks tonight and how in the summer I *love* blueberries in yogurt and then I picture the quivering yogurt and am in a spread-eagle all-fours position and feel a little worse for wear.

"You okay?" Robinson asks from underneath me.

"Now I've got you where I want you," I say. His face is slightly blurred in front of me.

"Finally," he says, and I'm not sure whether he's joking or not, and his left hand moves to cover mine on a green circle. He looks up at me, serious, and I could fall into his arms, lie right down on his strong chest.

But instead, just like the Radio Love Gods song predicted but with the wrong guy, I'm . . . I'm Coming Up. Make that throwing up. In one powerful heave I splash blue icy chunks all over Robinson's shirt, face, and the left side of his head. Cordelia stumbles to get me and we drunk-girl walk to the bathroom, leaving a revolted Robinson and a riveted audience behind.

But the trouble is, even cleaned up and washed off, I can't drive and neither can Cordelia, and Lila's nowhere to be seen and I don't even think to look for Jacob (and his pink sweater girl is gone, too), and I can't not go home.

So I call Mable.

And, like the good person she is, she drives out to fetch me, and Miles, her now official fiancé (emerald-cut, two baguettes on either side), drives my car back to Mable's. Miles leaves us there, in the safe haven of Slave to the Grind, amongst the comforting smell of beans, and says he'll come by tomorrow.

"I've already phoned your dad; he knows you're staying here."

"Did you tell him why?" I swallow the Tylenol Mable hands me.

"No," she says. "Not exactly. I mentioned that the party was over and you needed to talk, which is true."

I slip into one of Mable's oversized flannel nightshirts and pull my knees up against my chest on the couch. She lectures me about drinking and about my behavior—somehow she knows I slept here after the open mike night.

"I mean, you did fall asleep in the chair that *faces* the window, Love. Honestly, did you try to get caught?"

"No," I say. My head hurts and my tongue is a wad of dry paper. I will never be able to smell blueberry anything without wanting to barf. Bye-bye Pop-Tarts and fruit salad.

"Well, you act like you did. In fact, I think you've been crying out for some attention, which isn't like you."

"If I have been—which I seriously don't think so—it's not. Well, you haven't exactly been in shouting distance," I say and feel guilty. My aunt should have a love life, even if I don't. Even if it means ignoring me. "I mean, you didn't even *thank* me for hosting that night—all so you could be out with Mr. Coffee."

"Miles," she corrects. "And I'm sorry. You're right. I should have been more appreciative. But I need to have a life. And so does your dad."

"What does that mean?"

"It means . . ." She drifts off. "Nothing. Nothing. Just that you need to be aware of my limitations, that's all. And I love Miles. I do."

We segue into her relationship, and I hear all about their dates and trip to Vermont and the proposal. And I fall asleep only vaguely aware of the mess I've left not just on the Twister mat, but in my social life.

I drive back in silence the next day. No RLG, no ads. Just me and my five speeds and blue whale–splotched pants. Shift, clutch. Back home. When I walk in the door, my dad whispers something into the phone and then hangs up.

"Was that Mable?" I ask, thinking she's spilled the proverbial puking beans.

Dad stutters. "No, no. It wasn't." He gives me a hug and retires to the study for his Sunday evening symphonies (probably no one professes the perks of maxi-pads on that station).

Upstairs I shower and do a seaweed and cucumber face mask in the hopes that, as the package suggests, it will purify me. Or at least my pores. I sit with the algae-colored goop on my face and check email. Nothing. Check again five minutes later. Nothing. I Google "Robinson Hall" and get nothing except some genealogy thing about his maybe or maybe not relatives from two hundred years before. But then I try "JC Hall," remembering the conversation I had with him about how if he ever becomes a famous director he'll be JC after Joseph Conrad, who wrote *Heart of Darkness,* which became *Apocalypse Now,* which all guys (Channing, my dad, Chris the MLUT) adore.

Bingo. The all-time jackpot. Better than an old school photo online or a message posted to some pathetic dating site, JC Hall has a blog.

And, according to entry one-thirty-one, dated three days ago, I'm in it.

> So I have to say, I'm glad to be back at school for one reason only.
> The food. No. Love. Love gets me every time, pulling me back from
> wherever I've been and bringing me into the moment.

Okay, okay. He could mean Love the thing, the emotion. And I can't
go any further back than a week's worth of entries so there's no way
(damn!) to find out what he thought (if anything) all fall. But a week ago:

> Cheesy and gooey, flavorful, you bet—all the toppings you can eat
> and easy to order and get—Pizza Plus—we deliver and . . .
> The girl I like is a voice-over goddess, and just hearing her sexy extra
> cheese voice makes me want to do inappropriate American Pie sorts
> of things to pizza.

And that is how I know that ROBINSON FUCKING HALL, the
one and only, LIKES ME. Or at least he did before I slimed him.

I check email just to make sure he hasn't written. And Robinson
hasn't. But DrakeFan has. I click on the message and open it.

> Who ARE you, anyway?

I crawl, still hungover and weirded out and happy and confused, into
bed, snuggling under the covers and breathing in the cold air from the open
window. On the one hand, Robinson could still have feelings for me. On
the other hand (or face), I threw up on him last night. And whoever Drake-
Fan is—Robinson?—I'm not sure whether to interpret the message as "I'm
really curious to find out your identity" or "Who the hell do you think you
are?" My sense is that it's the second of these choices. He could have witnessed, played an active role in, or just heard about the party fiasco. But the
worst part about the whole thing is the image I have of myself—drunk and
sloppy and playing the game I said I wouldn't. Am I one of *those* people?

CHAPTER 14

The first time I heard it, I thought I was hallucinating; the second time, I figured I was inserting my own paranoia into the dining hall chatter. Now, after the third time hearing "Puke-owski," I am fully aware that the rumor mill is churning full force and I am its subject of choice today.

I long to escape the memory of the stomach-meets-alcohol incident and free myself from the knowing glances (Colorado, Cordelia, Harriet Walters) and glares (Colorado, after being informed some blue vomit stained her white Marc Jacobs shirt, Jacob in English—at least I think it was a look of disdain, but his hair is growing out over his eyes so it's hard to tell—and goddamn Thompson in Math, as if she knows what's going on beyond the blackboard).

With my newly purchased air-cushioned Saucony sneakers on, I flee and find myself running a totally different route than ever before. I go past the health center, behind the faculty lot, and up into the woods near the end of the cross-country trail. When I hear footsteps crunching behind me at a similar pace, I pray it's not a murderer, cursing the horror movies that take place in the woods for giving me the creeps on a perfectly pleasant jog—and am relieved, though very surprised, to find Lila looking like Cameron Diaz, a mesh of glamour and sport.

We run alongside each other until I nearly knock myself out on a tree and we stop short.

"Sorry," she says.

"I'm okay," I say, and pat the oak.

"No—I mean, not about that. About, you know. The other stuff." When I don't say anything, she keeps going, taking her hair out from its clasp and letting it fall to her shoulders. She loops the elastic around her middle finger and leaves it there. "You probably have figured it out by now, but I'm not pregnant." She lifts her shirt to show me her tanned, flat belly for proof.

"That's good, right?" I say. I lean up against the tree and stretch my legs.

"Sure—yeah. I guess I didn't say anything before because—well, first I didn't know, and then I finally got my period and I felt so fucked up over it."

I turn to her. "Of course you did. It's a really big thing that you had hanging over your head."

Lila shakes her head at me. "No, wait. I mean, what I want to say is that I never—Robinson and I never did it. We never had sex."

"So it would have been an immaculate conception?" I say, trying to make light or sense of this moment. They dated for nearly two years (a marriage in high school terms) and never consummated their deal . . . interesting. Unlikely, but interesting.

"I never felt ready with him. I wanted to—or I thought I did at certain points. Once at his parents' house in the Hamptons, but I'd had too much wine. And then, what am I going to do, lose my virginity in a dorm? No thanks."

"But so, why the pregnancy thing?" Is Lila crazy? One of those horribly misinformed women who don't understand the mechanisms of female anatomy? Or is she secretly an attention-monger, longing for the drama a missed period can bring?

"Well, this is the thing, Love. Please don't be mad. Okay?" I nod.

Sure. Why not. "I've been sleeping with Channing for, like, almost three months." I try to count backward to figure out when this started, and Lila can see what I'm doing so she preempts my math. "Since after you and he kissed. A couple of weeks after."

"What if I'd wanted to go out with him?" I ask. It was entirely conceivable that Channing could have won me over with persistence and ardor, and then where would I be?

"But you didn't." Lila sighs. "Anyway, I just hope you're cool with it. And that it's some consolation that Robinson was never a part of the EPT fiasco."

I'm unsure why she's going into all the details, but I'm glad to be her confidante. To have a running partner. We jog back, and she tells me the Puke-owski debacle will fade in a couple of days as soon as someone else does something gross or brainless or typically teenagery.

"Want to go shopping on Newbury Street this weekend?" Lila asks.

"Sure," I say. "There's a really good place for lunch I went to with my aunt—near G-Spa."

"Let's go there. I need to find something for the V-Day Dance." There's a new boutique hotel in the old leather district (think less S&M, more leather coats and belts) where the Hadley Hall Valentine's Dance will be held. The tickets raise money for some fund or other, and it's supposed to be fun. If, say, you're asked to go. But I haven't been.

Lila deposits me at the front door, and I head inside to procrastinate reading for English and History. I quickly do my Spanish homework; I write several whole paragraphs describing my house and my room (I live in a house yellow. My room, she is on the second floor and is having a green rug). Then I allow myself to check email.

Still no DrakeFan. Is it over? I write in my journal about our letters back and forth and read through some of the unfinished songs, including the one about Jacob and that night. The whole evening, all those hours and that sweet drink we made up, it all feels far away. Like it happened to someone else. Someone else in a movie. Pretty perfect, I guess. Maybe too much so.

Being the blog-spy that I am (and what other reason to have a blog if not for people to find it and read it. Antithetical, by the way, as to my own journal-keeping reasons), I check JC Hall's and find out that . . . dum-da-dum . . . JC/Robinson is going to ask me to the dance.

I head to the mat after dinner and find him there in the dark. The weight of Lila and guilt are lifted, and it makes me more nervous than ever—no excuses. But Robinson's there and smiling.

I'm immediately embarrassed by my mind-Polaroid of puking on him, and I try to excuse my actions. "Look," I say, teeth slightly chattering, more from nerves than cold. "I'm so—I am really, just really sorry about . . ."

But Robinson, god that he is, doesn't make me finish my crawl through shame village. Instead, he says, "Don't worry about it, seriously." And gives me a hug. We stay like that, on our knees, hugging on the cushion, until my hands are frigid.

"Want to come to the V-Dance with me?" he asks, whispering it into my ear and not looking at me. At first, I keep waiting for him to mention the Puke-owski incident. Everyone else has, and my actions affected him the most probably. But he doesn't.

I can't speak. I think if I do I will scream. Or puke. Wait, I did that already. So I just nod into his chest. And then I pull back to see his face, and he puts his fingers on my lips, not shushing me, just feeling my mouth. It's the sexiest thing I've ever had done to me, and he moves his hand down the side of my face and neck, resting it on my collarbone. I wait for him to make a move. He doesn't.

So, plenty of fodder for bedtime thoughts. No kiss, but an invite to the dance. I never really betrayed Lila more than she did to me. I kept my principles somewhat intact. No worries about being compared to Lila in the sack should it ever come to that (which would be impressive, since there has been no lip-to-lip contact). And in my head, words that could be lyrics or could be nothing. Possibilities. Principles. Potential.

The next morning on the way out the door, the phone rings. We still have one of those old yellow ones that's fastened to the kitchen wall, its cord a tangled and loopy mess. Dad runs in to get it and charges past me, which I find abnormal, since I'm the daughter (daughter = phone-answerer in the dictionary of family).

"Oh, hi," he says into the receiver, his tone dipping. "It's Mable." His arm extends the phone to me and I take note of his letdown—who'd he expect?

"Listen," Mable says, with the whir of the milk frother in the background. "Want to host an open mike night together? Just as a way of, you know, doing something fun." As opposed to drunken lectures, feelings of abandonment, and diamond ring ogling.

"Definitely," I say. Then, when my dad points to his watch and heads outside, I say, "Guess what? Radio Love Gods guy, Robinson? He asked me to the Valentine's Dance."

"I always knew RLG would tell you the truth," she says. "Just let them see the real you and the rest is history." True, if the real me constitutes a massive hurlage session.

"I'll go to the art room tonight and get supplies for posters," I say.

"Use glitter," Mable instructs. She's a sucker for all things shiny—and this way, the posters will match her high-heeled silver glitter boots from the first time flares were in fashion.

"Nice butt crack," Lila says to Cordelia, who takes the low-rise fashion to the extreme.

Cordelia hikes her black pants up and shoots back with, "Cleavage much?" Cordelia smirks at Lila's rather obvious push-up bra (and the resulting pop-up boobs), which is visible even through her double-layered tees.

They look to me for reassurance. "Your ass is great," I say, smiling, to Cordelia. And to Lila, "Babies and upperclassmen alike will fall at your feet. I mean breasts."

Lila does a mock push-up bra by squeezing her arms together. "Better?" she asks.

"No," I say. We swivel on our snack bar stools to see who's just come into the student center. Freshman. Back to us. It's funny how time has slipped past and I'm one of the watchers instead of just the watchee.

"I'm thinking I might get a tux for the dance," Lila says.

"How Annie Hall of you," Cordelia replies.

"Very andro," I say, and then, "If anyone can pull that off, it's you."

Lila does her best Melissa and Joan Rivers red carpet interview. "And who does Love have on tonight?"

"Well, even though Zac Posen and Armani both sent great dresses, I went with this smart little number." I stand up and pirouette, smoothing my imaginary gown. "I ended up going with an antique Dior."

"Oh, vintage. Very cool." Cordelia nods as if I'm really in some fantastic beaded number.

Then she and Lila stop talking and nudge me. "Someone wants you," they say. Lila blushes a little and waves. Robinson, of course.

He walks me to English and, in the long corridor near Chaucer's room says, "Listen, I have a plan."

"Oh, yeah?"

"Meet me tonight."

I put on my shocked face, hand over the mouth. "You mean, at the Bat Cave?"

"Sort of." He grins. We're in that John Hughes high school position with me leaning back against the wall and him propping himself up on one hand, tilting down to me. "Come to Whitcomb tonight."

"Oooohhh . . . parietals." Everyone jokes about how nonillicit the parietal hours are: seven o'clock until eight forty-five. Not one minute later. Not exactly the witching hour, nor the after-midnight and letting it all hang out kind of situation. But it's better than nothing, I guess.

"Not exactly." He tells me to sneak in through the upstairs bathroom window, one of those full-length ones that opens onto the flat section of roof seniors use in the spring for sunbathing and listening to music. All at once I am flustered and flattered and flummoxed. Yes? No? Maybe? I feel like I need one of those kid's games (one potato, two potato, for example) to help me decide if I'm in or out.

"Maybe," I say. I know I sound coy and perhaps cooler than I really am, which is fine, but the real reason behind my hesitation is that four-letter word starting with "F". No, not that—FEAR. "What if I get caught?"

"You know how many people do this *all* the time?" he asks. "Tons. And you know how many disciplinary actions there've been for sneaking in? One in the four years I've been here."

"And what happened then?"

"A stupid mistake. First two weeks of school this girl Juniper— a Fruckner House boarder, the kind of It Girl that year—climbed up into her boyfriend's bed and got through the whole night without incident."

"So how'd she get caught?"

"Overslept. Classic. The trick is you've got to be up and out by four-thirty, especially since the Von Tausigs get up at five just to see if there'll be a snow day. Four-thirty totally covers all asses." He smiles at me and traces my cheek with the side of his finger. "Anyway, with Juniper, dorm parents wound up doing a bed-check thinking someone was sick or something when the attendance office reported back. And the rest is *you're frucked* history."

"That sucks."

"But what I'm saying is, be smart and we won't get caught."

I spend the first seven-eighths of English class pretending to focus on symbolism and gender references while really wanting to crap myself (no, not literally—if I did that, between the Shiney Hiney and the puking, I'd be done for) out of excitement and *fear*.

The bell rings and Jacob, for the first time in ages, comes up to me.

"Hey," he says. How is it that guys can make single words come laced with innuendo and meaning? Or is that just my female interpretation? In my mind, the "hey" is a truce or, more aptly, a retraction for his distance.

"Hey," I say back, and am sure it comes out just as mere salutation. I flash forward to climbing in through a window and into Robinson's arms. Then I flash back to laughing my ass off with Jacob in the kitchen at Slave to the Grind. "I'm hosting another open night mike." I stutter. Blush. "Mike night, I mean."

Jacob does a nod and tiny smile. "What's your point?"

I put on faux bravado. "My point is that if a certain someone had real talent and wanted to display it, that someone could make an appearance."

"Point taken," he says. The second bell rings and Jacob and I become cattle, part of the bovine herds that clutter the hallway. Just as we're about to get separated by throngs of underclassmen (selves included), I tell him that I'm making posters in the art room tonight. I don't phrase this like a question as in would he want to join me, but it's out there—I'm out there. Or my future whereabouts are (until midnight, when who knows). He nods and gives an over-the-head wave.

"I'm going to the art room," I inform Dad as he's spooning rum raisin Häagen-Dazs from the pint and watching two old guys in suits spar about the current state of economic affairs. In the mode of "think globally, act locally," I'm more concerned with my own affairs—or lack thereof.

"Paint well," Dad says, even though I've told him twelve times I'm making posters—most likely not with paints. He looks up and gives me a wink. "And by paint, I mean glue and glitter well." He knows me too well. And to think I could pull one by him. . . .

I turn on only one of the rows of lights so that the massive art space resembles the kind of New York loft apartments depicted in architectural magazines; metal chairs and drawing boards, a gorgeous wall mural somewhere between Monet and O'Keeffe—flowers and swirls of mauves and blues, the very clear lily right in the center. I plant myself across from the white bloom and lay out the supplies. Then I decide I need tunes to make it through kindergarten paste and plan 101.

The ancient "boom box" (I call it thus because written in Wite-Out across the front two tape decks are the words "boom" and "box," probably circa 1984, when the thing was made) uses a twisted coat hanger for an antenna. I fiddle with it until WAJS comes on. Lucky for me, I don't have to hear any of my own ads—no feminine protection or beds. Just the nighttime "Desert Island Discs"—songs callers have written in to say they'd take on a *Survivor*-type excursion. Mable's Time-Life series comes in handy for shows like this: There are always groovy songs from the seventies, like "Hot Child in the City" and "Tonight's the Night." And then there are some I don't know—but Jacob, who appears in the doorway, does.

He sings along with the radio and ventures over once I've given him a smile. He produces from his backpack three bags filled with confetti—glitter confetti.

"Musical notes! Fun!" I say, a junior Martha Stewart (minus the prison stint). Then there's regular sparkles, and moons and stars. "A for effort."

"E for effort, no?" Jacob pulls a chair over, and we begin the session by using Popsicle sticks to spread paste onto the edges of thick paper. Soon we're back into the swing of the coffeehouse evening, with me spilling my guts about loving trashy chart hits from the bell-bottom era and Jacob—when pressed—giving details of his first kiss (baseball game, seventh grade, popcorn aftertaste). The red glitter I shake onto my paste pile makes me think of Valentine's Day, reinforced by the radio's selection of love songs.

"This is cool," Jacob says, pulling off the direct emotion by avoiding eye contact and focusing on sifting stuff onto the construction paper. "Maybe I'll even do you the honor of attending this open mike night. I heard the last one was pretty great."

It's the first time he's addressed the fact (or alluded to it, anyway) that we spent the night together (why does that sound more torrid than it was?) and had a kick-ass time.

"Yeah, it was," I say. "So I hear," I add, covering my ass.

Jacob shifts in his seat and then stands up. He comes over to me and puts himself in front of my face. We're almost the same height this way.

"You're sparkling," he says.

Can he see me blush in this dim light? "Really?"

He nods and swipes a piece of glitter from my cheek. "There. That's better."

I can feel the tracing of his finger on my face and wish he'd put his hand back on me. In the comfort of this room with him I can almost forget about a boy in a dorm room waiting to see if I'll have a clandestine meeting with him later. Will I?

How could I risk everything if I'm having so much fun with Jacob? I am emotionally schizoid. Must be. Or just won over by Jacob's sincerity and the way he listens. And his shoulders. And his voice.

And just as I'm about to be wooed into momentarily forgetting about Robinson and fling myself into my mini-movie of me and Jacob writing songs together (chart hit #1 being his ode to me, of course) I get the dreaded:

"Well, my friend, I have to go—work to do." Now, hearing he has work isn't the issue. Nor is the leaving part. That's all fine and par for the course (golf imagery even though I've never played—thanks, Dad!). The key problem with his sentence is the *my friend*. Could this be a casual conversational device? Maybe. But more likely Jacob sees me as his cool friend. The girl he can talk to—welcome back, Friend-Girl—but the one he'd never make a move on. After all, he let an entire night slide by, unparented, unwitnessed, and didn't act. Clearly he can't feel anything but the effects of Friend-Girl's magical powers.

And right then and there, I decide to throw caution to the proverbial wind and potentially chuck my future out the window by climbing into one of Whitcomb's.

"Hey," I call to Jacob, who finishes washing his hands in the industrial sink and dries them on the rough brown paper towels. Since I'm now in official nothing-but-friends mode with him I ask, "Ever snuck into anyone's dorm room at night?"

Jacob grins. "Wouldn't you like to know."

"That's why I'm asking."

"If what you're asking is if it's a smart move or not, then I'd have to tell you it depends entirely on the situation at hand."

I figured he'd say something like that. "I get it."

"You have to follow your heart, right?"

It never occurs to me then that he might have thought I was suggesting a Romeo and Juliet encounter with him.

With each hollow night air step, I hear an imaginary warning "Big mistake! Big mistake!" and then, when I make myself nuts, I say out loud, "Fun and great!" instead. I'm just stretching my boundaries, exploring the territory of the teenage mind. Ah, justification feels good.

I turn back and look at my house. Dark and turreted, I can picture my dad sound asleep and secure in the knowledge that his only daughter is safe upstairs. Guilt. I am guilty—or will be. But then I calm myself down by remembering that at four-thirty in the morning, when I do the campus "creep and crawl" (as Cordelia's explained the walk of shame is called at Hadley), I'll be back in my room with my dad none the wiser. Thank God for mandatory fire escapes and WD-

40 (the oil I sprayed on the latch and hinges of the ancient window in my room).

Fear is lurking around each bush and tree root I trip over, sending shivers and waves of nausea over me, but I push it all away and focus on Robinson's mouth, the way his face lighted up when he asked me to come over. I can finally step into the romantic phone booth and bid a semifond farewell to Friend-Girl. If this works, it'll be the first time I've made this transition from confidante to girlfriend. Dance date. Prom date? Whoa. Slow down.

I do. I slow down and cringe as each boot print crunches on the icy grass. Around the back of Whitcomb where I saw Robinson playing Frisbee months before, I follow his instructions and climb the back stairs to the flat roof. Instead of indulging in horrific fake headlines (PRINCIPAL'S DAUGHTER FALLS FROM ROOF WHILE FALLING FROM GRACE), I focus on the positives of this situation: I'll be in the warmth of Robinson's arms (and bed?) soon, I'm following in the tradition of my Hadley Hall hornies before me, and for once, I'm putting fear away and acting on impulse. Okay, not impulse (and thank God not smelling like it), since impulse implies acting quickly and this took me the better part of a day and evening to sort out.

"He's waiting for you," Channing says, the decoy sent to the bathroom to fetch me. Scrunching into a ball, I dangle my legs over and narrowly miss the seatless toilet. Channing picks me up and I follow him one door down from the bathroom to where, in an also unlighted room, Robinson waits for me.

Cue the not-yet-super-famous female singer-songwriter's future hit single. Cue the blue moonlight. Cue the doves. Okay, no doves, but pretty damn close. Robinson watches me check out his room. One wall is covered with an Indian print tapestry (typical Hadley Hall decor); a large bookshelf jammed with paperbacks and texts is on the far wall. He's cleaned up—I think—since the room is free of guy evidence (balled-up underwear, drapes of clothes over chairbacks). Noticeably lacking are the movie posters I expected. Instead, in frames, are three script covers from award-winning films, all signed and with penned words such as "Robinson—You the Man!—[insert famous name here]." Very cool.

"I've visited a lot of sets in the past, which was really exciting," Robinson says quietly, nodding to the script covers in reality and no doubt his producer dad in his mind. "But none of that compares to right now."

He walks over to me and unzips my coat. With his hands on my waist he pulls me into him and we press against each other. He lifts my hair up and puts his lips to my neck. Then he pulls back and looks at me. This is it—the moment. The ultimate film-worthy essence of what I've been wanting.

I tilt my face up to Robinson's. He drags his fingers through my hair (points for prior conditioning treatment). Then he leans down and BAM! ZING! CRASH!

No, these are *not* the sounds of love and mayhem in my head, nor the sounds of hormones and bodies clashing. Rather, these are the semitragic (in my case possibly not semi, just total) blarings of the fire alarm.

In an instant, all of Whitcomb's emergency lights flash on—think putrid green with a touch of bright white—and the hallways are filled with shirtless boys and the dorm parents, the dreaded Von Tausigs, flinging open doors to do bed checks and rid the entire house of its occupants.

"Fuck me!" Robinson says, and it's sadly not a command.

"What the hell am I supposed to do?" I ask. "Window?"

"No way," he says, throwing on a pair of unlaced boots and a sweatshirt. He looks panicked. "You can't go back the way you came—it's a trap. We're supposed to meet out back by the grill. There's no way you'll get down in time." Not even if I jump in one last dramatic plea?

"I could hide," I say, and crouch down near the (unused) bed checking for space underneath.

He shakes his head. Shrieks from the hallway. Channing bursts in and directs his sorry grin to Robinson. Leave it to him to be succinct and totally accurate. "Dude, you are so fucked."

Oh, like I'm not?

For the record, I owe my demise to Clive the exchange student. He got high with some stoner senior and freaked out, pulling the fire alarm handle and thus submitting me to torture in the form of my father who, as the dean of students, arrives bathrobe-clad and concerned at the back of the dorm. Needless to say, surprise understates tenfold the expression on his face upon seeing me between two irate dorm parents. I told Robinson and Channing to leave me in the room—in the hopes that there wasn't a real fire, just a drill—and save themselves. I'd just say I was acting on a dare. Which, in a way, I was—a dare from myself to stop being so cautious. And look where that got me.

I was busted alone—caught actually heading into Robinson's closet to try to hide by the Dorm Parents of Doom, making their way through each room (thanks to the overly litigious/paranoid board of trustees, each room has to be cleared lest any heavy sleepers burn in a blaze).

I had to endure the "Well, who do we have here?" from them—pure evil—and fought the urge to say "whom."

So, alone and in mucho trouble (have not yet learned how to say trouble or busted in Spanish), I trek back through the wintry grounds with my principal—I mean my father—and into my house, where he wordlessly sends me upstairs and I panic my way into a light sleep.

However, instead of waking up to screaming and yelling from my parental source, I wake up to the feeling, or at least the sounds, of nothing. Quiet invades the gray morning light, seeps into my unset alarm clock. Snow day? I prop myself up and look outside. No plows, no piles of white. I look again at my clock and then, noticing it's already eight o'clock and I am absolutely triple-screwed if I receive a tardy from Math Hell Thompson and her assembly attendance tally, I fling on some clothes and sprint down the stairs. Out through the kitchen, the only thing that gives me pause is the white piece of paper taped to the door.

> *Love—As per the decision of the disciplinary council (myself included) you are hereby suspended from Hadley Hall for two (2) days. Considering the parietals and the hour at which they were broken and the assumed intent by which the rules were disregarded, you are also banned from attending the Valentine's Day formal dance. Of course, this will be part of your permanent record.*
>
> *I'll be back after school.*
>
> *Dad*

Thoughtfully, this little poem of love was written on Dad's Hadley Hall emblemed and titled stationery as if I weren't privy to his role here—at school and in my life. And I hate the way he wrote out "two (2)" as if I might misunderstand what that meant. I pull the note down and read it again, fuming.

Assumed intent? Who are they to know what my intent was sneaking in. *I* don't even know! I mean, sure, my intent was to visit a boy, but more than that, who can say? So while I won't be getting any tardy slip today, I won't be getting any dress or going to the dance this weekend. I hate the note.

Mainly, I hate that I got caught. Little sniveling English boy Clive and his pot-induced paranoia make me want to send him back to the land of kings and queens. His way of blending in has been to befriend the stoners and Phish-followers, sticking labels from the supermarket bakery on his baseball cap and the back pocket of his jeans, the most common one being FRESHLY BAKED followed closely by BAKED DAILY. Three cheers for cultural enrichment! Hopefully, whomever St. Paul's sends next year will not enrich my life in the way Clive has. Knowing my luck, the girl will be his sister, who will rat me out for doing something I can't even fathom as of yet.

I watch morning TV. Chirpy newscasters are completely unaware that in a town outside of Boston a girl named Love is miserable. Lifetime sends out mushy messages of lost mothers (which I have), sexual issues (which I kind of have, if not having any sex qualifies as an albeit small problem), and possessive fathers (sort of have this base covered—more sports analogies!). Then the Weather Channel provides solace. Somewhere, not here, it's warm. Somewhere, not here, public school kids are getting ready for vacation. Hadley, like all private schools, follows the prep school calendar and has March factored in as midterm break, and so even though February is technically the shortest month, for me, this year anyway, it's the worst.

When I tire of celebrities promoting themselves and morning videos fail to make me wanna get up and shake my thang, I ooze upstairs and get in the shower. "All By Myself," "Owner of a Lonely Heart," "Don't Leave Me this Way," "Live to Tell"—I pound my way through whatever songs come to mind, belting them out at full force, even when the shampoo leaks into my eyes and I scurry like a blind hamster toward my washcloth.

I am of myself, I am of the world. I am of myself, I am of the world. I repeat the words in my head and then say them, seeing if any brilliant essay ideas charge out of my brain. No such luck. Sometimes it's hard for me to believe I have a future in writing anything at all with the way the words seem to halt themselves on the page. But maybe I'm just passing the buck (is that originally a sports analogy? Note to self: Look it up) and it's not the fault of the words but solely mine.

With my towel wrapped toga-style (hey, I'm not going anywhere for two (2) days, I may as well settle in), I sit at my desk and ponder the meaning of the school motto. Based on the reality-slap I've been given, I should have profundity coming out of my ass (an interesting image), but I don't. I have only *disciplinary action,* alarms ringing, and the smarmy Muzak from that baby diaper rash ointment (kudos to morning television) stuck in my head.

Even though I have good intentions—I sit with the pen poised and plan on writing the essay Chaucer's so insistent I attempt—I can't find any words. I can't seem to live up to the expectations in my own mind.

CHAPTER 15

Disc four (aka the Sad and Mopey one) spins out melodramatic monologues of pining and pouting—I feel right at home. Like Eric Carmen's "All By Myself." Like "When Will I See You Again?" Like "Just When I Needed You Most" (this one I sing while crying, a seriously pathetic memory of myself I will have to flush down the toilet—and then clean with Shiny Hiney).

I wish I had occasion to play disc six (aka Happy and Horny) and thump around the room readying for a big night out with Robinson, but I'm not. So instead of dancing to T. Rex's "Get It On" I'm pulling an Olivia Newton-John "Hopelessly Devoted to You" and sinking—wallowing, more like it—in my own stupidity and self-marginalization.

Never will I have golden hair, nor will it be trellis-strong and long enough to merit a prince climbing on it—besides, I think I've had enough window action for a while but from my Rapunzel-esque tower I can see the bus waiting to take people to the Valentine's Day dance. And like the lame-o fairy tale girl who just sits there, I do the same. Just my luck that today is actually the fourteenth—so I don't even get a makeup cheese-fest holiday session in school. No chocolate hearts from the Student Government trying to earn some money, no love notes on the day. I haven't left the house in forty-eight hours and won't until this evening.

Boys in tuxes stand puffing the cold air out, eyeing the girls who would rather show their strappy dresses off and freeze than cover themselves with jackets. A couple have wraps that will get trampled on and snow-soiled, particularly if they claim a seat at the back of the bus. I'm not filled with contempt, just longing.

Lila texted me from Newbury Street today as she slipped in and out of shift dresses and empire waists (a look I will never pull off—chesty and small = no boob-emphasizing formal wear). She finally settled on a simple celadon-green silk number that no doubt brings out her incredible eyes and complements her skin tone. She sweetly said she kept finding things she wanted me to try on. I didn't text back my poutiness. Where would I wear a gown?

At times like this, I've always wondered what it would be like to have a mother whisk in and give her sage advice. Sure, Mable's on her way to get me for our open mike night at Slave to the Grind and she'll insist on doing RLG in the car, or making me sing my ads or show tunes to encourage a smile across my face, or she'll tell me how she was stood up for the prom one year—but it's not the same. Wouldn't a mom try not just to distract me from my misery but make me feel like everything will work out in the end? And my dad won't try to appease me, not tonight. He's been moping as much as I have. And he made it perfectly clear to me that the only reason I'm allowed to go to the open mike night at all is because I made a commitment to Mable and he needs to reinforce my following through. Sometimes it's impossible to imagine him as a young guy, being cool and laid-back. Maybe he never was. But if he still had some of that when the school year started, he's packed it away for the winter.

I feel like I have no perspective. I can rattle off explanations and justifications about dances being a tiny blip on life's radar or my punishment not meaning the end of my promising (promising = not mathematically bound) academic career, but the fact of it is that tonight still sucks. One thing I really hope changes as you get older is the feeling that every day encompasses a year's worth of emotion and change. When I had pneumonia in the seventh grade, I was out of school for a week, and when I came back, it was as if the entire world had shifted. People I thought were my friends decided they weren't, classwork made no sense, and the boy I thought liked me (surprise surprise, I was his *friend*) had already kissed and declared "going out" status with Olivia Greenbrier (who later moved to Idaho, but I digress).

In some ways, that's how chapel Sunday night will feel. We'll all be in our proper outfits and blazers, eating family-style dinner (think massive plates of manicotti you inevitably drop onto your white shirt), and the talk will be of the dance. Who wore what, what songs played, funny incidents and coded stories, all going over my head. And while I wish—at least I *think* I wish—I were someone who would shrug this whole thing off to life experiences, I'm just not. At least not yet. Maybe with some more effort in the "personal development department" (the only department store Dad is fond of) I will reach the Zen-like status of Sting, able to cleanse myself of triviality and the trials of teenage-hood. Whatever. Fuck.

"Oh, my God," Mable says when we're in her car. After I got the Saab, she went and bought the next in a long line of cars under a couple of thousand dollars. Mable's always working out deals, like if you give her five hundred off the car, she'll give you a coffee pass, which basically entitles you to free coffee for life. Or she'll do your gardening or sew curtains for your office. This time, her transport is an old orange Volvo with room enough for cases of filters and milk in the back, or, when the backseat is down, some drummer's giant bongos.

"What? What's so great?"

"Guess who's opening the show?" She turns off the radio for concentration.

"Elvis?"

She gives me a soft hit on the shoulder. "Seriously."

I shake my head and look out the window. Somewhere, Robinson is slow-dancing with a pretty girl. Will he think of me? "I don't know, Mable. Who?"

"Jonatha Brooke!" Mable squeals. A real squeal. She and I have had a thing for Jonatha Brooke since we first heard her on a local radio station. Now she gets lots of airplay, but she's from a suburb near Boston and is about the coolest singer ever to emerge from our locale (apologies to Steven Tyler).

"How did this happen?" I ask.

"She's come into Slave before, you know, just to grab a soy venti and run. But I guess she saw the poster and is back home for the weekend and called up to see if it was okay."

Regardless of my mood, I have to let myself be excited. She has the sort of music career I'd love to have: not in it for the fame and fortune, just making really great music and developing a fan base that is so loyal. But I wish I didn't have the lurking dread of disappointing my dad hanging over me. When you're the only child of a single parent, there's so much extra pressure to be great, to be like this rock for them. Sometimes I feel like Brick, my bummer of an alter ego, stems from the responsibility I feel to just make everything work out okay for Dad, even though I am an aware enough person to know whatever my mother's deal was had nothing to do with me. But it affects my dad and thus dribbles down to me, and thus the psychiatrists of the world make enough money to go on vacations. But anyway. Back to Jonatha!

"Ugh," I say out loud. "I hope I manage not to drool on her and act like a stalker fan."

"You'll do fine," Mable says, and smirks like she's got some plan up her funnel-shaped sleeve. "I hope we get a good crowd."

Mable didn't have to hope too hard. Slave to the Grind is filled to capacity and the steamed drinks are flowing, each topped off with either a chocolate heart on top of the foam or a sprinkling of red cinnamon powder. The posters look great and make me think of Jacob, who—king of kings—shows up with his guitar and plays a song that the crowd loves but which I miss half of by being on the door collecting the five-dollar cover charge and handing out vouchers for future lattes (Mable's way of ensuring repeat customers). I catch the end and go up to him.

"You're really good," I say.

"That one's kind of Rufus Wainwright meets James Taylor. I just wanted to try it out." He looks around. Did he just check out that woman in the jean jacket? Wait—not my problem. Friend-Girl step into action.

"She's cute," I say, and nod to the girl.

Jacob nods. "I guess." He smiles. "Anyway, I asked Mable if I can close tonight. You think you'll stick around?"

"Of course," I say.

"Good. I want you to hear this one."

Just then, Mable grabs my arm and leads me over to the back table near the kitchen where, unbeknownst to me, Jonatha Brooke is sitting quietly sipping and chatting away with a friend.

I'm introduced and then Jonatha plays to a happy crowd and the mike is open—some funny singers (tone-deaf yet enthusiastic) and some serious (Is there a record scout in the audience?) take the stage. A couple of hours later, Mable and Jonatha lure me up, but I'm too embarrassed to sing. I know I've done it before, but the idea of singing a cover tune again makes me feel like shit. Why can't I write my own song and get up and show people? But then Jonatha asks me to sing with her, and this I can't refuse.

She plays guitar and I stand near her, singing her song "Better After All." The words and melody flow out of me, blending well with her voice, and the whole thing seems so poignant I might cry. Later, Jacob listens to the music and I wonder if he dissects the lyrics. If this were Radio Love Gods, whom would I be singing to? Robinson? Jacob? Someone I've yet to meet? Splitting myself into two people—the Love on stage and the Love observing the scene from the corner—I project myself into the words and wonder.

I am trying to read your mind . . . I won't beg and I won't barter . . .

It seems like she's singing my life, or something like it, but the song is so good I don't feel misty-eyed. Jonatha says a quick thank-you and I realize that unless I make myself just do it (no, please not more sports references), I won't have a complete song.

But Jonatha's is. Complete, I mean.

With lyrics that last a page and a tune that carries its weight. With the applause comes a blush and the feeling of both shame at myself for not committing to following through with my own writing and still feeling proud at my efforts here. Then, as the crowd asks for more, I notice something—someone—outside at the window.

Still in his tux, Robinson has one palm pressed to the glass, the other cupping a single rose. With the streetlight in back of him, he looks illuminated and otherwordly. He is otherwordly, from the planet of dances and formals from which I've been banned. He motions for me to leave the stage and come outside. I thank Jonatha and replace the microphone and try to squeeze through the crowd to get out to the sidewalk. Clearly, all the signs I posted—two in the student center included—did the job of spreading the open mike at Slave. Yay for glitter. And for me, I think as I smush against people to get to tux-clad Robinson.

Amidst the accolades and the coffee spills, I maneuver my way toward the front door. With a breath of freezing air, I'm outside—alone. Robinson isn't there anymore, but the rose is leaning against the building. The flower is apricot-colored, not dissimilar from the summer version of my hair. I'm glad it's not red or pink, although I'm sure I'd be psyched about any rose at this point. But the unusual tone reminds me of—me, I guess. Maybe Robinson really did pine for me (do guys pine?) at the V-Dance. Possibly he held onto a girl he wished were me, twirled her and spun the edges of her dress out, all the while imagining me in his arms.

I take the chilled and slightly wilted rose inside with me. Packing up, all the singers and coffee aficionados begin to clear out.

"Your friend left," Mable says.

I smile. "Yeah, but look what he left." I hold out my non-corsage.

"No," Mable says. "Not that guy—the other one. Mister sensitive artist." And when I clearly look befuddled she adds, "The guitarist. Jacob."

Jacob. I didn't hear his song. "Did he play again?"

Mable wipes up the crumbs and spills from the counter with a rag. "He sort of vanished, to be honest."

We stack saucers and fill massive black trash bags with the soiled paper cups and heat-sleeves (Mable had hers printed up to read: CAUTION: HOT DRINKS ARE HOT—YOU SPILL IT, YOU DEAL WITH IT), napkin wads, and sugar packets.

"So, what's the deal with you and these men?" she asks.

"There's no real deal," I laugh. "I wish there were." Mable raises her eyebrows, disappears to the back where she flicks on a disc, and comes back. "Did you ever just wish your life would be spread out in front of you where you can see it?"

Mable sits down in the chair. She looks really tired. With her mouth twisted she shakes her head. "What's the fun in that?"

"I don't know. Maybe I don't want fun. I know, I'm sixteen, I'm supposed to want to, what, frolic? But I just want to know what happens."

"What you think is going to happen won't, and what does actually occur will be better and worse than you could have predicted."

"Worse?"

"Sometimes. Sometimes life spins out of control and sucks." I wait to see if she explains this, but she doesn't. "And other times—most of the time—it's pretty great. Pretty great mixed with the mundane."

We set the chairs upended on the tables and Mable mops. "How's Miles?" I ask. "How come he wasn't here tonight?"

"Costa Rica," she explains. "He comes back this week. And then, let the planning begin."

Mable has yet to inform me of the date or details of the future wedding ceremony—part of me wonders if it will actually happen. Not to be a bitch or downplay their love, but I could see them just being eternally engaged; two of those children of the seventies who stay together and breed and bond without a license. Who knows.

I end the evening by singing her my latest jingle—an ode to the Beach Boys and surf scene with frothy lyrics about soapsuds and summer breezes. Outside, it's still below zero.

CHAPTER 16

*S*unday morning is noticeably devoid of pancakes of any size or shape. Dad must have left early, since he wasn't up to see me in last night when Mable dropped me off and isn't home now. I take a cup of coffee and a toasted Eggo waffle with nothing on it upstairs and nibble my way around the crispy edges. This is how I'd eat everything, given the chance (and if manners and social graces were not a part of my world at all). In the comfort of my room or with Mable or a friend, I'll eat the sides of a Kit Kat bar, then gnaw my way through the wafer layers. Or I'll eat the middle of a brownie and save the edges for last (note to self: must find life-mate who prefers middles, since I like all things crispy and crunchy).

I log on and go right to JC Hall's blog. This time, the entry looks different. Where it usually opens with a movie quote, there's a blank banner. No date, no time. No paragraphs of thoughts. Just these words:

> Meet me there.

Am I a dumb shit for thinking these are instructions for me to follow? Does he know about my blog-snooping? Or just a hunch? I take my chances and, without a shower or thought to attire, I lace up and run to the blue high-jump mat. And, wait for the bells to chime. Nope. I find myself alone. But before I can wallow, he's there.

Robinson, just like in the movie theater of my mind, strides purposefully over to me and lifts my face up so it's angled perfectly for kissing. Which is what we do. Finally. And it lives up to all the coming attractions. You know those small moments in your life when things seem to come perfectly together? This is one of those. I know I will look back on this kiss and smile. It's the kind of kiss Mable talks about two decades later. The kiss from the boy you never thought you'd get. The kiss I hoped—but never counted on—having just for myself.

Still in my kiss-haze (read: me, dreamy, floating around like a moth), I get on with my Sunday night. After the seemingly endless communal postchapel dinner, I go to the library to study. Study = make out with Robinson in between the Women's Studies and Russian History stacks. I feel sure the dictators and female heroines are watching from their literary vantage points and cheering me on. At least I'd like to think so.

We've actually brought books so we can do our best mock-studying, and while I flip through Fitzgerald's *This Side of Paradise,* Robinson highlights nearly every line of his physics text.

"Let me explain gravity to you," he says.

"Oh, Professor, please do," I say, leaning in. My feet are on the rungs of his chair.

"Things fall," he says and cracks himself up, pulling me in to his mouth while laughing. We kiss and read and try to compose ourselves when anyone walks by. As I read about the guy in my book (and by read I mean mainly repeat the same sentence over and over again until it's devoid of meaning), my heart is flipping around in my chest cavity. I am—we are—one of those library couples. The kind you see when you've come to look up some boring something or other and stumble upon holding hands. In the movie version of right now, the camera would be on a crane, fixed and held two stories up against the library window, focusing in on us, revealing how we look from the outside.

"And how does Fitzgerald explore the quest for self-identity in *Paradise*?" Mr. Chaucer asks. A week shy of spring break and everyone's distracted. Thoughts of leisure days and sun-filled afternoons cloud the intellect. Not that I'm heading anywhere particularly warm nor exotic. For now, I'm in Robinsonland (like Disneyland but with very different rides). I've been the subject of Colorado's gossip wheel and Cordelia's half-nice, half-vicious questioning (Do you love him? Did you guys really do it in the library bathroom? Yeah. I want to lose my virginity with the smell of industrial cleaner under fluorescent lighting). I've been the subject of fawning (Robinson has left notes in my mailbox, but not cheesy ones). He'll print out whole scenes from movies and recast us in the roles. He scanned my face and his into movie posters from *Casablanca* and *The Breakfast Club* (I was the prom queen—unlikely— and he was the rebel—also unlikely, but cute).

"It's the duality of his position," Harriet Walters is saying when I tune back in. "Fitzgerald is toying with the reader, a typical male sensibility of politicizing the personal."

Jacob butts in. "I disagree. I think it's pretty simple. He's trying to find out who he is because without doing that, happiness is impossible. Fitzgerald dangles the possibility of fulfillment and joy, but doesn't let the characters have it unless they've put in their work."

He looks at me when he says this, and the combination of his navy blue stare and his words gives me chills.

"Maybe Fitzgerald . . . imagines the perfect-case scenario, but by doing this, blocks the reality of his everyday life," I say, talking about a long-dead writer and myself at the same time.

"And?" Chaucer prods.

"And by doing this, he numbs any potential pain. But I think he also negates the possibility of finding something extraordinary."

I blow off lunch and go to the computer lab, where I've only poked my head in before. Sitting with a view only of people's feet (the room is in the basement), I start to write. Four pages come out before I even check the time. I may be late for math (*again*—crap!), but I'm finally on my way to writing my personal essay for the Hadley Hall awards.

Shock of the world. When I get to math, even though the period's ten minutes under way, Thompson is nowhere to be found. We sit on the tables and hang out, wondering where she could be.

"Pulling the pole out of her ass?" someone suggests.

"Seriously," Penelope Parker says. "That woman needs laxatives just to make room to breathe." And, from what Cordelia says, Penelope would know, having a slight tendency to overpop those pills.

Thompson never shows and, as per the handbook, after a twenty-minute grace period, we are free to leave. This rule is some remnant from when a horse and carriage were responsible for providing teachers with the cross-campus commute, but we take advantage of it and head out before Thompson can return.

I walk home, done for the day, and wander around the house like it's someone else's. And maybe it still feels that way. Not all of the furniture is ours—in fact, a lot of it lives here permanently—and I realize, sitting in the formal chintz armchair, that all of this stuff will outlast us. I will go to college or whatever and Dad will stay here for however long and then we'll be shipped out like the people before us and this same flowery chair will be the host to someone else's ass.

All this seems very depressing—ah, notes from Brick—and not even the note in my pocket from Robinson makes me feel better. I look for the remote control (the CCC come through once a week to dust, mop, and rearrange the semiorder Dad and I try to have around the house). It's not in the coffee table drawers, nor is it perched atop the television. Unused side table? Yes, along with an old-fashioned key, one of those that looks as though it's supposed to reveal a treasure map.

And it sort of does. Either boredom or curiosity pushes me to unlock the sideboard door. In back of some huge silver serving pieces for dinners my father has yet to host, I find a small pile of old photos and slips of paper. White-edged and slightly water-stained, the first photo is my dad at maybe twenty years of age. Was he at college then? His shirt is like something from the vintage store Mable took me to, open-necked, gauzy yellow cotton. He's looking down in the photo as if something or someone is nearby and catching his gaze. Another picture contains a youthful Mable with hair down her back, tawny ringlets and coils all looped on each other. Her arm is around a guy I don't recognize with a full mustache and beard (may that look never completely return). Instinctively, I know what I'm looking for. Not a what. A who.

Is there a photo somewhere of a woman with my shaped lips? The points at the top? Does she have red hair that spills from its bun? Or a pixie haircut like Mia Farrow in that scary baby movie? I'm paging through this pile like an FBI agent, trying to make sense of what I consider to be clues to my past. Where is the lawn these people are sprawled out on? Did Mable introduce my parents? I hardly ever think of *them* as my *parents*. And the yellow legal pad pages with obsolete phone numbers (they are obsolete, right? Like if I try them, would a voice on the other end of the line be my mother's?). What do they mean? Why were they saved? I check my watch. Dad will be home any second. And though I hate to put the stuff away, I do. If he riffled through my drawers and journal I'd be pissed as hell, and maybe this is the equivalent for him. But it directly impacts me.

During our baked cod with breadcrumbs, broccoli, and sweet potato, I broach the subject with my dad.

"Do you ever miss being young?" I ask. He doesn't mind my hypothetical questions or past-searching, as long as I veer away from the touchy fringe of my mother and her whereabouts or history.

"Sometimes I do," he says. "I'm more tired now, that's for sure. But I like being where I am."

I eat a mouthful of fish and think back to our conversation at the seafood restaurant the night before school started. "And do you really believe that everyone changes—forever? Like you never get to a point where you just are?"

"Best case is that you always evolve. Stagnancy is death." Okay. Serious. Dad, meet Brick. Brick, Dad.

"It just sounds exhausting," I say. "In fact, I'm kind of exhausted just from all the mini-dramas and minutia of my daily existence." Dad laughs. A big, happy laugh. He likes when I just let it all out and complain or talk about my teenage life, I guess.

"What brought all this on?" he asks, and puts a broccoli spear into his mouth. "Remember you used to call them 'little trees'?"

I nod. I used to imagine little broccoli forests populated by those marshmallow yellow bunnies—Easter Peeps. "Those pictures . . ." I look at Dad. He chews and swallows and doesn't eat more. "The ones in the cabinet—when are they from? Who's that guy with Mable?" Dad says nothing. "Don't you get it? I need to know this stuff. Everyone has a family history, right? And I'm like supposed to be this educated, confident person—isn't that who you want me to be?"

"I want you to be who you are, Love, not what I want."

"Well, in order to do that, can't you just give me something? Is she alive? Did she, like, die some tragic death or become a man or what?"

Dad stands up and clears his plate. With the water running, he says, "Are we going here again?"

"Yes," I say, and bring my plate to the counter. Water splashes from the fish pan onto my arm and face where the droplets feel suspiciously like tears. "We're always going to end up back here."

"Like it or not, Love," Dad says and faces me, "this is your family history." He points to himself and to me. "We're it."

So much for further lyrical inspiration and impetus for finishing my Hadley Hall essay. I spend the rest of the night online, IM-ing with Robinson and Google-searching for cool things to do this summer. With the knowledge that I'm likely to be reaching into tubs of mint chocolate chip and cookie dough to serve up smalls and double cones from the JP Licks in town, I'm trying to figure out a way to do something with music. Not band camp or anything, but teaching singing to kids or finding a kick-ass internship at *Rolling Stone* (never mind that this is never going to happen) or working more open mike nights at Slave to the Grind. I take out my journal and make lists of jobs and activities that sound good, provide at least some income, and get me out of the house.

Robinson slides his hands up my back and we kiss to the sounds of Roxy Music's "Oh Yeah." I love this song, even though it's always struck me as sad rather than sexy. In this context, a dog food ad would make me excited. It's Robinson's first time in my room and he's impressed by the books and the breadth of my CDs, not to mention my double mattress. This last item he eyes more than once.

"Get your mind out of the gutter," I say. He kisses me again. "All right—my dad's coming back in an hour and I'm not taking any chances."

I walk him out and we sit on the porch. Muddy clumps of earth and tire-treaded slush line the driveway. Farch (Farch = combo of February and March, the netherworld of seasons).

"Have fun in the sun," I say, intentionally rhyming.

"I'll try," he says. "But I'll miss you."

Spring break starts tomorrow, and by this time then Robinson will have landed in St. Barts and be well on his way to sipping rum-enhanced drinks, slathering on the SPF of his choice, and maybe ogling the bikini-clad hotties.

"Picture me in a bikini," I say, even though I'm more of a boy-cut short and bikini top kind of swimmer.

"I always do," he says, and we kiss good-bye.

The next morning as the campus clears out, I swing by the student center to empty my mailbox of the various slips of paper I've let accumulate. I usually take Robinson's notes out and shove the other crap back in. Today, I take the lot of it out and stand over the wide mouth of the trash can, chucking out old notices for play tryouts and movie nights on campus. Then I come to a small packet, inside of which is an unlabeled CD. A Maxell, electric blue, eighty minutes. Probably mine or someone's misplaced papers. I take the disc home and am psyched to find that it's a mix—Robinson's proof of missing me already—with some songs I know, some that I don't. Already, just the first time through, I know I'm going to love this CD.

CHAPTER 17

My love life is no longer decaf. I am officially in a relationship, one that's spelled out for me in music via the mix I am now putting through overplay. I write Robinson an email that I don't send after rereading and deciding that it is way too mushy and more of a journal entry to myself, talking about how all the songs are amazing and oddly a handful of them are on my private list of favorites and how he just gets me, and how comforting that is.

Right before driving over to meet Mable for coffee, I check my account and find, to my surprise, an email from DrakeFan! A line of the message replays over and over again as I start the ignition. *It's been a long time—I've missed you.* I've missed DF, too, and now have the old feeling of looking forward to the next message again.

Mable wants to discuss my maid of honor dress—I guess the wedding is actually happening—and shows me fabric swatches in citrus hues.

"I'll look like a mango," I say, and neg the first one.

"You look great in orange and yellow," she says.

"Are you wearing white?" I ask.

"Planning on it. Why? You think I'm not pure enough? Too old?"

"I was kidding. But now that you mention it, I could see you in more of a flowy kind of . . ."

"You mean hippy, weird gauzy thing," she cuts me off. "Not this time."

"This time? You mean there've been others?"

Mable sighs. I wonder where she went inside her head. Then she explains. "A long time ago. I was married for about five minutes."

"Did he have a green Volkswagen van?" I ask, suddenly remembering mustache man and the photo with the camper van in the background.

Mable's face changes. "How did you know that?" I can't tell if she's pleasantly surprised or feels betrayed somehow, like her secret past is now not so undisclosed.

I mime photographing and say, "I found some stuff."

Mable nods and bites at her fingernails, considering something. She sighs. "Yes, as a matter of fact he did have a green VW. *We* did."

"And what happened?" This is better than movies or TV. How crazy that people have these enormous histories that just lurk underneath and you never know.

"David, his name was David. Davy back then. I don't know." She chews on her coffee stirrer. "He just wanted to hang out and go to California, surf, and do God knows what. Not anything productive."

"But you loved him?"

Mable sighs again. She looks so tired these days—even wedding planning seems to take its toll on her. "At the time I thought I did." She sips her drink. "But I think I liked the idea of love more than actually being in it." She sits up and shakes off the memory. "But I do love Miles, and it's a different kind. More real."

"You mean mature?" I ask, putting on a teacher voice.

"Something like that," she says. We go back to nuptial talk, and settle on having a dress made for me in a teal color that matches some of the flowers Mable wants to carry.

"You should give little gift bags of coffee beans or something," I suggest.

Mable perks up. "Good idea. I think I'll put that on the list of Things Miles Can Organize."

I want to say sorry for looking at my dad's old photos and stuff, so I try to find him on campus. Most buildings are locked, so I hunt around for him. His note on the kitchen table says he has a faculty meeting, which I assume means he'll be with the other administrators in his school office, but he's not there. I check the student center (locked) and the dining hall (faculty meetings often involve baked goods and lukewarm coffee) but to no avail. On the way back, I try to cut through Rollinson Hall, reminiscing about that first day of school with Robinson, who is now my boyfriend. Too funny/weird. The back door is open, so I go inside and past my bad-vibe math room. Only when I see people inside do I backtrack.

Thompson sits grading tests, circling errors with her red pen, and behind her is none other than my father, who leans down and kisses her cheek.

Bucket, please. I don't need a Blue Whale Beverage. I'm going to be sick just at the sight of them.

Faculty meeting, my ass. Who's breaking the honor code now? That'd be you, Dad. I decide to confront him when he comes home, which he does only after my solo dinner (Stouffer's French Bread Pizza, still a classic in my book). Plopping down next to me on the couch he asks about Mable, about my day. I tell him Mable seems tired and he nods, saying how tough it is to run her own business, how maybe I should work there for the summer to help her out. I neglect to mention my musical ambitions and focus instead on being the bearer of news.

"So, how long have you guys been dating, then?" I ask. It's clear from my tone and my dad's surprise that he's more than a little embarrassed at being found out. I don't wait for him to answer. "I mean, not that I haven't tried to get you to have some semblance of a romantic life—like, forever—but with her? She's so not who I'd picture you with. Not to mention that I figured you'd tell me when you had a—you know—a . . ." I can't make the word come out. I can't say "girlfriend" in reference to pole-up-ass Thompson and my dad.

"Love, I'm sorry. You're right, I should have said something. But I—we . . ." Gross, they're already a *we*?

"I just don't get how you can expect me to be all forthcoming with my thoughts and feelings or whatever but basically be dishonest yourself."

Dad agrees with me and we sit with the sound off on the TV and slowly chisel away at the details of our respective love lives. Skirting around the details of the parietals incident, I talk a little about liking Robinson and how it sucks to be here on campus while everyone—even Cordelia (who wrangled an invite to Colorado's Anguilla beach house)—is on vacation.

Dad stretches his arms above his head like he's dunking an imaginary basketball and launches into his paternal version of the MTV confessional room. "I liked Patty right off the bat." Could he have more sports analogies?

"Really?" I say, and it comes out shocked, like how could he possibly have had good, warm feelings about Trig Witch immediately when the rest of the world—okay, the Hadley campus—thinks of her class as a prison sentence?

"Really, Love, she's not that bad." He watches my face for signs of life. "At least, not out of the classroom." I give him the half-laugh he's looking for, some assurance I'm not going to disown him.

"So," I say, leaning in, "give me the dirt. You know, the behind-the-scenes look at the weird and wonderful world of Patty Thompson and . . . my dad." When I say it, I can hardly fathom the reality.

"She speaks very knowledgably about wines." Apparently, this is an adult aphrodisiac version. "She lived in Italy—Portofino—and—" He stops. "And . . . and the upshot is, we like each other. A lot."

And . . . and . . . I'm half disgusted and half happy for him—maybe not in that order. But I know, I've seen and been around him my whole life and he's never seemed lonely, but maybe he is. And I can't wish that on him, even if it means accepting his offer to join him and Thompson, Patty, for dinner.

I stand up and pull him up from the couch. We hug and I say, "I'll consider it, but only if we go for Chinese." There's lots of chopstick handling and pancake rolling, which could make conversation less of a necessity. But I add, "I just can't get enough of that Changsho pea-pod dish." I walk to my room, knowing full well my lame *maybe* is a *yes*.

Change just keeps happening, I guess, whether you're up for it or not, whether you feel prepared or vulnerable.

My feet drag on the stairs and, without warning, I find the inspiration I need to finish the Hadley Hall essay. I write about the evolution of song and self, from Gregorian chants and not knowing who you are to classical and folk and expressing oneself through lyrics and notes. I try to relate all this to my own life, to the parts I imagine and try to predict, how I am my own constantly morphing song.

At three in the morning, when I'm finished, I save the paper, email it to myself for safekeeping, and go to bed. I dream of California and being in the sun, singing, with citrus-colored flowers and giant ripe oranges. Robinson is there, and various people I don't recognize. Just when I am about to drive a green Volkswagen van, I look down and see that I'm topless. I have to choose between covering up or steering the van, and just when I'm about to veer off the road, Jacob takes control. "Don't worry," he says. "I didn't see anything."

Waking up to the sounds of birds enjoying the first days of spring makes the whole dream come back to me, even the part where Jacob and I got together. I semi-dream-cheated on Robinson and now have that weird postnocturnal intimacy feeling. Not only was I subliminally unfaithful, I also got it on with Jacob and know that I have to face him in class. That's always so bizarre, when you get into a fight with some-one in a dream and then see them the next day and recoil, or if you get it on with some random guy and then see him—it's like it really hap-pened, even though it didn't.

It didn't, I remind myself when Robinson comes back from break a day early (praise be to the foul-weather systems that moved through the tropics and returned him to New York and then to me) and he sucks up coming back to campus early just to hang out with me. We go to the Museum of Fine Arts and take turns sounding educated (note the brushstrokes and how Chagall conveyed his message through the im-ages and the medium by which they were delivered) and stupid (oh, my God! Check out the ugly dude in this painting!), stopping in the Egyptian wing to make out by the ancient urns and vases. Our kissing is witnessed only by mummies. I have one of the songs from the mix stuck in my head and I proceed to sing bits of it during the day. Robin-son finally clamps his hand over my mouth and smiles. "I get it," he says. "You like that song. I'm glad. But we've got to find something else for you to sing."

"Don't *you* like that song?" I ask.

He shrugs. "It's okay, I guess." If it's just okay, why would he put it on my mix to convey his feelings to me? This bugs me on the drive back to Hadley Hall from the city, but then I let it go.

CHAPTER 18

T hompson tries to break the ice by sliding a box toward me. Inside are retro postcards, most with movie images from the original film ads, including my favorite, *The Philadelphia Story*.

"Thanks," I say, and put the box next to me on the booth. Isn't it too soon for bribe gifts to the daughter?

"Your father mentioned you liked old movies." She smiles her toothless math teacher smile and takes a sip of her wine. At times like this I wish we had a legal drinking age of fifteen. I swirl my straw in my Coke and try mind-melding to will a splash of rum—anything—into the liquid to make the night more palatable. Kudos for the cool postcards; they will be good for summer correspondence. But she could've given me the promise of an A in math and I'd be happier.

To make my dad happy, I make small talk and only escape to the bathroom twice; once for actual lavatory purposes and once to call Robinson. We talk for all of three minutes and then I have to go, retreating to the alterna-world of school and home life becoming one.

Now that spring has sprung and I have my car and driving privileges reinstated, I take meandering routes on the weekends and back from

WAJS. Lila, with two college acceptances (Vassar and Amherst) and one wait-list (Brown), comes with me to drive along Massachusetts Ave.— all the way from Cambridge and where we double-dated this fall to the far end where Berklee College of Music is located. We sit at a café and watch the students heft their instruments from practice to home. They all seem content, sure that this is where they want to be and what they should be doing.

"You'll have to start looking at schools next year," Lila says. "Any thoughts?"

"Not really," I say. "It sort of depends on the music thing—if I want to study formally or go out to L.A. and try to be an idol or jingle-rocker. Or if I drop it all."

Lila rolls her eyes. "It's impossible not to see you doing something with music." We sit and watch the smokers exhale and cough into the sunlight, and Lila tells me about her uncle, who is somewhat connected in the music industry. She reaches into her wallet and pulls out his card. "Here," she says. "Just in case you ever get out there. I saw him over break and thought of you. Can't hurt."

"Thanks," I say, watching her clip and reclip her hair. "I'll miss you next year."

"I know. Me, too. It's so weird to know I won't be back here in the fall. It's like starting over."

In this way, I don't think college will feel that new to me. I'm sure the freedom will, but the newness, the clean-slate part won't. I've done all that before. And, just like with this year, it always turns out differently than I first expect.

"So," Lila says, flinging her hand in the air to get a bee to go away, "you like him, huh?"

We haven't really spoken of Robinson much. Just the sort of quiet acknowledgment that it's okay between us. "Yeah," I say. "I do."

"Just be careful," she says, instantly annoying me in the way that only a parent or the girl who got to your boyfriend first can. I nod and crunch sugar granules in my back teeth. "Did you go to New York during break?"

"No." I am pea-sized. She had two years with him; I've had like a month. She's slept (not with him, but in close proximity) in his beach house, the town house, God knows how many state lines they've crossed together. "Not yet," I add for good measure.

Lila raises one eyebrow and gathers her hair into a messy-sexy pile. "Well, let's talk after you do." What is Lila hinting at? I raise my eyebrows back at her, but probably look dorkier than she does in this gesture. Lila responds with a cryptic, "Let's just say that Robinson isn't . . . totally organic." I wonder if this is a reference to some obscure drug addiction or a potential love of aspartame and processed cheese or just Lila's way of being just a tad jealous.

"Sure," I say, wondering if I will ever go home with Robinson. "I'll tell you if and when it ever happens." We sip our drinks. "When will you hear from Brown about the wait-list?"

Lila sighs. "Don't know. Maybe a couple of weeks?"

We stand up and leave the table, both of us feeling like we are second choice, the alternate who moves up the list only when someone else drops off.

World Hunger Day. To show solidarity with struggling nations and teach the privileged students of Hadley Hall an ephemeral (SAT prep has begun: ephemeral = fleeting) lesson, the dining hall is split and segregated. Upon entering the room, we each draw a little piece of paper from a raffle box that informs us what world we're a part of: first, second, third, fourth. Participation in the exercise is optional, but everyone does it (e.g., theoretically optional). You then get a meal (or lack thereof, if you're fourth world) that represents what you'd have if you lived anywhere but here. The actual numbers are eye-catching. Only a handful of students get a first-world ticket—just like the real percentage of people who live in the U.S.

and Europe. Most people get third world and a scoop of rice or beans.

Of course, the anorexics among us are quite thrilled by this, as are the vegans, and there's ample opportunity for ticket-trading. Most noticeable aside from the third-world students sitting cross-legged on the floor is the sheer disarray of the usual social patterns. Cliques are temporarily disbanded, jocks sit next to their stoner peers. The preppy girl with all things Burberry makes do with her beans, wedged between two members of the school Anarchy Society (no symbol—thus being even more about chaos) and the frozen-yogurt machine.

I, however, am sitting drinking from a goblet (one of those plastic ones with the detachable stem) at the first-class table. The few of us first-worlders are seated around a linen-draped lunch table. We tuck into our hot meals. Watching the mounds of rice and glop of pureed lentils on the plates nearby, I'm overwhelmed and guilt-ridden for eating the chocolate-covered strawberries in front of me.

"Oh, who the fuck cares?" This from Colorado, who has a berry in each hand (miraculously, nothing up her nose).

"I do," says one girl.

"This is so random," one guy says, and pushes his plate away. I kind of want to abandon my fancy table and go sit with Lila, who is eating rice with her fingers (utensils are for second and first world only). But I'm not allowed. There's no mixing of worlds. And I'm right back where I was at the beginning of the year: alone. I shove a strawberry into my mouth and lick my fingers. Then I see Jacob sitting in a mass of second world eaters. I blush at the sight of him, my dream rushing back at me. As if on cue, he looks up and stares, then focuses on his lap-held plate. Across the room, Robinson waves and points to his meal with a thumbs-up.

Later, he tells me it was just like going out for Indian food, minus the chicken tikka masala.

"Isn't that the point?" I ask.

Robinson walks me to math, where Patty/Thompson/stick-butt has chosen today for a pop quiz. Students complain about their empty stomachs and say they can't think straight for being hit with hunger pangs.

"Poor you," she mock-sympathizes. And then, since she saw me at the first-world table, she says, "Shouldn't be a problem for you though, Love."

Of course not. And it shouldn't be a problem for you if I still wish you weren't dating my dad. I roll my eyes at my lame inner-monologue comment and put the note from Robinson in my lap to read while trying to complete the quiz in the time allotted.

The note is a handmade coupon good for one round-trip ticket on Amtrak's fast train from Boston to New York. On the bottom, like a disclaimer, Robinson has written in tiny print that this ticket comes with no expectations (expectations = Love loses virginity atop Empire State Building, etc.), just hopes for good fun, food, and a chance to hang out with him on his home turf. I notice there's no expiration date—good until the end of time? Whoa. Slow down.

I prepare for the debacle of asking and pleading with my dad. I figure I will have to run him in illogical circles about why it's so important to me to go to New York with my senior boyfriend for Memorial Day. I come up with several routes that might lead to "yes." Among them, my chance to have a firsthand tour of the city with a person who grew up there, a chance to explore the cultural aspects of the place (and by cultural I mean the Guggenheim, MoMA, and CBGB, where Blondie and Tom Waits and the Ramones played, not a walking tour of Robinson's naked bod). If all else fails, I figure I can wink and say that it's a chance for my dad to have the house to himself (even though what that implies makes me feel ill).

But I never have to pull out those stops. My dad, smiling after a phone call I can only assume was with Thompson, comes to the dinner table and sits down.

"Dad, look, I just want to tell you something that's important to me. I've been invited to go to New York for Memorial Day weekend, and I really, really want to go."

"With Robinson?" he asks. I nod. "I don't want you navigating the roads, Love."

"No, I'd take the train." This seems to satisfy him and he considers it.

"I assume the Halls will be there, chaperoning?" Um, this I'm not sure about, but I guess.

"I think so," I say.

"I'd like to speak with them, but then I don't see why not," he says. "Sounds like fun."

Why, yes. Yes, it does. The parental negotiations prove easier than I thought they would be, but I know that if I asked unprepared for the worst, he totally would have needed to be convinced.

Now departing from track two at the Route 128 Station—Love Bukowski on her first real solo trip to see a boy in a city she doesn't know very well. And maybe sleep with him. Or near him. Or not. With no chance of fire alarms and parental interruptions (Robinson has mentioned pointedly more than once that his parents are very mellow and won't care where I sleep), I have game-show-type fear. Will I pick the correct door? Will I spin the wheel of fortune in the right direction? Buy a vowel?

Landscape whizzes past, first city then the beaches of Rhode Island. Lila's family house is near here in Newport. Wonder if I'll ever see it, or if our friendship will give way to distance and circumstance. I'm sitting enjoying my view and a grossly large and overpriced chocolate-chip cookie from the dining car when I see a curly-topped head of hair I know to be Jacob's. I'm at one end of the car and he's at the other, his head bobbing slightly to the music coming through his earphones. He doesn't see me. When he goes toward the snack bar, I go to his seat with the intent of dropping a funny note there. Gripping the seat in front so I don't fall over, I first examine the CD on his tray table. Then, when I look at the liner notes inside, I'm too freaked out to do anything but bolt back to my seat. He's got a copy of the CD Robinson made for me. Who knew Jacob would be a stalker. Or maybe it's a dorm thing and Robinson handed out copies to whoever wanted one. No, that's really lame. I debate whether I'd rather cool Jacob be a creepy stalker or find out that Robinson so doesn't get the mix as a personal thing that he'd hand out copies to whoever wanted them.

There's nothing like the feeling of being swept off your feet in the middle of a train station or airport. Okay, I don't have the airport experience, but the train station part rocks. Robinson shows up with a little tacky snow globe of a mini Manhattan and shakes it so I can see the snow glitter fall. We kiss for what feels like an hour and then run outside, my bag slung over his shoulder, and jump in a cab heading uptown.

I wish I'd paid more attention to Monopoly properties, because then the Park Avenue value would have registered prior to my showing up at his doorman building and being greeted by name (name = Miss Bukowski). We don't need keys because the elevator opens directly into the entryway of his apartment.

"It's actually two apartments we combined," Robinson explains on the tour. He points out where the division line used to be, where now there's a double-length living room and a kitchen that looks like something out of a magazine.

My room—Robinson shows me this with a wink—is a mélange of creams, beiges, and blues, with ironed sheets and bolster cushions, heavy drapes that pull back to reveal a view of building tops and toy-sized taxis. I want to ask Robinson what it was like to grow up here, in Manhattan, but also in this apartment. I want to know his memories and the meaning behind some of the framed artwork that hangs on the wall. But there's no time to sit and chill out.

As soon as I drop my bag and wash my face, Robinson whisks me into the library, a paneled room with an entire wall of leather-bound antique volumes and speakeasy-style club chairs that face an entertainment system worthy of a Coppola. And then I remember his dad *is* like a Coppola and I feel better.

"We can screen something later if you want," Robinson says, noticing me noticing the full-size movie screen.

Rather than the family meal I pictured for tonight, I get a full five minutes with his mother, Belinda—Bissy—who casts a subtle, practiced eye over me and my casual-yet-put-together outfit.

"I gather your father is rather a well-known figure on campus," Bissy says. She slides a tiny tray of sushi toward me like it's a normal afternoon snack and I take a California roll to be polite. Then I try to speak intelligibly about Dad and my summer plans while chewing on seaweed.

"So, yeah," I conclude. "My ideal world would be a *Rolling Stone* internship, but I'll probably wind up babysitting or . . ."

Bissy interrupts and tilts her head to Robinson. "Who do we know at *Rolling Stone*? Does Marcus still work there? What about—what was that one with the long hair—Genevieve?" Robinson shrugs and eats another piece of ebi.

I'm about to be excited; maybe she's a real connection to a summer that doesn't suck. But then the glimmer of hope is extinguished when she drifts off toward the kitchen and forgets all about it. "Well, you kids have fun tonight, and Love, you must come to the Hamptons this summer."

"Will you?" Robinson asks, when we're waiting for the elevator to take us downstairs and way downtown to some club.

"Do you want me to?" I ask, knowing full well he does. He nods and does a fake puppy dog pant. We haven't spoken much about his plans for NYU in the fall. I mean, I guess we could keep going long-distance, but didn't most senior-sophomore relationships end shortly after graduation? Right after a roll in the infamous sand at the Crescent Beach party?

"Maybe," I say. "If you play your cards right."

Den of Cin (as in cinema) is this fun place downtown where you get to basically do karaoke but with movie scenes instead of songs. This is my introduction to the world of Movieoke. The person who started it made a film in school where the main character could only communicate in movie lines (which I could totally relate to), and now we all (all = me, Robinson, and his New York posse), write down scenes we want to do and wait for them to be cued up.

At the table, we pick at tempura vegetables, dipping them in spicy mustard and soy sauce. I take my time chewing so I can survey Robinson's group. Paul is the nicest, an English guy who had retained only the slightest lilt after moving here when he was fourteen, Plant (whose name is something like Peter Ficus, but who has been deemed Plant forever), and a couple of girls. One Robinson doesn't know, and sadly, she seems like the most down-to-earth. The other two are Kai (like Chai, only not as sweet, with cropped hair and a bright-red mouth) and Lindsay Parrish, whose moniker sounds diminutive and possibly sweet and chaste, but whose personality and form beg to differ. Lindsay Parrish introduces herself as Ms. Manhattan to Robinson's Mr., and from there, I can tell it's a battle brewing.

Not that I did anything except show up to inspire the claws and fangs I feel sprouting under the table from Lindsay's long fingers and limbs. Everything about her seems stretched—wide smile with blinding teeth, her impossibly long jean-clad legs, her bangled wrists. She's too cool for me; a flat celluloid image. Flat except for the boobs. Those are 3-D (literally).

"You're up," Robinson says. He ventures in front of the screen with me and, with his friends, we redo the scene from *The Breakfast Club* where Claire (me, even though it was obvious that Ms. Manhattan wanted it, but she got the Ally Sheedy role and then pronounced it far more important anyway) puts lipstick on via sticking the tube of it between her breasts.

Well, I figure, I've certainly got the correct anatomy for the role, and the scene goes well. Maybe too well. With Robinson fake-clapping the Judd Nelson part and real lipstick (Kai's red—a bad choice for me) smeared on my lips. I step down and wipe my mouth.

After a few more rounds, we head to some bar where Kai and Lindsay Parrish double-kiss a plethora of identical boys in black T-shirts who wander in and out of conversation. Robinson makes sure I'm well oiled (his words, not mine) with martinis but leaves me periodically to chat with leggy women and guys from grade school or the Hamptons or wherever people like this meet. English Paul keeps me entertained with a running commentary of people's downfalls and connections. For example: "That's Billy Katchum, who used to date Lindsay, but who shagged that girl—the one with the obvious implants—last summer. And next to her is Sydney, who just got out of rehab, but who, from the looks of it, needs a round-trip ticket."

I'm amused, but hollow by the end of the evening. I want so much to hang out and just talk, eat pizza, and chill at Robinson's house, getting to know people who know his old stories—the non–Hadley Hall ones. Then, it occurs to me, as we're split up for the ride back uptown, that this might be the non–Hadley Hall Robinson Hall. A mouthful—but not in a good way.

"You coming in?" Robinson, drink in hand, T-shirt and boxers on, stands in the doorway. He's so gorgeous. I motion for him to come over to me. "So, what'd you think of them?"

"Your friends? They're nice. Thanks."

"That's it?" he asks, let down. "Isn't LP just the best?"

"LP?"

He rolls his eyes as if I'm clueless, which I am. "Lindsay Parrish. She's been in my life since nursery school—you know, that girl that used to pull on my hair and I'd push her down."

"Puppy love?"

Robinson wraps his arms around me. "No, nothing like that. We just go way back, that's all. She's been there for me during some rough patches and I'd drop anything for her." I know this should make me feel like I have a loving boyfriend who is so concerned with another's well-being that he'd run to her in a time of crisis, but what I feel is funny. Not ha-ha. Odd. Suspicious. Would he drop me to run to her?

"What's the plan for tomorrow?"

"Brunch a little ways from here and then maybe a walk in the park if it's nice? Or a museum? What sounds good?" Just like that, regular Robinson is back. I picture us having omelets and home fries and walking hand in hand.

"Any of it—all of it," I say, and then I let him lead me into his room. We kiss and lie down on the bed, kissing more with his shirt off, and then in one experienced motion my own shirt is flung to the floor and I'm looking up at Robinson above me. He kisses my neck, and when he moves, he gives a clear view of the picture frames on his side table. Him with Lindsay on the beach as young teenagers. Lindsay with her hands on his chest, looking up at him. Lindsay Parrish alone, in front of some European monument I don't know.

I sit up and reach for my shirt. "What's wrong?" Robinson asks. He's breathing heavy and has the glazed-over look of a guy with a booty mission.

"Nothing," I say, but I stand up. "I'm just really, really tired." Robinson hugs me.

"Stay here?" He pats the bed.

I pretend to consider it, although I know damn well I need to be alone tonight. "Not tonight," I say. He walks me back and we kiss more. Then he tucks me in and turns out the light.

I draw back the blinds and look at the night view of New York. Everything still looks small—distant.

"Rise and shine, Love." The scent of waffles and fruit rouses me before I even open my eyes. Is there anything sexier and more appetite-stimulating than a half-naked Robinson Hall holding a tray of breakfast goods?

"Thanks, that's so sweet," I say and sit up. Robinson puts the breakfast-in-bed tray on my lap and we nibble at the Belgian waffles, dipping them in a warm pot of syrup. He's even put an apricot-colored rose on the tray. I point to it. "Did you get this color on purpose?"

"I went out to the grocers this morning," he says, and gives me a sticky kiss on the mouth.

"I thought we were going out for brunch," I say. And then, in case he thinks I'm disappointed, "But this is better."

Later, we're taking the promised walk in Central Park amidst the joggers and baby strollers. The leaves are unfurled and the crocuses are blooming. A horse and carriage trot by.

"Newlyweds, ugh," Robinson says.

"What—you have a problem with them?" I ask.

"No." Robinson puts his arm around me. "I just think those carriages are so cheesy. So touristy."

"Yeah." I nod. "But they could be fun."

Robinson suddenly drops his arm from around my shoulder and runs to catch up with a spandex-clad person ahead. "Linds!" he calls. The leggy runner slows down and turns. They double-kiss (um, are we in Europe?), and Lindsay Parrish, breathy and aglow with cardio-induced endorphins, strides to me.

"Morning," she says. "What brings you two lovebirds out here?"

"I've never been to Central Park before, I just wanted to check it out," I say.

Lindsay nudges Robinson. "A first-timer, huh?" I get the feeling she means more than a Central Park virgin. I watch a young family, mother, father, shaggy dog, two kids. Then I think about my dad and suddenly am hit with how lonely it must have been for him taking care of me by himself. I want to talk about this, share it with Robinson.

"I'd love a cup of coffee," I say.

"Great." Robinson nods and takes my hand. And to Lindsay he adds, "See you later?" I'd bet good money it wasn't a question so much as a statement.

At Piccolino, a small Italian place with pastries and frothy drinks, we sit outside and watch the passersby. I try to express my thoughts coherently, a challenge in itself, about my family, my Dad, even how he's dating Math Thompson. Robinson listens—I want to say politely, but doesn't really push for details or comment the way he would if we were talking about the latest movie.

I switch gears, going from emotional digging to girlish poking and prodding. I'm filled with a certain amount of self-loathing when I do this, but I am too curious not to. "So, does Lindsay go running on that path often?"

Robinson doesn't take my bait. I thought he'd say something like yes, every morning, and then I could accuse him of taking that route just to bump into her. But he says, "I don't know. I mean, she's on the cross-country team at Tate Academy." My face is blank, so he goes on. "That's probably the best girls' school—it's right near where we live." We meaning the collective Upper East Siders.

"Oh," I say. And making a concerted effort not to be bitchy, "It's funny to picture it as *cross-country* in Manhattan."

"Well, she might transfer," Robinson says. "I keep telling her to go to Hadley Hall next year."

"I thought she was a senior." Is that jealousy, panic or coffee acid in my stomach?

"No, sophomore, like you." Robinson leaves money on the table and we go off to explore the windows of Fifth Avenue.

Over the course of the next twelve hours we have moments that register as filmlike in my mind, or like Robinson's black-and-white summer snapshots. Kissing by that fountain near the opera, each of us trying on wigs in some transvestite-populated store in the Village, Robinson wiping my mouth free of mustard after a hot dog at Gray's Papaya.

We head home in the early evening for a recuperative change of clothes. He heads off to shower, and I change, then explore the house a little, choosing a room to read in. I snuggle into an oversized armchair and begin paging through one of the movie scripts on the shelf. I read a couple of scenes from one that says *Perchance to Dream (working title)* on its cover. Then, tired of the epic nature of that one, I choose another. This one, weirdly, is called *Apricot Rose*. I'm drawn in from the beginning, especially when I read scene two and Chester, the main character, tries to woo Lucy with an apricot-colored rose. In the stage directions, it calls for Chester to hold up the rose to a window where Lucy sits painting in the formal drawing room.

Fine, so it's set in Great Britain in the late 1800s, but it pretty much mimics Robinson's visit to Slave to the Grind, with Chester disappearing before Lucy can thank him. This makes her long for him. Like I did. I quickly skim for more likeness. Nothing, nothing, tea in a shop, formal dinner party, and then—boom—the breakfast-in-bed scene. Chester delivers toast and poached eggs to Lucy after they've had an argument.

I want to page ahead, find out what else lies in store for me (me and Lucy), but can hear Robinson talking on the phone, walking this way. I slide the script back in among the others, and wonder if this is what Lila meant when she talked about Robinson in New York. And maybe why she never slept with him. I mean, I love the cinema and obviously spend a bit too much time camera-angling at myself and my life, but I still want something real.

And this doesn't feel like it is anymore.

"Ready?" Robinson asks. I almost want to call him Chester, but I don't.

"Sure," I say.

We head downtown to meet up with—surprise, surprise—English Paul and potentially Hadley-bound Lindsay and Plant. Another bar, another round, another night of being on the outskirts, and then tender Robinson at home. In the morning, I'm up and dressed and packed.

"I wish you'd stay and just come back to school with me Monday night," he says as we try to hail a cab for Penn Station. "We could have another whole twenty-four hours together without parietals." He smirks. "A night . . ." This last word comes out as a question, to which I shake my head.

"I know," I say. I put my hand on his back and know I'll feel weird on the train having left early. "But I have to do work and you should see your friends."

Robinson puts me in the cab and leans in the window for a kiss. "You'll have to come for a week this summer. The Hamptons, baby. You'll love it."

On the train back, I think about Chester and Lucy and movieoke. I think about other scenes we could have acted out. Maybe the *Dirty Dancing* one with "Nobody puts Baby in a corner"—except the reality of it would have been that I was.

Screeech, halt. I'm woken up from my train slumber not by motion but the lack of it. The conductor comes on to announce we are stuck.

No shit, really? Passengers, me included, look out the window as if this will give us a clue as to what's going on. We're informed that shuttles will take us into Providence and from there we'll be given vouchers for a bus ride back to Boston. I'm fairly sure that this was not in the *Apricot Rose* script.

On the shuttle I am squeezed in next to an enormous man with a cat in a carrying case. I sneeze before we've begun the journey, and he glares at me.

"I'm allergic," I say.

"So is Muffy," he answers. "To people who aren't cat people." Why do I always find my way to the freak shows? Why can't there be someone nearby with whom I actually want to converse? I'm wondering this and blowing my nose on a waxy napkin I find in my bag when I hear a familiar cough.

From behind me I hear: "I'll trade seats with you." Much to my surprise, the voice and cough belong to Jacob, saving me from welts and hives and wheezes.

"Thanks," I say, and stand up. I reach for my bag and Jacob says not to worry about it. "What're you doing here?"

Jacob doesn't answer, but I quickly move two rows back to avoid further congestion and splotchiness. Nothing more appealing than a hive- and welt-covered woman. Not that I care how I look in front of Jacob. Okay, not a total truth.

When we park in Providence, I stay still, letting the shuttle bus clear until Jacob and I are the only ones left.

"My dad lives in New Haven," Jacob explains, as if we've just been talking. "So I go to the city now and then." He looks directly at me. "What's your excuse for slumming?"

I think of Robinson's fancy apartment—hardly slumming. This time it's my turn not to answer. Instead I stand by his seat and get my bag from where it's wedged between his knees and the row in front of him. "You're my hero." This comes out more forceful and weighted than I intend, and I cover it up by blowing my nose and laughing about the cat guy.

"Hey," Jacob says when we're on the sidewalk. "Let's check our bags at the bus station and walk around." It's like we're both apologizing for something, the way we've entered and slunk back from each other's lives.

"Sounds like a plan," I say.

We have all intentions of seeing the whaling museum and walking around Brown University campus, but we wind up finding a diner housed in an old cable car, and once we've ordered, we end up sitting and talking for three hours straight.

Grilled-cheese crusts strewn aside, fries eaten, Cokes drunk, we convince the waitress to let us sit while she cleans and closes up.

"First love . . . I remember it," the waitress with piles of bright red hair says.

This makes me crack up and Jacob look like he's going to pass out.

"We're not . . ." I try to explain. The waitress holds up her palm.

"I've heard that one before," she says, and fills the salt and pepper. "Tell me another one."

The light fades on the bus ride back to Boston. Dad will pick us up at the station, and it occurs to me I might need to explain leaving to visit one guy and returning to campus with another one. Jacob starts to nod off.

"Can I listen to your CD player?" I ask, totally forgetting he has Robinson's CD in there. Jacob hands it over and falls asleep.

Watching the nondescript office buildings and warehouses and listening to the mix, I feel let down and confused. How could such great music come from a guy who used a script to figure out how to have a relationship with me? How could such a cool person like Jacob need to live vicariously through a dormmate's mixed disc?

Jacob's head lolls onto my shoulder. I don't shrug him off. His hair smells like vanilla. Yum. I press STOP on the player. This wakes him up.

"You like it?" he asks, pointing sleepily to the mix.

"Actually, I wanted to say, I think it's kind of bizarre—and by bizarre I meant creepy—that you have this. I mean, are you even friends with Robinson? Does he know you have it?"

Jacob sighs and shakes his head, annoyed. "You're really something, aren't you, Love?"

"What's that supposed to mean?" I ask. The bus stops in the station and people collect their bags and walk down the narrow steps. I can see my dad leaning on a pole, reading the Sunday paper while he waits.

"You really thought this . . ." He grabs the CD player and coils the headphones around it. "Was from *him*?" I'm dumbstruck.

"Passengers off, please," the driver calls back.

Jacob stands up. I follow, and we take our bags. Dad starts over to me.

"*I* made this," Jacob says. My heart stops, starts, jumps. "For you." Of course. Of course. I am the biggest ass ever. Of course Jacob knew me well enough to know the songs that would hit home so hard. The ones that made me swell with—love?

"Jacob—I didn't—I just assumed . . ."

"Love," Dad interrupts. He hugs me and I stare at Jacob. All this time I've given credit to Robinson for pouring himself into the song list. "Ready?" Dad takes my bag and starts to walk away, presumably to the car.

"You coming?" I ask Jacob.

"No," he says quietly, and stares at me with his dark blue eyes. "I think I can make it back by myself."

I stand there for a moment hoping he'll change his mind, but he doesn't. I back off first and follow my dad to the car. In my head I hear some of the lyrics from the mix and imagine them like subtitles over the marathon conversation Jacob and I had at the diner. Should I run after him? Make my dad follow him and insist on giving a ride?

Should I make him a mix? Too many easy options. And this time I have to take the tougher route and just explain how I feel myself. Without props.

I fiddle with the radio and consider doing RLG and then think better of it and turn the thing off.

"So," Dad asks when we're back on Route 128 and the sunset has fizzled out, "how was the Big Apple? Did you take a bite?"

CHAPTER 19

I got in! I got in!" Lila rushes up and hugs me, practically swinging me around. "I'm going to Brown!"

"That's great! You rock!" I say.

"Now I'll only be, like, forty-five minutes away next fall. You totally have to come and hang out with me. We'll have a blast." This sends me reeling back into my post-Providence slump.

After my colossal mix mix-up and my distaste for all things apricot-flavored, I've been sloughing through work and trying to forget my woes. I would have told Lila about Robinson, but I didn't want to talk about Jacob. And I would have told Cordelia about my dad dating Thompson and how he's "really quite taken with her"—blech—but she would have made it campus-wide news. And I would have told Mable about most of it but she's been unreachable—too wedding-absorbed to call me back. So instead, I pour it all out in an epic email to DrakeFan. The whole Jacob/Robinson conundrum, the Dad saga, even how I'm determined to finish one song before the academic year is through. I don't know why I want to complete it now, I just want to know that if something's important to me I can get through it and not shy away. That I'm not just the friend in the corner waiting to be liked, nor am I Love Puke-owski—I'm just Love. Not just. My name and who I am speaks for itself.

Rummaging through my journal and messy desk drawers, I find the lyrics Jacob printed out for me to "Which Will"—that song he played at the coffeehouse so long ago. I shove them into my journal and then check email.

Like the heroine in a teen flick, I should be overjoyed right now after reading Robinson's message asking me to go to the senior prom with him. The prom. Isn't it supposed to be a dream come true for sophomore girls? The perfect dress, the perfect guy, the perfect theme song and—it's enough to make me want to stop seeing movies altogether.

The next day I find a disc in my mailbox. Not a mix, thankfully, since I don't think I can take having to decipher lyrics and meanings at this point. It's a real disc, a purchased one, still in its wrapper: *Way to Blue,* by Nick Drake. Oh, DrakeFan. Nick Drake Fan. I guess I bypassed the singer and thought of Drake's the snack food. I put the CD in my bag and go to class, thinking how nice it will be to listen to something unfamiliar. I remember Mable talking about Nick Drake and how she crushed out on him back when she listened to vinyl, but up till now I've never listened to his songs before.

I call her from the phone box at school using the Nick Drake info as my ruse for making contact. She's been so out of it—not even my dad knows why. He just says she'll call or stop by when she's got the time. Maybe her business is faltering. She used to run a greeting card company and that folded—maybe Slave to the Grind will, too. But instead of bearing bad business tidings, Mable gives me the lowdown on her love life.

"Anyway, to cut to the chase: I'm calling off the wedding. I hope you understand."

"What? Me? Don't you mean Miles?"

"For someone who wasn't exactly jumping for joy during my dating process, you seem kind of upset," Mable says. She sounds far away.

"I'm sorry. I'm sorry," I say.

"No," she says, "I'm sorry. I shouldn't be laying all this on you. It's just—Miles and I . . . listen. Relationships are different when you get older. More complicated."

"I know about complicated," I say, and then wish I hadn't.

"Well, if you think things are complex now, just wait."

I hang up a few minutes later after saying I'll return the fabric for the maid of honor dress, to which Mable replies that none of it matters. It's no big deal and she'll sort it out. She's seriously down and I don't know how to help her. Part of me wonders if it's more than Miles, more than the wedding that's the issue. But probably I'm wrong and it's just the complexity of love that's got her down. We'll have to see.

With the disc safely tucked away, I realize I'm a tad freaked out with the DrakeFan scenario. On the one hand, the guy could be my long-lost soul mate. On the other hand, he could be a psychotic weirdo with intentions to track me down and . . . Well, at the very least, he knows *way* more about me than I ever thought I'd reveal to a total stranger. Which leads me to my next thought, which is that maybe he's not a total stranger; maybe he's someone I kind of know. And just as I'm thinking this, I spot Chris the MLUT across campus and it dawns on me: guitar player, musical, kind of known to me, flirty. Shit: I could have revealed my inner life to the sluttiest guy around. Or maybe, like in a John Hughes movie, he'll turn out to have a heart (or some other body part) made of gold and the slut thing is just his protective coating. Or maybe DrakeFan isn't a student at all, but some creepy slacker hacker online. Or a teacher. Mr. Chaucer? I shake my head at the thought. How can you ever really know what's going on in someone's head, what drives them to act in certain ways or share their bizarre thoughts? Everyone tries to manipulate or come across in a particular way, right? Robinson, the one I thought could have been meant for me, clearly had an agenda. And look where that got me.

I meet Robinson by the pole-vaulting mat but I don't sit down. I don't lie down and look up at the bright blue sky. Nor do I relish in the weather and the way the sunlight gleams off his hair, sending glints of blond into the atmosphere. I am about to break up with him.

He walks over and puts his hands on my shoulders. I'm not nuts, I remind myself. Hot and fun does not mean it's the right fit.

"Listen" I say. "I got your email. And about the prom . . ." I try to find the words to say thanks but no thanks, but Robinson interrupts.

"Wait. I shouldn't have sent that—it was like a guilt-reaction."

I try to follow as I figure out how to say what I want to say. "Robinson, I liked you right away . . ."

"Love—I fucked up."

Maybe he will admit to his scripted actions, his Mr. Manhattan attitude.

"No," I say. "It wasn't just you—it was me, too. I think I wanted it to happen so much that I . . ."

"I slept with Lindsay Parrish." Why the hell he feels the need to use her full name I don't know, but it annoys the crap out of me. But more importantly . . .

Five words. A figurative slap. It doesn't matter that I was going to dump him—he cheated on me. When he thought I still liked him. I will not cry. I won't cry because I don't feel sad, I feel revolted. Mr. and Ms. Manhattan—now they can be Mr. and Mrs.!

"She found out she's accepted to Hadley for next year and we were celebrating and—if you hadn't left New York early maybe we . . ."

"Oh, my God! Don't you even think of blaming this on me. The fact that I was on a train . . ."—okay, sitting sharing a soda with Jacob in a diner, but still—"while you were screwing your 'just an old friend' makes me sick."

Robinson tries to hug me. I bristle. "So why even bother inviting me to the stupid prom?"

"I don't know. Guilt?" It's his honest reaction, but it makes me so mad that my first prom invite is based on guilt rather than romantic desire.

"Why don't you ask Lindsay Parrish? I'm sure she'd love to come."
I start to walk away.

"Love, don't leave it like this," he says. He's right. I should be the
bigger person here. The more mature. Sucks that it feels so good to be
petty. I walk over and can't face the good-bye hug he so obviously
wants, the one that would make him feel guilt-free. I reach forward and
sort of tousle his hair like he's a retriever or a kid. He takes my hand
and tries to hold it and I pull back. Of course, not before Jacob and a
group of his friends walk by and catch the rather intimate gesture. Did
I detect a glare from him?

"Good-bye," I say to Robinson, my campus hottie, my photo lab
fantasy. "And by the way—out of curiosity, what happens to Chester
and Lucy? Do they attend a formal ball together?" Robinson is horrified and blushes. "Maybe with an apricot rose as the corsage?"

The End. Roll credits.

I could have tried to sprint after Jacob to explain my hugging Robinson was a parting gesture, but I don't. Instead, I sprint home and open
my journal. Words come flowing out of me: not angry words of being
cheated on, not words of disillusionment, just feelings. My feelings
about Jacob. An hour later and the only thing that's missing from my
first song is a title.

CHAPTER 20

"Welcome to the last open mike night of the season," Mable says, and tries to quiet the crowd. I do a quick Jacob scan. No dice. "We'll be closing for inventory after this, but come back and see us in two weeks." Two weeks? This strikes me as very peculiar, since inventory takes a day or two at most. Maybe Mable's heading for a midlife crisis in the nullifying of her nuptials.

I listen to performers and serve iced coffees and lemon sherbet in tall glasses with long spoons, and enjoy the breeze through the open windows. In the spring and summer, the entire front façade opens up and lets in street noise, making for great people-watching.

This time I don't wait to be asked or urged. I write my name down like everyone else and bring my guitar up. I'm still not good enough to completely accompany myself, but I can sufficiently strum chords and make slow changes. Heh—just like in life. I look into the crowd and see a couple of people from WAJS. Mable must have asked them to come, since they are habitual caffeine consumers. I'm happy to see familiar faces as I play my first original song.

How can I explain what I never have before?
Who is there to blame for what was once an open door?
The more you walk away, the more I want to follow

But I've been down that road before and it leads to only hollow
Tell me once and tell me more
I'll be the one who knows you to the core
Say you'll stay and let me learn
How to put out the fire and keep the burn

There was a night I felt so sure of it all
And a bus ride, a diner, nights I never called
Say you'll stay and keep me warm
Tell me more, I promise no harm
I'll explain what I never have before
That where there's Love there's an open door

The applause is nice, but what hits me in a way I never would have expected is how good it feels to do what I said I would. I wrote it. I sang it. And hopefully, it's not a one-off and more will follow. I leave the stage, and before I can serve another drink, Mable tells me to go outside. In front of the blooming apple blossom tree, standing in the confetti of the strewn petals, is Jacob.

"I used to think I was one of those people who wouldn't find anyone worth being with in high school—or college—maybe never," Jacob says.

"Tough critic?"

"I guess." He reaches up and clasps at the leaves above him. A hailstorm of petals rains down. "But right away, that first Chaucer class, I wanted to know you. What you're thinking, what makes you happy." He moves toward me, but doesn't touch me. "What makes you sad. Where you come from. And I knew it wouldn't be easy."

"Sorry I made you chase me." I smile at him and let my hands find his. They're warm and soft.

"Are you kidding? I'm still a guy, despite the affinity for acoustic music and poster glitter. I won." He pauses. "Right?"

I'm well aware I'm not a prize, but I feel so good right now that maybe I deserve to be the blue ribbon. "You won," I say. "But it wasn't a competition. It was just . . ." I try to find a coherent way to tell him. "I feel like I won, actually."

Flowerless and without prescripted dialogue, he isn't perfect. He's real. And, according to him, really more than ready to kiss me. Which is what we do for the rest of the night.

At home, I look out my window and see Jacob waiting for me to wave. He's near the walkway lamp, and I can see his smile from where I sit on my bed. He waves back and walks toward the dorm.

Only one thing left to do now to put everything in order. I log on and write to DrakeFan.

> Writing to you has helped me through this whole year. I haven't had the chance to listen to the Nick Drake CD, but I'm sure it's as great as you are—or are via electronica. I hope you understand when I say that I can't write anymore like this. I have someone I can talk with face-to-face, and I feel like it wouldn't be fair to any of us to continue . . .

I go on for a bit more and thank him and click SEND. Can't get it back. Then, to commemorate the moment, I open the Nick Drake CD and put it on. The songs are lovely and sad and contemplative—and then I get to one called "Which Will," and my mouth drops open.

I get an IM from DrakeFan and take a risk writing back: *You're Jacob?*

He answers: *The one and only.*

Jacob is DrakeFan; life is good. Sophomore year is almost over, and the pieces are falling into place. I just have to figure out what I'm doing this summer (aside from swooning over Jacob), and then I'm all set. I even let my dad know that Thompson might not give me a good grade, and he was okay with it. He's clearly so besotted with her that he's blind to her classroom evils—and who am I to judge? Maybe she'll prove to be a nice distraction for Dad this summer. Time will tell.

Graduation starts in seven minutes. I've SPF'd myself from head to toe and slide into my sandals before heading out the door. Underclassmen are wedged together, row after row of us in white dresses and blue blazers, listening to the speakers while we roast in the sun and check to see which seniors are crying on stage. I can see Robinson and Channing, and Lila gives a small wave from her seat far down on the left. She looks amazing, of course, and was completely horrified when I told her that Lindsay Parrish/Ms. Manhattan would be joining the Hadley Hall ranks next year. After the NYC debacle, Lila admitted her issues to me: She'd had the hardest time with Lindsay, and felt all along with Robinson that he wasn't really a whole person, just a movie poster boy who didn't know how to be real. When I asked her why she didn't tell me that day in the café, she asked me if I would have believed her or just thought she was jealous. And she was totally right. When you're blinded by lust and visions of perfection, there's no use sprinkling reality dust anywhere; it'll just blow past. Anyway, in terms of Lindsay Parrish, at least I have the summer to enjoy before seeing her face again—especially knowing that she bedded down with my first real boyfriend. Lila wants me to visit Newport for a weekend and I just might. I'll miss having a friend around like her. My hope is that come September, I'll find the friend I've been looking for, but for now it's wishful thinking.

My father leads us all in the school hymn, "Green Though It Yet May Be," and I watch the student body form words in unison. Thinking back to the opening day ceremony in the chapel, it's funny how much has happened and still how seamless the year is from then until now. When we get to the part about lush hills and blossoms, I can feel tears welling up, and I'm not sure exactly why. Maybe I'm more sentimental than I think I am. Picturing Hadley without the current seniors feels foreign, but then again I know once I'm a month or two into junior year, it'll be hard to remember what it felt like to be a sophomore. My dad's cheeks are sun-reddened and I watch him sing the last verse. When we all sit back down, the air is full and humid, and I'm officially ready for summer.

"Love Bukowski!" Applause. Huh? I'm so busy reflecting and recalling the past nine months like the valedictorian asked that I don't know what's happening until Clive the English exchange student turns around and hisses at me. Am I graduating early?

"Are you a bloody idiot?" he asks. Clearly the pot has been traded in for something else. I take a nanosecond to hope that next year's exchange student comes with more tact, grace, and charm. "They're calling you. You won."

I won? What did I win? I'm on the way up to accept the award in my honor when I realize that I have won the Hadley Hall English Essay prize. My father, from behind the podium, hands me the award (which he clearly knew I won prior to now—no wonder he didn't mind my potentially lackluster grade in math) and smiles. Instead of shaking hands, we hug, which feels reassuring, not embarrassing. From the faculty rows, Mr. Chaucer gives me the thumbs-up. I walk off the stage and find my way back to my seat, noting the already crispy feeling on my shoulders from the strong sun. Attached to the frame-worthy piece of paper is a letter detailing how my essay will be published in an alumni magazine. For the whole year I assumed that this would mean a Hadley Hall magazine, but as I read on I learn that the alum for my essay is the editor of *Music Magazine*. And my piece will be published in the August issue for new voices on the music scene! I'm the female Cameron Crowe! Whoa. Slow down.

My dad's closing remarks about self-discovery and knowledge of our surrounding worlds is both beautiful and hypocritical. How will I follow these life instructions without him easing up on hiding the details of my past?

At home, I aloe myself and change into shorts and a T-shirt. It's summer. I am free from ringing bells and parietals and papers until next fall. Three whole months. On my bed I find a present with a card that just says LOVE, DAD. Inside are letters dated 1985 to 1988—all from my mother to my father—and then some photos with dad's writing on the back explaining where and when and who . . . and an old tape. I don't even read them now. I don't look now. I know I will later, tonight or tomorrow or next week. I have some clues to my maternal mystery. Not everything, I'm sure. But the beginnings of figuring it out.

"Get your butt out here!" Jacob cups his hands to his mouth and yells up to my window. He's holding two dripping Popsicles, and I rush down the stairs to meet him. I poke my head out the window.

"One sec," I shout.

"I'm going to have to eat your raspberry ice," he warns.

"Save me the last lick then," I say.

Outside, in the shade of the elm tree, we sit and wipe our sticky hands on the green grass. Jacob leaves in two days to go back to his dad's house in New Haven. I've been wondering if another Amtrak excursion is in order.

"So," he says with a massive grin.

"What?" I laugh, and give his shoulder a push.

"Want to spend the summer with me?"

"Um, yes, please."

Jacob reaches for something in his pocket. "I'm serious," he says, and shows me a photo of a house with a tumbling garden in front, hills in the background.

"Details?" I ask.

"Come to Europe with me. This is my mom's house in the South of France. We can hang out there for a while and then meet my dad in Rome and tour around."

"You want me to tour around Europe with you?"

Jacob nods. "Dad told me I could bring a friend—his treat. My choice of company."

"And you choose me?" I smile and plant a kiss on his lips. He pulls me in.

"Always," he says. The phone rings inside and I stand up to get it. "But you have to tell me by tonight at eight o'clock. The tickets are on a twenty-four-hour hold, and Dad's insisting on buying them today."

I give a whoop and run inside, heart racing. Would my dad say yes? I can't even think of all the things rushing through my brain. And then I pick up the phone.

"Love Bukowski?"

Hoping I'm not being offered a free sample of something or for my political affiliation, I say, "This is she."

"Hi." The voice warms up. "This is John Rickman, editor of *Music Magazine* in New York."

Fluster, fluster, composure. "Oh, hi!" I say.

"We wanted to call and congratulate you on your success. You must be very proud of your essay."

I think back to how long it took me to write it, and the struggles on and off paper. "Yes, I am." Outside, Jacob is trying to make me laugh, dancing like a robot and then trying to flee from a bee. I suppress a giggle.

"The editorial staff and I were pretty taken with your writing—especially for someone your age."

"Thanks—thanks a lot. I just want to say that I'm a big fan of the magazine and really am excited to have something published in it," I say, hoping I'm not coming off as a giant kiss-ass. Small kiss-ass, fine. Just not Cadillac-huge.

"Sorry, Love, would you mind holding for a moment?" He clicks off and I give Jacob the two minutes sign. Jacob shouts back that it's no problem, not to rush, and sits down in the grass, stringing together a chain of dandelions that will no doubt be given to me.

"I'm back," John Rickman says. "That was Elton John on the line. Had to take it."

"Yeah, I can see that you'd have to." I laugh. So does Rickman.

"Listen—the reason for my call is this: In our staff meeting yesterday we were reviewing student internship proposals, and it dawned on me that you're every bit as qualified as the high school seniors who've applied."

I draw a breath and sit down, pulling the coil of yellow cord with me. I don't say anything, and he goes on. "Anyway, we're wondering if you've got the time and interest to join our staff for the summer. I'll be honest and tell you the position doesn't pay much. Just a stipend, really. And you'll have to research facts and get coffees and run errands for Eminem or Sheryl Crow when they come for interviews."

Drool, drool, composure. "I see. And, ah, where and when and . . ."

"Our central offices. In Manhattan. I have to say, I'd be thrilled to have another Hadley Hall person here with me. So you think about it and let me know."

"Wow, sure!" I say. "Should I call back to let you know or—"

"We can give you some time," he reassures me. "I know it's a lot to take in suddenly." I breathe a sigh of relief. Between the phone call and the offer to go to Europe with Jacob—I can totally see falling in love among the trains and travel—I'm overwhelmed. "Why don't you think about this for a couple of hours and give me a ring by the end of the day—say, seven o'clock tonight?"

I hang up and step outside to the porch. Up the driveway, I can see my dad and Thompson holding hands and walking this way. First I think Dad looks really happy; then I notice the slump of his shoulders and the way Thompson pats his back—not out of love, more like an action of sympathy. I start to walk over to them, and Jacob joins me.

"So, mademoiselle, are we going on our world expedition?"

Next to me is Jacob, who slips his arm around my waist and offers me the world. In my head, the *Music Magazine* clings to me. And in front of me stands my dad, whose face tells me that something is wrong.

This is the moment that freezes like a photograph image—the start of my summer. The start of the next song in my life. The next version of my life as I know it.

AND THEN . . .

Dear Lila,

    The train is just leaving Route 128 and I'll be seeing you in Providence in about twenty minutes, but I thought you'd appreciate a real letter more than just email cloggage in your inbox. As you can imagine, the summer flew by. Who'd have thought my life would turn so fast? I can't wait to see you and tell you about my crazy couple of months, love, and the pursuit of musical glory. Not to mention the shocking news I just can't seem to put on paper—seeing the words written will make it too real. But I'll tell you everything when we're face-to-face. I can't believe what you told me in the postcard from London. What's so amazing about Clive the lame English exchange student? If you say his sister's cool, then I'll take your word for it—until I meet her myself this fall. Did you get my letter from—oh, wait, we're here and I can see you out the window! What did you do to your hair??

    More soon—
    Love

Coming soon—*Piece, Love, and Happiness,* the second in the LOVE chronicles, available fall 2005. To preorder, visit Love online at www.emilyfranklin.com.

Don't you just love cool new novels like

THE PRINCIPLES OF LOVE?

Now here's a preview of two books just like it that rock!

Turn the page to sample

Trish Cook's
SO LYRICAL
(on sale now)

and

Liza Conrad's
ROCK MY WORLD: A Novel of Thongs, Spandex, and Love in G Minor
(on sale now)

SO LYRICAL
Trish Cook

"Trace!"

I stuck my head out of my locker and scanned the between-class mosh pit. A blur of faces surfed by, none of which seemed to belong to anyone in desperate need of me. Taking a deep breath, I went back to my excavation. I finally found what I was looking for underneath a week-old lunch bag.

"Gotcha," I muttered, unearthing my trig book. Pens, crumpled papers, and unwashed gym clothes all came flying out after it. I tossed the scrambled mess back inside, slamming the door and throwing myself against it for good measure. I could totally understand the escape attempt. It reeked like tuna and old sweat in there.

"Trace!"

There was that voice again, only louder and more pissed off this time. I scoped the halls until I finally spotted the screamer—otherwise know as my best friend, Sabrina Maldonati. Her body-hugging skirt and sky-high heels made navigating the polished marble floors of Northshore Regional High School a tough proposition. Think beached mermaid and you'll get the picture.

If I could only fast-forward her, I thought, glancing at my watch and hoping I wasn't going to be late for class. Brina made her grand entrance a moment later clutching a piece of paper to her more-than-ample chest.

"Stop bitching and start reading," she said. "Because this is the most unbelievable thing ever."

I faked a big yawn. "Can't Harvard just take no for an answer?" the more over-the-top she gets, the more I like to yank her chain.

"Not funny."

"Your mom wrote a note so you don't have to face the fat calipers in gym today?"

Brina shook her head so hard I thought brains would come flying out her ears in wrinkly pieces. "Wrong again. And anyway, you know how I feel about the *F* word."

"What, fu—?"

"Uh, uh, uh. You quit swearing, remember?" Brina said, interrupting me just in the nick of time. "And the word I was referring to is 'fat.' Last night, my mom offered to get me liposuction for my eighteenth birthday."

"You're so full of—"

"Trace, you're gonna have to try a lot harder if you're serious about cleaning up your language."

"I was about to say 'malarkey.' "

"One of us is lying," said Brina. "Here's a hint. It's not me."

She was right. I wouldn't be caught dead saying anything remotely like, "You're so full of malarkey." That meant the lipo story must be true. Brina's mom, being the anorexic lunatic that she is, probably decided fat-sucking cash was the most thoughtful, generous gift in the history of mankind.

The reality is this: Brina has an eye-popping, curvaceous bod. But instead of realizing that boobs and a butt are normal—even desirable—parts of a woman's figure, all Mrs. Maldonati can see is rolls, rolls and more rolls. In her wildest dreams, Brina suddenly turns into whichever Olsen twin is the dangerously skinny one.

"Don't hold your breath" and "not in this lifetime" are two choice phrases that come to mind, but Mrs. Maldonati refuses to give up hope just yet.

"So if it isn't from Harvard and it's not a reprieve from the claw, what *is* the most unbelievable thing ever?" I asked.

"An anonymous note. Signed by 'slp.' I don't know whether to be flattered or call the cops."

So maybe this really *was* something worth getting excited about. "Hand it over," I told her.

Brina passed the note my way and breathed down my neck. I could almost hear her lips moving behind me as I read.

> *Brina,*
> *I like to watch you from afar*
> *Always know just where you are*
> *But not where this might lead*
> *Maybe you could walk with me*
> *slp*

A lone bead of sweat trickled down my back. Was I jealous? Hell, yeah. Here was some pretty awesome poetry, sweet without being sickening, warm without losing its cool. And once again, I was relegated to the lumpy, frumpy sidekick role—Quasimodo next to Brina's Esmeralda.

"Honestly? It's amazing," I admitted.

"That's what I thought," she said, folding the paper carefully and zipping it into a little compartment in the front of her notebook. I hated how she could be so neat. I also hated that her boobs were so big, and that mine were so nonexistent.

"So what are you going to do about it?" I asked her.

"Do? Nothing." We took a couple more steps before she said, "Why? What would you do?"

"I'd go walk with him."

Brina rolled her eyes.

"I'm serious," I told her.

"Oh, please. Why would I want to stroll around with some loser who's too scared to ask me out?" Brina said, doing a quick one-eighty and dismissing slp as yesterday's news. "Let's just forget about it."

I cleared my throat as a new thought came to me. This would be a kick if it actually turned out to be true. "Maybe slp is a she," I suggested. Brina may have had all the guys in school drooling after her, but up until now she hadn't done a thing for the chicks. "Your Sss-sss-secret Le-le-lesbian Puh-puh-pal." I emphasized the letters so she'd catch my drift.

Brina didn't even stop to consider my theory. "Sorry, Trace. It's just not my thing. If my pal's a gal, we're gonna have to stay friends."

I took one last crack at it. "Have you ever considered it might just be Some Lovesick Puppy?"

"Shut up, Trace, and walk. We've gotta get to trig."

Brina and I slipped into our seats as the final bell was ringing. I kept rereading the note in my mind, trying to figure out who slp might really be. And why he—like every other guy I knew—found Brina so intriguing, and me so not.

Stanley Larsen Pratt?

Spencer Louis Perog?

Shawn Leonard Pearsall?

All great guesses. If any of these names belonged to anyone we knew, that is. And they didn't.

Minutes passed before I, being the incredibly brilliant person I am, solved the slp mystery. There he was—Sam Parish, a cute enough guy if you could overlook his constant sniffling—slumped down in his seat with his feet stuffed under Brina's chair.

I got all excited and passed her a note.

Brina:

Don't look now, but I think slp's behind you. If his middle name is Lester or Langley or Lancelot or Lars, it's him. Identity crisis over.
Trace

P.S. Maybe it's not an allergy or drug problem like we thought. He could just be trying to inhale your pheromones, or whatever they're called.

She read it and scribbled back.

Trace:

Good detective work. Let's see if he passes the test.
slp's girlfriend

While the rest of the class was trying to calculate the Pythagorean cosine tangent of the something or other, Brina casually leaned back and whispered, "What's your middle name, hon?"

Sam pointed to his chest—honestly, he looked a little scared—and mouthed, "Me?" Then he just sat there staring at Brina with his mouth hanging open.

She finally patted his arm and whispered, "That's OK. You can tell me later." Brina turned her attention back to the nasty problem at hand, and Sam scrunched down even farther in his seat. He looked like he wanted the floor to swallow him up because he'd just ruined his one big chance with Brina. Or who knows? Maybe he was just trying to hide a huge boner.

Scratch, scratch. Fold, fold. Brina chucked the note back to me.

Trace:

Don't think it's him. Far too shy to have the balls to send me an anonymous love note. He might write one, but I think that's about as far as it would go.

   B

Maybe, maybe not, I thought. He could also be embarrassed at being outed so quickly by gifted me. Scribble, scribble, toss, toss.

   B:
   Let's keep him on the list for now. I'll put it right next to the one about my dad on my locker door.
   T

The other list was necessary because, unless his name really was Mike Graphone like it says on my birth certificate, I don't know a thing about my father. And as cool as my mother is in other respects—especially compared to my friends' parents—she's unbelievably uptight and close-mouthed about everything related to Daddy dearest. The only suspects I've been able to pinpoint so far are total shots in the dark: the guys I see hugging my mom in pictures hung around the rock-and-roll shrine otherwise known as my house.

Scritchy-scratchy. Flitter-flutter. Plip-plop. Mr. Flagstaff's eyes darted around the room until they came to rest on the note Brina had just thrown my way. It was just lying there on my desk looking guilty.

"Care to try your hand at the board, Tracey?" he asked.

"Sure thing, Mr. Flagstaff," I said in as cheerful a voice as I could muster. Maybe a little enthusiasm would make him forget I hadn't been paying attention for the past half an hour. Since day one, if I'm being totally honest.

But nothing could have saved me. I had no clue how to even start the problem, no less solve it. I stumbled and bumbled with the chalk, creating a powdery mess that made no sense. Not nearly soon enough, the Staffman put me out of my misery.

"Perhaps some extra homework problems will help you catch up to the rest of the class, Miss Tillingham. Your notes tonight will have a lot less to do with your social life and a lot more to do with trigonometry now, won't they?"

I gave him my best conciliatory look and saw a night of terminal boredom and frustration in my future. Once again, Brina had been my partner in crime and I was the only one captured.

Why wasn't I the least bit surprised? Because it happened all the time. Farty old Mr. Flagstaff probably had a crush on her, like every other man on earth. Having the world's most desirable girl as my best friend was really beginning to suck the big wazoo, no matter how much I liked her.

I went directly to my room after school and changed into my workout clothes. I thought maybe a long, hard run might help me focus on the fact that I was not, contrary to what my mind would have me believing today, the world's biggest loser. Me, my Brooks sneakers, and my beloved green iPod mini were all halfway out the door before my mom stopped me dead in my tracks.

"Hey, Bebe," I said, grabbing a Balance bar and shoving it down my throat. Though my mom's real name is Belinda, I've called her Bebe since I could string a few sounds together. She says that at the time, "Mommy" was just too weird—after all, she was still a teenager herself— and the whole shebang proved to be too big of a mouthful for one-year-old me.

"So Brina got a secret love note today, huh?" Bebe asked.

I swallowed fast. "How'd you find that out?"

"She called and when I asked how her day was, she said, 'Great! I got a secret love note today.' "

"Subtle."

"So what did it say, anyway?"

"Something about watching her from afar and not knowing

where things will lead," I said. "Oh, and that maybe Brina should walk *with* him."

Bebe ran her fingers through her hair, looking a little puzzled.

"What?"

"Nothing," she said. "It just sounds familiar and I can't figure out why."

"Right. Well, wouldn't you know it, even the sensitive, poetic types are falling for Brina now."

"Pisses you off, huh?" Bebe put her arm around me and squeezed my shoulder.

"Yup," I said. "I guess I should be happy for her?" I didn't mean to, but it came out as a question.

"Nahhhh. It would piss me off, too." It's almost eerie how Bebe always understands exactly how I'm feeling. The fact that we've never been through that "I hate you" phase most mothers and daughters hit at some point during high school makes me extremely lucky—I know. But when your mom: (*a*) is younger than everyone else's parents by at least ten years, (*b*) was a groupie back in the eighties (regardless of whether the overwhelming majority of bands she worshipped were kinda sorta lame even then and definitely ancient history now), and (*c*) has morphed herself into a successful author of Harlequin-ish romances starring fictional musicians, it's easy to see how we'd relate better than most.

Bebe mercifully dropped the subject of me being caught hunching alongside Brina yet again. "You going for a long one today?"

I gulped down some prerun water. "Eight miles. Why, you need me?"

"My agent always thinks going to a show will inspire my next book, so he bribed me with these," Bebe said, waving a couple of familiar-looking rectangles at me. "Got tenth-row tix to see the luscious Hall and Oates tonight."

"Who's luscious?" I asked her. "Hall or Oates?" I can never keep them straight.

"I don't play favorites," Bebe said, licking her lips, just in case I didn't realize she thinks they are fine, so divine. Believe me, I got it well before the spit dried.

"Can't go, Bebe," I said, thankful for my math punishment now. I mean, yikes. No one's heard from those guys in twenty years. "Flagstaff caught me passing notes in trig class and I ended up with extra home-work. Brina got off the hook, of course."

"Don't sweat it. Your teacher was probably blinded by her boobs." Bebe put down the tickets and picked up the phone. "I'll just call Trixie to come with me," she said, hitting the speed dial. Trixie is Bebe's one and only Winnetka friend.

Bebe ended up here—in the world's most conservative suburb— once it became apparent that she had picked up more than just waitressing experience at the shore during her eighteenth summer. Once she started showing, Bebe got shipped off to Great-aunt Betty's house in Winnetka under the guise that it would do her some good to get out of New Jersey for a while. The truth is, it made for a lot less explaining. Never mind the fact that Bebe's par-ents—my grandma and grandpa Tillingham—are so cute yet so clueless, they're probably still wondering why Bebe hasn't been nominated for sainthood, what with her having had an immaculate conception and all.

To this day, Bebe says living in Winnetka is her sacrifice to me; she wanted me to have as normal an upbringing as possible, given the cir-cumstances. And I can't imagine a better place for a kid to grow up, or a more unsuitable one for Bebe. I mean, she just doesn't blend. Instead of wearing tennis whites and listening to NPR in the luxury SUV, Bebe has holey-kneed jeans and cruises around in a beat-up Beetle cranking Quiet Riot or some other band that horrifies both me and the Winnetka ladies, though for different reasons. I'm embarrassed; they're disturbed by the noise.

"Sure, Trace would love to watch the kids until John gets home from his meeting," Bebe was saying into the phone a minute later, winking at me. And I was pretty grateful for the job—even if she didn't have the courtesy to ask me first—because I might as well make some money while slaving over my math punishment.

The slp note, trig torture, and my nonexistent dad kept rolling around in my mind when I first started my run. But after a mile or two I went into the brain-dead zone, happily listening to my latest and greatest playlist and singing along whenever the spirit moved me.

My mind made it back to the land of the living when I noticed an extremely cute guy jogging alongside of me. OK, he wasn't just jogging: he was laughing. At me. I stopped singing and started scowling. What a reality slap—there was no soundproof bubble surrounding me when I had headphones on like I'd always imagined.

I shot the guy my best pissed-off Jersey Girl look—honed during our annual two-week summer vacation at Long Beach Island with my sweet 'n' ditzy grandparents—and kept running. He didn't seem the least bit intimidated and stayed in stride with me.

"You like Jimmy Eat World a lot, huh?"

I ignored him, even though I was impressed. They're not the world's most well-known band—not yet, at least.

"Know how I guessed?" he asked, belting out their song "The Sweetness" in way too good of a voice. Even all the whoa-oh-ohhh-ohhh-ohs sounded right. And to think, his ears were the recipients of my most recent off-key, a cappella solo. Even worse, after hearing him sing the right ones, I was pretty sure there was a place waiting for me in the Misheard-Lyrics Hall of Fame.

"See?" he said, grinning at me.

"Sorry I offended your virgin ears, Mr. Rock Star." All the good comebacks would no doubt torture me tonight while I was tossing and turning in bed, trying to sleep.

"Not offended," he said, flashing a killer smile. "Not a virgin, either."

Hard as I tried to stay mad, I ended up laughing instead. He took it as encouragement.

"I'm Zander O'Brien," he said, sticking out his hand.

I stared at his long, tapered fingers, not sure what to do with them. After all, we were still moving at a nine-minute-mile pace. I just couldn't imagine the mechanics of the whole thing working out.

Zander gave up on the doomed handshake thing, using that arm to pump again. "How long you running for?" he asked, panting.

By now, the adrenaline shooting through me had picked my pace up to sprint. "Almost done. I'm on my last mile."

Zander seemed like he was about ready to pass out. "Want to hit . . . Starbucks . . . so we can talk . . . without me . . . gasping . . . for . . . breath?"

"Sounds great, but I gotta get home. I have to babysit tonight so my mom can go to the Hall and Oates show."

Zander stopped short. "You do?"

I stopped, too. "Yup."

"I don't think my mother has ever even been to a concert. And the only tunes she listens to are by guys who died a million years ago. You know, like Elvis and the Beatles."

"Not all of the Beatles are dead," I had to point out. "There are Elvis sightings all the time. And Hall and Oates haven't had a hit since the eighties."

"Whatever," Zander said. "At least you don't have to leave the house whenever your mom puts her music on."

If he only knew. "I wouldn't go that far," I told him. "But I will admit, my mom is pretty unique. And we're both really into music."

That's a gigantic understatement. My mom spends her days writing and cranking out tunes that everyone else—with the exception of those retro shows—forgot decades ago. A dilapidated jukebox in the corner of our basement plays Bebe's prehistoric 45s. The portable turntable left over from her childhood spins the stacks and stacks of albums she spent her entire allowance on growing up. And her boom box, circa 1989, plays the songs contained on the seventeen thousand little cassettes that keep threatening to take over the attic someday.

Thankfully, a brand-new, state-of-the-art home entertainment system in the living room takes care of our continuously growing mountain of CDs. Because I want to save my music from any premature aging, I've separated the CDs into two piles: hers and mine. And it's easy to tell whose is whose. Bebe owns the ones only Oldies 101.5 would play; my bands rock MTV2.

To further prove her musical fanaticism—and make us the biggest freaks in all of Lilly Pulitzer–wearing Winnetka—almost every wall of our house is plastered with photos of Bebe and her now-aging idols. Autographed ticket stubs, T-shirts, and a bass round out the mix. The absolute kicker is in the family room: a drum set–turned–coffee table signed by all of Dexy's Midnight Runners. Whoever they were.

Whenever my friends come over for the first time, it's always a big freak-out until they realize they have no idea who or what they're really looking at. It's always, "Is that Slash from Guns N' Roses with your mom in this picture?"

And I say, "Nope, it's Billy Squier."

Then they say, "Who?"

And I tell them, "Never mind."

Next they study the autographed bass. "Whoa. Nikki Sixx signed this?"

And I say, "Actually, Keith Scott did."

Then they say, "Who?"

He played with Bryan Adams, but they don't need to know that. Instead, I tell them, "If you don't know now, you never will."

Finally, they spot the drum set/coffee table. "Don't even ask," I say before they get totally confused.

Though I normally dreaded this whole routine, I thought I might actually enjoy running through it for Zander. I prayed to the ancient third-string rock gods he would come over for a visit soon.

Meanwhile, he was right next to me in the present tense, trying to make small talk. "You know what? We have a lot in common."

"We do?"

"Yeah. For one thing, we're both into running."

You could have fooled me, I thought. I just watched you and it wasn't pretty. "You're a natural," I said. Obviously, my brain was working just fine—it was only my mouth that refused to let all the good lines out.

"And music. We both love music." Zander gave me a slightly crooked smile that reminded me of Ashton Kutcher's. I was getting sucked in despite the fact I'd sworn off guys just last month. "I'm in a band. Want to hear us play sometime? Maybe you could sing backup or something."

"Ha-ha." I dug my fingernails into my arm really hard, just to make sure I wasn't dreaming. Red half-moons appeared, proof positive I was awake.

"If you're afraid of being alone with me and the guys, you could bring a friend along," he said. "C'mon, I don't bite. Not unless you want me to."

"I might be able to arrange that," I said, hoping I sounded sexier than I must have looked, with the sweat dripping down my face and all.

"Maybe later," he said, flirting like crazy. "After you've showered. So, do you go to Northshore Regional?"

"Yup. You?"

Zander looked slightly embarrassed. "Nope. Country Day."

"Ahhhhh. One of them." Them unbelievably rich people, I meant. Yikes. This guy was so out of my league, I might as well quit now while I was ahead. "Well, gotta run, Zander. Nice meeting you."

He reached out and put his hand on my shoulder to stop me. "You haven't even told me your name yet."

Finally, something I could answer without feeling the need to be clever and witty. "Trace. Short for Tracey."

"So, Trace," Zander said, twirling my name around in his mouth. "You want to come see my band play at the rec center on Friday night or what?"

It was time to admit it: Wild horses couldn't keep me away. "Sounds good, Zander." My tongue must have swollen to gigantic proportions over the past few minutes, because it came out sounding like "Zounz-goozandah."

If he noticed, he didn't mention it. "Hey, in case you don't make it, what's your last name?"

"Tillingham," I said, my tongue returning to its normal size instantaneously.

I started the short run home, making it a full block before I gave in to my screaming mind and turned around for one last look at Zander. By then he was peanut-sized. Figures he'd pick now to turn into a gazelle, I thought.

"Good run?" the back of Bebe's head asked me as I banged through the front door. My mom's face was buried in the computer screen, as usual.

"Great one. I just met the hottest guy from Country Day."

Bebe twirled around in her chair and stopped working on whatever her latest novel was going to turn out to be. "Someone who can cure the T. J. blues?" T. J. was my last boyfriend—the one who dumped me for that slut Claire Russell the day after declaring his undying love for me.

"Could be. It's too early to tell."

"Gonna see him again?"

"Yup. He invited me to watch his band play Friday night."

"Hey, maybe I'll come along!"

I crinkled up my nose at the thought of it. "I don't think so. Not only would that mortify me, but they don't play oldies. Not your style at all, Bebe."

"I'm too cool to be mortifying," she said, clearly delusional. "And Duran Duran is playing the House of Blues, anyway. They can probably still blow the doors off your new boyfriend's band."

"Probably," I said, though I sincerely doubted it was true. I grabbed a water bottle from the fridge and took a chug, wondering if Bebe even realized what a musical time warp she was in.

ROCK MY WORLD:
A Novel of Thongs, Spandex, and Love in G Minor
Liza Conrad

"And on the Sixth day, God created Nick Hoffman's voice, Liz Phair's lyrics, Kurt Cobain's angst, and Lenny Kravitz's guitar licks. And he saw that it was good. So He just said, Screw it . . . tomorrow I'm resting."

I looked across the table at Carl Erikson, *Rock On* magazine's editor-in-chief, as he put down my essay, "Creation of Rock and Roll," that had run in my high school newspaper. I held my breath.

"This is really quite clever, Livy," he said.

I relaxed a little. "Clever" is a lot better than "What were you thinking, slacker?" or "Cheesy"—and I so wanted this summer gig. I tried to picture Carl forty pounds lighter. With hair. And an earring. In tight jeans. With eyeliner. Back when he was cool, or at least not bald and "pleasantly plump," back when he and my father used to hang out after Babydolls' concerts and smoke an ungodly amount of pot. And Lord knows what else. Trying not to laugh, I simply said, "Thanks."

One time, my father said, when I was four years old, Carl stripped naked and played air guitar in our living room during a party. I don't remember that, which is just as well. If I'd been able to recall Carl's flaccid—my father remembers that detail perfectly—penis, I was quite positive I would have fallen on the floor in hysterics and wouldn't have been able to do this interview.

"You know what we're asking you to do, right?" Carl raised an eyebrow, his reading glasses perched on the end of his nose.

I nodded.

"Good," he said. "I like the way you write. At seventeen, you're better than half of my staff, and I mean that—though don't tell them. *Rock On* is for the MTV set. We're not like *Rolling Stone*. They cover the whole spectrum, and they're oh-so-self-important." He took his glasses off and laid them on his desk. "We want readers mostly your age . . . and into their twenties. We've got gossip and lots of photos. Backstage candids. Interviews with actors. Do you read *Rock On*?"

I nodded, even though I didn't. I thought most of it was crap.

"Of course you do. All teens in your age bracket do."

"Sure," I said convincingly.

"Well." Carl leaned back in his enormous leather chair, a view of the New York skyline behind him. "I don't have to tell you what the Babydolls mean to rock and roll history. I'm sure you meet people all the time who tell you what an amazing musician and singer your father was—and is. And the reunion tour is going to be the hottest summer stadium ticket both here and in Europe."

"And Japan," I said. "That's where the tour starts."

"Yeah. The Japanese love them. And now he's got that American Express commercial. Hysterical. Comes across as uber-hip. And with the Wolves opening for the Babydolls on the tour . . . Jesus, I wish I was twenty again." He smiled, and for a split second, I could see the twenty-year-old Carl. His eyes were less tired, and his dimples showed.

"Well, Livy . . . I'm sold. What I want is a series of articles—you could make them like journal entries—from the road. Places like Madison Square Garden, L.A., London . . . Wherever they are—wherever you are. And then mingled with that, I'd love to read the story of the Babydolls . . . and your life with your parents and the band and so on. I'd love to connect this tour with readers your age—they'll be able to relate to you."

"Like Kelly Osborne without the pink hair. And the foul mouth— most of the time."

"Yeah. Minus the pink hair and the f-word." He smiled at me. "I like how you think. You're quick—like your old man. I'll give you my email, and Rob's—he's a very sharp editor. He's good, and he's excited about this."

"Great."

"I'd also like you to take digital pictures—candids—of the tour bus, the jet, the crowds, the band, the Wolves."

The Wolves were opening for my father's band. Nick Hoffman was so good-looking that grown women got wolf paw tattoos on their breasts. I remember being five or six and seeing women throwing baby-doll pajamas on the stage at my father. Though tossing pajamas and permanently inking your body seem like two entirely different brands of fan obsession.

"Sure." Photograph Nick Hoffman? I could just imagine my best friend Cammie's response when she heard that: *Can we take his picture with his shirt off?*

"One story a week for the summer tour . . . We'll put you on the payroll for two hundred dollars a week; fifty bucks for every photo we use."

"Deal." I said it calmly, but I would have done the stories for free— just to start building up press clippings. My dream was to someday start my own rock magazine. Getting *paid* to write? That meant I could actually *say* I was a writer. For real.

Carl stood and shook my hand, then came out from behind the desk. Suddenly, and without warning, he enveloped me in a bear hug. "God, I remember when you used to toddle around the house in your diapers. Can't believe it. You look like a model, and you're taller than I am."

"That's not hard, Carl," I said, looking down at the top of his bald head. I'm five foot eleven. He had to be five foot five.

He laughed and put his arm around me.

"So you think if I was as tall as your dad, *I* would have gotten all the groupies?"

"Not unless you put on some spandex back then."

"Oh, I had spandex."

"Well, you know how chicks dig musicians. And you can't play anything," I teased.

"I once played the tambourine on stage with the Babydolls. At Wembley."

We left his office in search of my father.

"Tambourines don't count."

"Yeah, well, I had hair then, too." He looked over at me and winked.

Down the hall, I heard female giggling. Lots of it. Along with a cooing sort of fawning. It could only be for my dad—women still fall all over him. He says it's because he kicked hard drugs, so he didn't age like Keith Richards, the walking cadaver—though that's giving cadavers a bad name. They don't make the corpses on *CSI* look that bad. My father still looks young. He wears his hair to his shoulders, and it's as thick and dirty blond as when he was twenty-one. He has blue eyes and a lanky build, and he speaks with a raspy voice like some light-night DJ who's chain-smoking through the night shift. He wears boot-cut jeans, custom-made lizard-skin cowboy boots, and tight black T-shirts that show off his body. He looks, all the time, like what he is: a rock star. All my life, girls tried to be friends with me because of him. It's beyond creepy to go to a friend's house and see a poster of your father in her bedroom—when you know in her fifth-grade mind she's kissing him. *Gross!*

Carl opened the door to *Rock On*'s conference room. And there was my dad, Paul James, black Sharpie pen in hand, signing the left breast of some woman, her top unbuttoned to her belly button. She blushed and covered up. The other women were laughing. Not just women my dad's age either. There were interns there who looked just a couple of years older than I am—college girls. I rolled my eyes, and Dad came over and kissed me.

"Well, baby?"

Carl smiled. "She's hired. We worked it all out. Have some paperwork to fill out, but it's all set."

"Cool. That's my girl."

We hung around the office, took care of the paperwork, and then Dad and I went downstairs where our limousine waited. My father got his fifth DUI before I was even in junior high. After that, he never bothered to get his license back again. It's kind of pathetic when you have to drive your own parents around. My mother's from England, and she never did learn to drive on our side of the road. What a pair they are. At least, however, I have a convertible. I mean, if you have to drive your father around, might as well drive something you're not embarrassed by. And when I don't drive, then it's the limo. Toby is our driver/bodyguard. He used to drive me to school every day until I got my license. He also keeps all the liquor in the house under lock and key.

In the back of the limousine, Dad grinned. He has this lopsided smile women have been swooning over forever.

"You're all grown up, Livy."

I rolled my eyes. "*Please* don't get all mushy on me."

"Well, it seems like yesterday. I mean, holy shit, I can barely remember you when you were small. And now you've got your first job as a real writer. Next thing it'll be college. One year. Christ, just one more year. Then next thing you know you'll be hosting *Total Request Live*."

"Dad, I'm a writer, not a TV host. They read cue cards."

"Well . . . where did the time go?"

"The time went down the sucking vortex of drugs, Dad. You can't remember me because you pretty much went through the 1990s in a blackout."

"Ahh, yes. And now, unfortunately, I'm constantly reminded you're way too clever with words, courtesy of that very expensive private school you go to . . . so you can mouth off to me—and I get to remember it all because I have no blackouts to help me forget," he sighed. "Anyway, I'm sober now."

"Yes. Now."

"What's that supposed to mean?"

"Dad, sometimes I don't think you really . . . think things through. Have you thought about this tour, Dad? I mean really thought about it?"

"Yeah. . . . At least I think so. Why?"

"Sex, drugs, and rock and roll, Dad. . . . You're going back on tour with Greg Essex and Steve Zane. Neither of whom has ever met a drug he didn't like. And you and Charlie have been trying to go to AA. Have you thought about what the tour bus is going to be like? What backstage is going to be like? Not to mention the whole Paris incident. The stuff of legend, Dad. Are you sure you can handle this?"

"Since when did you get so fucking smart?"

"Since I raised myself. Toby went to more of my school events than you did."

He leaned his head back, shut his eyes, and pretended to sleep. I could see Toby in the rearview mirror and knew he was hoping I'd let it drop. I watched my dad fake-sleeping, trying to remember a time when he was responsible, and pretty much recalling none. We rode back to Nyack in silence, and Toby pulled into the gate and up our long driveway. Dad pretended to wake up. As we got out of the car, he grabbed my hand.

"I love you, Livy. You're my girl. I hate fighting."

"I know."

Dad let go of my hand and went into the house. I got my purse, feeling aggravated. I was one of those big "surprises" in life. Mom was a backup singer who had fallen in love—like the whole world—with Greg Essex, lead guitarist of the Babydolls with the biceps and forearms of a sex god. They were together first, then he broke her heart when he suggested a threesome with another woman. She ran into the arms of his best friend, my father and lead singer, and five months later—just starting to show—my mother married my dad. There was some question about my paternity . . . but I happen to have my father's blue eyes. They are this weird icy blue. And I'm his. Much as I sometimes wish I wasn't.

Our house—for a couple who never had any other children—is way too big. Eight bedrooms. Which is okay, I guess, since there always seems to be *someone* crashing—usually a musician. I once spent three months sharing a bathroom with David Drake, the bassist from the Kung-fu Cowboys. He had a nervous breakdown and spent the entire summer building model airplanes. Whatever.

Our house is on the Hudson River in Nyack, New York. Kind of trendy. A perky talk show host who never ceases gabbing about her children on the air lives next door. Guess what? The kids are raised entirely by nannies. I'm surprised Ms. Perky Talk Show Host even knows their names. But we can barely see their house for the big pines that surround our property. Our house is pretty, with a big back lawn that touches the water. My room is on the third floor, in what used to be the attic. My parents finished it off so it's my own living room and bedroom. And no more sharing the bathroom with musician houseguests.

I shut the car door and started to head up to the front porch. Toby cleared his throat. "Liv?"

I turned around. Toby weighs a good 280—all muscle—and he shaves his head, but he has this enormous handlebar moustache that curls around his mouth and makes him look like some kind of weird Kewpie doll.

"Yeah?"

"He's trying."

"I know."

"Cut him some slack. He's going to need a lot of support on this tour."

I nodded. Toby was in AA, too, but unlike Dad, Toby had been sober for twenty years or something like that. My father pretty much fell off the wagon about every six months. Now he had nearly a year under his belt. I hoped he could stay out of trouble on the tour—no women, no drugs, no alcohol. The last tour ended with him in rehab. The tour before that with two nights in jail.

"I know, Toby. We're all just worried." I turned and climbed up the steps and into the house and then kept on going—all the way up to my room. When I was little, in my mind I used to pretend Toby was my father.

When I got upstairs, I turned on my stereo and popped a CD in— one I burned myself. I make a CD every week of all my favorites. That changes from week to week, song to song. Sometimes I can get into a "phase"—like only Nine Inch Nails for two or three weeks. Sometimes I hear an old song—like from my parents' generation, like the Rolling Stones' "Sympathy for the Devil," or from the Seattle grunge era—and I can literally listen to the same song two hundred times. It's in me, part of me, whatever. I put on my current set of favorites and started jumping up and down on my bed. *Holy shit! I got it! I got it! Rock On!*

I called Cammie, my best friend, who had talked her parents into letting her go on tour with us for two months. They thought it would be a great opportunity to see the world. I wasn't sure what they thought of my father's reputation, but I also knew they were so close to a divorce that maybe it didn't matter—just having Cammie away while they tried to work things out would be good. They were letting her older brother live in Boston that summer. He's going to college there. Anyway, her father could never say no to her. She had him twisted around her little pinkie.

"I got it, Cam!" I screamed into my cell phone. I had stopped jumping and flopped straight backward down on my bed. For some weird reason, I love doing that—except for the one time I hit my head on the wall and had to get stitches.

"Oh my God! That's *so* great!"

"They're ever *paying* me."

"Wow! Next thing you know, you'll have your own reality show. Paul James's daughter as rock star critic. You could call it *Livy's Real World*."

"No, I think my life has enough reality it in already."

"I'm so happy for you."

"I can't believe it. My name in print . . . in a real magazine."

"You'll get into NYU's journalism program for sure."

For as long as I can remember, Cammie and I have been planning to go to New York University together. She wanted to study film-making. We had visions of sharing an apartment in Greenwich Village.

"You excited?" I asked her. We'd been planning this summer tour together as soon as the Babydolls announced their concert dates.

"Two dolls and counting!" She sounded like she was hyperventilating.

"One suitcase, Cammie. You can't get nuts." I was picturing clothes from one end of her room to the other.

"I know. One *big* suitcase."

"Yes, one big suitcase. One carry-on. But it's not like the suitcase can be the size of your closet, so I don't know how you're whittling down all your crap into one bag."

"I'll manage."

Cammie was a major clothes horse. Juicy Couture and Abercrombie and Fitch—her two favorites. What she didn't have, she borrowed—from me. She was also a makeup nut, and I think she had no less than fifty-two kinds of shampoo in her bathroom. I kind of liked sleeping over at her house because I felt like I was at a spa—getting to pick shampoos, conditioners, soaps, cleansers. You can't see her bathroom counter, it's so full of stuff.

"Anything new on Operation V?" she asked me.

"I refuse to help you anymore."

"Oh, come on."

Cammie was determined to lose her virginity—in a scheme that made our history teacher's description of the landing at Normandy in World War II sound like a casual battle plan.

"All right. I just found out this morning that Steve Zane is not bringing anyone on the tour."

"No one?"

"Nope. His latest girlfriend left him."

"Operation V is going according to plan."

Cammie intended to lose her virginity to the drummer of the Babydolls. He's younger than my dad by maybe ten years, and he's a total slut. But Cammie had a theory about losing her virginity.

"Are you *sure* you want to go through with this, Cam?"

"Absolutely. As I have said a thousand times before, I have yet to meet a single person who ranked their virginity-losing partner as anyone great. I mean, sure, you think you're in love with some hot guy and you lose your virginity to him. Twenty years from now, he's just some dumb guy you lost your virginity to. Most people are lucky if they remember the guy's name. But if I lose *my* virginity to Steve Zane, even when you and I are ninety and have false teeth and side-by-side rocking chairs in the nursing home, I'll remember exactly who it was—and to top it off, he's probably quite good at it."

"Whatever, Cam. Just don't say I didn't warn you. Every nanny I ever had in my life quit because he'd sleep with her and then dump her a week later in a different city. They'd all go home crushed."

"But *I* know exactly what I'm doing. I'm losing my virginity for historical reasons. I can tell my *grandchildren* that I did it with Steve Zane."

"Yeah. I often discuss sex with my grandmother."

"Well, you get the idea. This isn't about a relationship. It's a quest. You can't tell me you don't think Steve Zane is totally fucking hot."

I admit it. He was. Brown hair, blue eyes, really full lips, high cheek-bones. He was the Babydoll the magazines said was "the pretty one."

"Cammie, you know my rule."

"Yes," she sighed. "Livy James's first rule of the opposite sex: No musicians need apply."

"Trust me, Cam. After a few weeks on the road, you'll never look at a band the same way again."

Sex, drugs, and rock and roll.

It's not always all it's cracked up to be.

But then again, it's the only life I've ever known.

books

COMING THIS SUMMER
A TOTALLY FRESH LINE OF BOOKS

May 2005
SO LYRICAL
by Trish Cook
0-451-21508-7

June 2005
ROCK MY WORLD
by Lisa Conrad
0-451-21523-0

July 2005
THE PRINCIPLES OF LOVE
by Emily Franklin
0-451-21517-6

CONFESSIONS OF AN ALMOST-MOVIE STAR
by Mary Kennedy
0-425-20467-7

August 2005
JENNIFER SCALES AND THE ANCIENT FURNACE
by MaryJanice Davidson
and Anthony Alongi
0-425-20598-3

Available in paperback from Berkley and New American Library

www.penguin.com